"Would I step in front of a bullet for you?

"Yes. Would I stand off a room f·ll ·f ·ngry were-creatures to  an eye. Does that fr········ ··u mean that much t·

"Yes."

He pulled ···· ··· ···, ·ungry slant of his mouth. ·ne straddled his lap, holding his face between her palms so she could return the urgency, the longing, the desperate need that always flickered like a pilot light just waiting to take flame. And just as that pyre of want was about to consume her, he fisted his hand in her hair to pull her back slightly so he could study her passion-flushed features, and she could delve into the glittery heat of this stare.

"Would you break your precious laws for me?" he asked with a sudden fierce intensity. "Would you look the other way while I broke them?"

Her mood cooled slightly, as did her tone. "I've bent them plenty already."

"The truth, Charlotte."

"Yes," she growled out. "It would destroy everything I built my life on. It would strip me of every ounce of dignity and self-respect. But I would do it, without hesitation, without regret, if you asked me to. That's how much you mean to me. And if you care for me even half that much, you would never ask."

Chased by Moonlight is also available as an eBook

ALSO BY NANCY GIDEON

NANCY GIDEON

Chased by Moonlight

POCKET BOOKS
New York   London   Toronto   Sydney

Pocket Books
A Division of Simon & Schuster, Inc.
1230 Avenue of the Americas
New York, NY 10020

This book is a work of fiction. Names, characters, places, and incidents either are products of the author's imagination or are used fictitiously. Any resemblance to actual events or locales or persons, living or dead, is entirely coincidental.

First Pocket Books paperback edition July 2010

POCKET and colophon are registered trademarks of Simon & Schuster, Inc.

For information about special discounts for bulk purchases, please contact Simon & Schuster Special Sales at 1-866-506-1949 or business@simonandschuster.com.

The Simon & Schuster Speakers Bureau can bring authors to your live event. For more information or to book an event contact the Simon & Schuster Speakers Bureau at 1-866-248-3049 or visit our website at www.simonspeakers.com.

Cover design by Min Choi
Cover art by Craig White

Manufactured in the United States of America

10 9 8 7 6 5 4 3 2 1

ISBN 978-1-4391-4964-5
ISBN 978-1-4391-5541-7 (ebook)

To my fabulous critique group.
Thanks for the encouragement, support
and well-deserved butt-kicking.
Love you guys!

Chased by
Moonlight

Prologue

A LOW RUMBLE.

At first she thought it was a motorcycle on one of the distant streets.

She continued to walk without worries, keys in hand, still smiling over a joke one of her friends had told just before she left the club. She tried to remember the punch line so she could retell it when she went home for dinner this weekend. Something about a farmer with a gallon of paint and an old lady carrying a chicken . . . She totally sucked at jokes. Her dad, who had a slickly perfect delivery, was fond of saying that the only thing with worse timing than hers was her ancient Volvo.

She drew in a deep breath of night air to chase away the fuzziness from her last drink—some fruity creation that guy at the next table had sent over in hopes of an invitation. But it was girls' night out, and some rules couldn't be broken. Only estrogen-bearing bodies were allowed at the table. She'd smiled her thanks, hoping he'd catch her at the door to get her number. But he'd been distracted by a very short skirt on the dance floor, and they'd been necking back by the johns before she'd even left. Oh well. That timing thing again.

She crossed Decatur and headed toward the parking lot where her dented Volvo sat in the darkness. The main lot had been full when she arrived after work, forcing her into the overflow boonies. She didn't mind the walk. The breeze coming off the Mississippi was cool on her arms and face, a treat after the sticky afternoon heat.

Her heels crunched on gravel as she left the paved area of the lot. She could hear the water and the lonesome sound of a big barge moving upriver. The muted revelry of New Orleans was behind her, but where she was headed, alone in the dark, it was silent. Except for her footsteps and the sudden deep vibration of that strange rumble again.

What *was* that? It sounded like the growl of some big dog.

She glanced over her shoulder and quickened her step, even though she didn't see anything in the deserted lot. Probably a hungry stray nosing around the overflowing trash cans, warning her off.

She should have asked one of the girls to walk with her. But she loved the spicy fun of the Quarter, and had never felt afraid after dark before.

She let out a breath of relief when she reached her car. Dim light from the other section of the lot cast her reflection in the car window, a pretty young woman—with something huge, dark, and indistinguishable rising up over her shoulder.

A squeak of alarm escaped and her keys hit the gravel as she turned, pressing back against the car. She was confused, then relieved by the sight of a man standing there. Because that's not what she'd seen in that brief, terrifying second, looming behind her with eyes red and gleaming.

No more fruity drinks! The vow pounded frantically on the e-ticket amusement park ride her pulse was taking.

He was tall, dark, and good-looking in a ruthlessly arrogant manner, and nicely dressed in black business casual. Not someone out to snatch her purse.

He smiled slowly with nonthreatening charm, his voice deep and pleasant. "I'm sorry, Sandra. Did I scare you?"

Hearing him speak her name in that warm conversational tone made her relax. Was he someone from the media looking for a quote? Oh, man, she didn't look like she'd had one too many, did she? Her dad would kill her. Or was he someone her father had sent to watch over her? She'd told him time and again it wasn't necessary. But with her heart hammering frantically along her rib cage as if knocking out a tune on a xylophone in a marching band, she wasn't about to question his wisdom now.

She expelled a nervous little laugh and admitted, "Just a bit."

"Just a bit? Then I'll have to do better than that, won't I?"

Still smiling, he gave her keys a kick, sending them spinning under the Volvo.

It took a slow, stomach-rolling second for the danger to register. He wasn't one of her father's employees. He wasn't from the press. And he was after something more than pocket change.

Her glance flashed about the lot, but they were very, very alone—just the two of them beneath the dark light pole. Then she noticed the broken glass from its missing globe littering on the loose gravel.

"What do you want?" she whimpered breathlessly.

"I want you to play a game with me, Sandra. You run; I'll chase you."

She stared at him, eyes round and bright with incomprehensible terror. He looked so normal, so trustworthy.

"I'll even give you a head start."

"W-what?" she stammered, not understanding. Until his smile widened, revealing horribly sharp canine teeth. And his eyes glowed, hot gold and red.

"Run!"

She screamed and bolted, slipping on the gravel to her hands and knees, where the jagged rocks cut her soft skin. Shrieking madly, she expected to feel his hands grabbing at her, those teeth tearing into her. But he waited, giving her time to scramble up, her blood trickling slick and warm, her breath sobbing from her.

"Give it your all, Sandra," he taunted as she sped away, dropping her purse. Hoping he'd stop to look through it.

But he wasn't interested in her spangly bag. He was appreciating the tangling whip of her long blond hair, watching her tight little butt work the snug seat of her capri pants as she wobbled on ridiculously high heels. The scent of her fear was as rich and potent as any perfume. Delicious.

He could taste her already.

"I'll be right behind you," he added with a mocking chuckle.

She ran soundlessly, saving her breath.

Following her frantic race through the lot and down the sidewalk with his unnatural stare, his smile returned, sharp and fierce. Because she was headed not toward the lights, where she might have found the safety of her own kind, but into shadows, where she foolishly thought she might hide.

Silly girl.

Then he chased her.

One

THE RING OF her cell phone dragged Charlotte Caissie from a very delicious dream. She scowled, trying to ignore the unwelcome summons intruding into her private world.

Go away. Leave a message.

Finally the ringing stopped.

Concentrate.

The breath sighed from her as she was skillfully coaxed back into the moment.

Oh, that's it, baby. Right there. That's the spot.

Chills of sensation skimmed across her flushed skin—and the phone began to ring again with shrill impatience. While her flesh was more than willing to ignore it, her well-trained mind was already lured to distraction.

Oh, for fuck's sake!

As her hand unfisted from sleek dark hair, a low voice came from under the covers.

"Don't answer it."

The request was punctuated by her body's greedy shuddering, but her hand was already on the phone.

"Caissie."

"Cee Cee, I need you to meet me on the Moon-walk."

"Babineau, I'm right in the middle of some-thing." Her testy, breathless tone resulted in a long silence on the other end. But having had to suffer through the details of her partner's new marriage *ad nauseam* for the last eight months, she didn't care if he was shocked. "And if you don't let me get back to it right now, I'm going to have to injure you badly. I am officially off the clock and unavailable. Got it?"

"Sorry, but the chief asked for you in particular."

She groaned, both in objection and delight as a chain of hot kisses moved slowly up her belly. "Where?" It was hard to hear his answer over the roar of her blood. Her back arched into a sensuous bow, then slumped to the mattress again. "I'm on my way." She threw the phone and then said gruffly, "I've got to go."

Her clever and oh-so-generous lover came up on his elbows, annoyance ill-concealed. "I thought we were already on our way to a very different destina-tion."

Being dragged from his bed, particularly at this suspenseful juncture, was the last thing she'd envi-sioned for the morning, too.

Her tone clipped tight, her manner all-business. "Duty calls. And it's not like we haven't been on this particular journey all day yesterday and most of last night."

A cool distance seeped into his expression, and

his voice grew brittle. "Excuse me, detective. I thought you were enjoying the ride. My mistake."

She returned his fierce, unblinking glower for a long minute, then with a laugh toppled him over onto his back, coming up astride him.

"I love it when you pout," she murmured against the firm set of his mouth.

"I'm not pouting. I'm being indignant." But his lips relaxed too quickly under hers to be convincing. "All right, I'm pouting. And in a minute, I'll be begging. I have no shame where you're concerned, *sha*. Don't go. Please."

She brushed her fingertips over the sharp angles of his face, adoring the strong, compelling lines. How easily she'd become addicted to him, to this. Once she'd surrendered to the drugging pleasures of his touch, she found it difficult to remember why she'd resisted him for so long.

She did a mental balancing now. Sex or murder? How was a girl to choose? He wasn't making it any easier, with that slow drag of his fingertips over the curve of her torso. "Don't make this harder than it has to be," she warned shakily.

His eyes crinkled with wicked amusement. "It couldn't be much harder than it already is. Are you sure you can't show pity for my unfortunate state and spare a few more minutes?"

"I'm surprised you can still muster up a . . . complaint, let alone move." She grinned. "You are an insatiable beast."

"You say that like it's a bad thing."

She pressed a quick kiss on the tip of his nose, then rolled out of bed while she still had the will-power. She heard his heavy moan of resignation as she said, "I've got to swing by my apartment to feed the pigs, shower, and grab some clean clothes."

"You can shower here."

The temptation was almost irresistible, just as he intended. Picturing suds and steam and more hot sex, she smiled wryly. "I'm afraid that would be counterproductive."

"It would save time if you'd leave some clothes here." At her sudden look of panic, he added silkily, "I promise not to wear them."

They hadn't discussed that step. Actually, they hadn't discussed much of anything. They'd only ventured from their den of lustful pleasures to for-age for food. Caught up in the right-now, instead of the week later where the rest of the world waited, she hadn't felt words were too important. Not when he possessed so many other delectable, nonverbal communication skills.

Bringing clothes over sounded suspiciously like setting up housekeeping, and alarms and whistles protecting her personal space rang. She said care-fully, "We'll talk about that later."

"Whenever you have the time, detective. What happened to your week's vacation? I had plans for every minute of it."

A warm tingle spread through some very well-satisfied places as she imagined what else he might have had in mind. A long, X-rated, clothing-unnecessary week of sensation and relaxation with the only person she'd ever wanted to share such things with. Didn't he realize she was as angry about losing any of that precious time together as he was? But one of them had to be reasonable, and he was too busy pouting. A dark, smoldery pout that had her heartbeat kicking up a notch. She was too new at the complexities of a relationship to know when it was better to run like hell rather than to attempt an explanation.

"Apparently the department cannot continue without me for more than one day." She started pulling on her crumpled clothes with rapid efficiency under his brooding regard.

"Neither can I."

The deeply pitched sentiment gripped her emotions like a fist. It took a phenomenal amount of determination to continue buttoning her shirt.

Seeing that he wasn't going to sway her, he said mildly, "Tell your partner I'll be making good on your threat."

"What threat is that?" she asked, strapping on her weapon.

"To injure him badly."

She glanced over at the long, powerful figure stretched out beneath well-rumpled Egyptian cotton sheets. His black hair was endearingly mussed and spiky, his unshaven cheeks smudged with morning shadow, but his stare was level, still and unblinking. For a moment, a reminder of who he was, what he was, and what he was capable of, shocked through her with a nasty little jolt. Dangerous. Deadly. A predator no longer answering to anyone.

She hesitated. Was he serious?

He showed his teeth in a wide, possible smile. "Just kidding."

Was he?

"You'd better be." She released a cautious breath. "I don't want to break in a new partner any more than I want to break in a new boyfriend. I'll see you later?"

"Oh, you can count on that." He stretched, arms over head and toes reaching for the opposite wall, the movement strong and as lazily sinuous as that of some big, powerful animal. Which, technically, was exactly what he was. "I might as well go to work, too," he grumbled, "since you've managed to suck the illicit enjoyment out of my day. I'll stop by your apartment so you can tell me what was more important than sharing this bed with me."

She couldn't imagine anything running even a close second to him, so in a moment of tangled vulnerability, she let down her guard. "That was the best one-day vacation I've ever had in my life. You're amazing."

"Thank you." His mouth curved, his smile smug, his gaze warming. "My pleasure."

She took one step toward him, then caught herself. It was madness to want him so much. A nearly uncontrollable madness. Time to run like hell.

"I'll see you soon."

"SANDRA CUMMINGS, TWENTY-TWO, single, a business student at Tulane. Apparently she went to a club off the Square with a group of friends. She left about one thirty and walked to her car alone."

"She should have known better." Charlotte looked at the plastic-draped form, frustration roiling. Why hadn't she known better? One too many drinks? The invulnerability of youth? How could her friends let her just walk out into the night by herself? What had they been thinking?

Unfortunately she had a pretty good idea what they'd be thinking when they heard the news. They'd be thinking it was all their fault. And then they'd have to learn to live with it. Lesson learned too damn late, and now just another grim statistic. "Stupid kids," she muttered almost angrily.

She glanced around, her cool, dark eyes efficiently detailing the scene, imagining it the way it would look late at night—not the way it did now, skirted by police tape and obscenely visible to those beginning to crowd behind it. After midnight it would be isolated, empty in favor of the jazz and dance-club party scene closer to the Square. A lonely, shadowed place to die. No place for a twenty-two-year-old student to be lying under plastic.

"What was so special about her that the chief

called me back in?" She glanced at her partner, alerted by his edgy evasiveness. Not much made Alain Babineau fidget. He was the epitome of cool and calm under even the most grisly circumstances. Together they'd seen all the ugly, shocking reminders of what man was willing to do to his fellow man in the name of anger, jealousy, madness, or just plain business.

"She's Simon Cummings's youngest daughter."

"Cummings?" She'd met the aggressively proactive mayoral hopeful at several professional functions. She'd liked his firm, hard line against crime. "A coincidence?"

Something uneasy moved in Babineau's face as he bent and pulled back the plastic. "I don't think so."

She stared down at the partially nude and viciously mutilated body of Sandra Cummings, seeing the signature MO. She didn't need to wait for the pronouncement of cause from the medical examiner, Devlin Dovion. She recognized the work.

Fangs and claws.

"Do you want to drive or shall I?" Babineau asked softly.

LEGERE ENTERPRISES INTERNATIONAL had its business office in a renovated warehouse along the wharf, close to the pulse of its many interests. And many of those interests had been under attack by Simon Cummings. His campaign had stepped up considerably since Jimmy Legere's death and the assumption of power by his long-time bodyguard, Max Savoie.

Savoie was an unknown quantity. Despite his highly visible stance at Legere's back, he'd stayed in the shadows as a silent, simmering threat to any who would dare cross his mentor. He literally hadn't existed on paper until Legere's high-priced lawyer arranged for the necessary documents to allow him to take control.

How he would run LE International, and his ability to retain his hold on the far-flung and allegedly illegal ventures, was the topic of much debate. Dangerous debate. And though the head that wore the new crown was uneasy, one wouldn't know it when looking at the sleek businessman seated behind a huge teak desk.

"Detectives, what can I do for you this morning?"

In unspoken agreement, Cee Cee remained quiet while her partner, Alain Babineau, squared up to ask questions. From the backup position she could study the elegant Savoie, looking beyond his beautifully tailored gray Armani suit and immaculate grooming to the sharp-edged killer he'd been until a few months ago. The aura of potential violence still shimmered about him, despite the careful composition of his ruggedly compelling features. Knowing how much more was hidden behind the steady arrogance of his stare had Cee Cee dreading the confrontation to come.

That, and the fact that she was sleeping with him.

"We're investigating a murder, Mr. Savoie. A young woman was attacked at her car, chased down the Moonwalk, overpowered, raped, and killed."

Max never blinked. "How unfortunate. And this relates to me how? Do I know her? Does she work for me?"

"Her father was Simon Cummings. Get the picture now?"

"Still out of focus. Fine-tune, please."

"Her throat was torn out. It appears as if some of her internal organs were . . . eaten."

"Ah. Are you asking if I suddenly got a craving for young coed and decided to go out for a snack?"

"Did you?"

A cool smile. "No. I'm afraid my girlfriend doesn't approve of me assaulting and devouring other women. She's funny that way. I try my best not to irritate her unnecessarily, even though she doesn't seem to have a problem irritating me. Nor do you, apparently, Detective Babineau."

"So you won't mind telling me for the record where you were between one and two this morning."

"I was at my home. In bed. Handling an urgent personal matter. I was not alone." His stony stare never deviated from Babineau's. "Did you need proof, detective? I'm afraid I don't have any Polaroids or video for documentation. Is that something you think I should consider doing, for future reference?"

Alain Babineau was a straight shooter, a good cop, and a tough one without being a hard-ass. His unspoiled good looks could have sold anything from toothpaste to boxers with his blue eyes, dimples, and compact athletic build. He was protective of his partner in a way that made Savoie grateful and uneasy at the same time. They would never like each other, because of the woman and the badge that stood between them.

"And your time can be vouched for all night?"

"Yes. Every delectable minute of it."

Cee Cee frowned. Max's gaze flickered to her for an instant, registering puzzlement, before returning to his interrogator.

"Any other questions, detective, or would you like to gut me right here to see if any pieces of Ms. Cummings come spilling out on my carpet?"

"I don't think I could get a warrant for that." But his scowl said he wouldn't be above asking for a sample of his stomach contents. "Can you deny that Simon Cummings has been causing you and your organization a considerable amount of trouble lately?"

"No. He's a tolerable nuisance. But then again, so are you, detective, and I haven't killed and eaten you."

They locked testosterone-fueled stares for a long moment, until a clearly irritated Cee Cee stepped between them. Her demand held a crisp neutrality.

"Did anyone in your employ, with or without

your knowledge, undertake the intimidation of Ms. Cummings in order to dissuade her father from continuing his vendetta against your businesses?"

Cold green eyes slashed over to meet hers. "Are you asking if I authorized the rape and murder of an innocent young girl because her father was annoying me? Is that what you're asking, Detective Caissie?"

When she refused to clarify the question, his mood grew glacial.

"The answer is no. This interview is over. If you have any other questions you can contact my attorney. I'm sure you know your way out."

"I'll say this for you, Savoie," Babineau stated in a parting shot. "You certainly are a quick study. You've gotten comfortable real fast behind that desk. Just remember where fast and clever got Jimmy Legere."

Without moving a muscle, fury vibrated through the new top thug on the block. "I'll remember. Detective Caissie, a word."

Charlotte wasn't fooled by his smooth manner. He was in a dangerous coil of temper, ready to strike. Still, she nodded to her reluctant partner and remained behind. She began with cautious impartiality, hoping to quickly defuse the situation. "I'm sorry for that, Max. You know it's just part of the drill. I can't help that you top our list of the usual, or rather the unusual, suspects."

But that wasn't what concerned him.

"What was that look for, Charlotte?"

Her competent cop expression puckered with confusion. "What look?"

"When Babineau asked about us being together all night, you made a peculiar face. I don't understand. Explain it to me."

She confronted him directly. "I woke up about quarter to two. You weren't with me."

"What do you mean?"

"You were gone. I didn't think anything of it at the time. I went back to sleep."

"But you're thinking something of it now."

"Of course not."

She was lying; he could practically hear the wheels in her cop brain whirring. His features registered the shock of it briefly before the impenetrable glaze returned. "You think I climbed out of the bed I was sharing with you, came into town to have forced sex with someone else after you'd been supplying it so generously for the previous thirty-six hours, killed her, made a meal of her, came back, washed up, and was all warm and ready to make love to you again?"

How awful he made her sound. It *was* awful. She felt awful, but trying to defend herself would have only made things worse.

She couldn't help remembering the past bodies she'd seen. She couldn't change the fact that she knew what had torn them into pieces. *Who* had torn them into pieces.

He came toward her with a purposeful stride. She held her ground, her heart pounding. She'd never been truly afraid of him, of what he was and what he could do, yet subconscious caution shivered through her soul. He came as close as he could without actually touching her, until she could feel his heat, his strength, his intensity. There was no man alive that she would let do that without thrusting up barriers to protect her space.

But then, Max Savoie was no man.

He asked softly against her ear, "How could you let me put my hands on you if you believed that for even an instant?"

His fingertips rested on the backs of her arms. And she flinched.

With a low oath, he turned away. "Leave, Charlotte. Just go."

The toneless quality of his voice scared her. "Max?" she asked softly, plaintively.

"What a monster you must think I am. How can you stand me?"

"*Max.*" She reached for him but he shied away, returning to the other side of his desk. When he looked at her again, his face was without expression.

"Don't keep your partner waiting, detective. I'm sure you have more important places you need to be."

Charlotte returned his gaze for a long, controlled moment, her stare flat and ungiving. He knew she wouldn't just slink away. Not with all that fierce, prideful arrogance that both fascinated and infuriated him. Didn't she realize she could destroy him with just a subtle shift of her expression, a betraying flicker he always prepared for that would plunge from desire to disgust? But she kept her features neutral—those bold, exotically beautiful features that could crush a man's courage with purposeful viciousness or conceal a vulnerable world of pain behind hard onyx eyes.

She abruptly broke her rigid stance and strode to the door the way she did everything, with a take-no-prisoners certainty.

After the door closed behind her, he let his breath out in a shaky spasm. He quickly took another one, deep and strong, to get on top of all the turmoil writhing around inside him. He'd deal with that later. For now, he had to take care of business.

He pressed the intercom on his desk. "Francis, come in here, please."

Francis Petitjohn was Jimmy Legere's cousin and had supposed himself the heir apparent to the fortune he'd helped make. Finding out that Jimmy had passed his vast holdings to the dangerous enigma he'd taken in as an orphaned child created a difficult tension between the two of them. Difficult and nearly deadly.

"Whatchu need, Max?"

"The truth would be nice."

Max sank back into the big leather chair that had been Petitjohn's up until a month ago. The chair he'd sat in to calmly watch Max twist on the floor in the grip of the poison T-John had used to try to kill him. When Max decided to take the disputed job and the chair instead of T-John's life, Petitjohn had no objections. But he didn't have to like the situation.

"Truth about what?"

"Simon Cummings. Someone killed his daughter last night in a way that was rather telling. Like a gruesome finger pointing in my direction. Whatchu know about it?"

Petitjohn shrugged, looking properly clueless. But then he wasn't exactly the soul of sincerity. Max knew exactly what he was: lying, sneaking, devious, and for the moment, a necessary evil acting as liaison between him and the cautious factions of their criminal world.

The fact that he resembled Jimmy might have had something to do with Max's reluctance to simply dispose of him. He had Legere's wiry build and sharp, cunning features. His voice held that same casual drawl of indifferent contempt for anything that wasn't making him money. He could be charming when he chose to be, or he could be merciless. Both sides made Max wary.

"I don't know anything about it, Max. First I heard."

Max tented his hands, resting his chin on his fingertips. His gaze was still, unnervingly unnatural. "Really? And that's the truth?"

"Yeah."

"Have you been leaning on Cummings?"

"Of course. He's a pain in the ass, like a boil that bothers you every time you try to sit down."

If he'd answered any differently, Max would have known he was lying. As it was, he couldn't be certain.

"Ask around. Find out who did this thing and why. Let them know I don't like it. It's not how I want to do business. Have Marissa send two sizable checks in the daughter's name—one to whatever department she was in at the university, and one to St. Bart's for their women's shelter. Have her reach out very lightly to the family with our condolences."

"That's not how Jimmy would have handled it. Jimmy would have used their grief to apply a little more pressure. He would have considered it a good business opportunity."

Max regarded him narrowly. "I'm not Jimmy. And I will not condone anyone ever harming a woman or child in my name or in my employ. Not *ever*. Don't make me have to repeat that to you. I shouldn't have had to say it in the first place, and you know why."

T-John said nothing.

Max sighed heavily and sagged back into the leather cushions. "I don't need this right now, Francis. I'm trying to establish a sense of trust here on the docks, and it's like trying to reach under a virgin's skirt while convincing her your intentions are honorable."

Petitjohn smiled slightly and Max realized he

was talking too much and to the wrong person. If he needed a confidant, the man on the other side of the desk was not the one to choose. Unfortunately the person he wanted to unburden himself to was equally unacceptable. And that chewed on him like a wharf rat.

"I've got some people to see. I should be back in a couple of hours. Don't talk to the police; don't make any statements to anyone. Deny everything. Make us sound like the aggrieved party. You're good at that."

As Max moved toward the door, Petitjohn drawled, "Whatever you want, Max. Happy to take care of it for you," echoing words Max had said in all sincerity to Jimmy Legere, twisting them with a touch of a sneer.

Max turned slowly to regard him. His voice was low, almost pleasant.

"Just because I let you go on breathing, don't think that implies any sentimentality or stupidity. I know exactly what you are—and the second you cease to serve a purpose on my behalf, I will rip out your heart and swallow it whole while it's still beating."

"I never doubted that for a minute, Max."

Max paused, gauging Petitjohn's response. The other man's pulse was racing. He was sweating, breathing in shallow fear-laced snatches. Terror was something Jimmy had taught Max to ply ruthlessly, and as long as T-John was afraid, he'd have a degree of control. For emphasis, he let his stare turn hot and gold while a bloody red swamped the whites of his eyes. With a blink, that look was back to normal.

"Good. Then we understand each other."

Something else occurred to him.

"And if anything happens to Charlotte Caissie— say, if a car runs over her, a safe falls from a second-story window on her, if she contracts some fatal disease, or gets shot in the course of a robbery—I will hold you, and *only* you, personally responsible. And, Francis," he added almost conversationally, "you'll beg me to eat your heart raw just so you can die. Got it?"

"Got it, Max."

He left the office, shutting the door softly behind him, then lingered to hear Francis Petitjohn mutter on the other side.

"And *you'll* get it, too, you smug son of a bitch. So don't get too comfortable in that chair."

Two

THE CUMMINGSES' HOME was on St. Charles in the Garden District. The sprawling house was tour book pristine with turrets, lacy wrought iron, and vivid splashes of color from bougainvilleas and crape myrtle. The interior was warm and filled with family touches. Photos marched along the mantels and tabletops; awards boasting everything from cheerleading and valedictorian to debate and the science fair were proudly arranged in lighted cases. A half-played chess match was laid out on a side table awaiting the next move.

Cee Cee imagined the rooms filled with laughter and conversation. Not this horrid, silent aftermath of death.

The interview was difficult. How could any conversation about the loss of a loved one be anything else? She and Babineau sat surrounded by reminders of life and joy, holding delicate cups of hazelnut coffee and plates with little crustless sandwiches Noreen Cummings provided with a fluttery hospitality that kept shock from settling too deep, too soon; watching stoically while Simon Cummings sobbed into his hands over the unanswerable question of "Why?" There was nothing to do but awkwardly balance those dainty dishes and wait.

Finally Cummings looked up as if seeing them for the first time, and the grief in his eyes gave way to anger. Even ravaged by sorrow, the charisma that would carry him from business to voting booths was present. A PR dream, Cummings was a tall, fit figure of Southern masculinity with his flowing white hair, chiseled jaw, and steely stare. He inspired admiration with his elegance and an everyman comfort with his fondness for family and humanitarian causes. Old ladies wanted to pinch him and young ones wanted to look up to him. The men felt unthreatened enough to hoist a beer and open their checkbooks. He was a man on the move—but at the moment, he was a father in mourning.

"Who did this to my little girl?"

"That's what we're going to find out," Babineau assured him.

Taking the opening, Cee Cee began with calm determination. "Mr. Cummings, we need to ask some questions to help us find who might have wanted to harm your daughter."

"No one, detective. No one wanted to harm my girl. Everyone liked her. She was sweet and smart and caring."

And trusting. Way too trusting. Cee Cee couldn't help but think of another girl who had fit that description, someone full of fun and spirit who'd been similarly crushed by a cruel twist of fate.

"Was she involved with anyone in particular? Had she broken up with someone who might have been angry?"

Dabbing his puffy eyes, Cummings shook his head. "No one serious, just lots of friends. She said she was too busy for a relationship. Busy— at twenty-two." His expression crumpled with renewed anguish. "She had school and work and volunteering. She wanted to be involved in my campaign. . . . Dear God." His gaze lifted to theirs, horrified with a new realization. "This is about me. It's about me, isn't it?"

Cee Cee shifted the focus gently. "Has someone been threatening you, Mr. Cummings? Threatening to hurt your family?"

He was silent for a long moment as he considered the awful possibility that his child was dead because of him.

"Has anyone in your family been approached directly, Mr. Cummings? I know this is hard, but it's very important that you try to remember."

"Those bastards," he whispered. "Those bastards."

"Who are we talking about?" Cee Cee pressed. "A name."

"Legere."

Why wasn't she surprised? "What kind of threats, sir? Made by whom?"

"We've always been at odds. I'd propose a project to benefit the community, and if he couldn't find a way to profit from it, he'd try to shut me down or make me pay through the nose for doing business. We were constantly tied up in court. It was a game to the old man, but his games came with harsh rules. He made no bones about wanting to measure me for cement; there was nothing subtle about Jimmy Legere. Victor Vantour was another one who was always blocking progress in the name of payoffs. But Legere and Vantour are both dead. Both of them were fighting my riverfront development program with everything they had."

"Everything including murder?"

His stare grew as sharp as a stropped blade. "Maybe. You tell me, detectives."

"Have you had any direct dealings with Max Savoie?" Babineau asked, drawing the man's attention away from his partner.

"No. I know who he is. What he is. I know he's ruthless and has the blood on his hands of anyone who ever got in Legere's way. Like I did." Suddenly Cummings's gaze settled on Cee Cee, and an ugly suspicion colored his expression.

Carefully Cee Cee put the delicate china on the table beside her chair and rose. "If you'll excuse me for a minute, I'm going to wash my hands."

Why did every damned thing have to circle back to Max Savoie?

Resenting the fact that she'd been forced to abandon the questioning, Cee Cee made a purposeful turn into the kitchen, where Noreen Cummings was putting away silverware and chain-smoking with a very unladylike intensity. She didn't glance up, but her hands started shaking.

"You do everything you can to keep them safe," she began in a casual way that invited Cee Cee to come closer. "You watch over them when they're young. You teach them to be smart and careful. But they never quite believe you, do they, detective?"

"About the things out there that can hurt them? No. They don't, Mrs. Cummings. I am so sorry."

She nodded her perfectly coiffed head. It became a struggle for her to sort the forks into dinner, salad, and dessert, rolling each into silver cloth with a meticulous care.

"Were you trying to protect your husband, Mrs. Cummings?"

Her gaze flickered up with startled apprehension. Noreen Cummings was the perfect counterpoint for her husband: willowy, graceful, Norwegian fair, from the best schools and the best family. Yet Cee Cee sensed an underlying core of toughness that immediately had her respect. She was wounded but was rallying for an attack.

"What do you mean?" Noreen asked.

"Did someone approach you or the children? Did they make threats that you were keeping from your husband so as not to worry him? Something insignificant, that you didn't take seriously?"

"Sandra told me someone had been following her—never getting close, just there in the background. I thought it was someone Simon had hired but hadn't told us about. He liked to pretend we didn't know there was danger involved in what he did. Sweet, silly man. Of course we knew. And we accepted it because it was part of what he does."

"Have you asked him if he hired someone?"

"I—I never had the chance. There was so much to plan, so much to do."

Cee Cee put her hand over Noreen Cummings's elegantly manicured fingers. "None of this is your fault, Mrs. Cummings. You're not to blame for what evil men choose to do."

Noreen's voice was quiet. "I never thought he was serious."

"Who, Mrs. Cummings?"

"He came up to me about six months ago at some charity event promoting development along the waterfront. Very polite but very . . . cold. He didn't identify himself but I knew who he was. He said my name, and he said, 'You must be proud of them. So young and innocent. It would be such a shame if anything should happen to spoil that because he cares more for his career than his children.'"

A terrible chill settled in the pit of Cee Cee's stomach. "And then?'

"He walked away."

"Did you feel threatened? Did he touch you or make you feel in immediate danger?"

"No. He didn't actually do anything specific, but he scared me because he was so . . . I don't know . . . *strange*, I guess, is the best word. I was so scared. I had both girls come home for a few weeks, pretending I was empty nesting." Her smile trembled.

"But you didn't say anything to your husband?"

"I was afraid he would act on it. I was afraid it would make things worse. We've had to deal with crazies since the first day Simon gave an interview. It's part of the job. He told me not to fret over what crackpots might say or do."

"And this man was a crackpot, a crazy?"

"Oh, no. He wasn't making idle threats to make himself feel important. He was warning me, and I didn't listen. If I had acted on it, Sandra would still be alive. I just couldn't believe he would actually . . . would actually harm one of my girls."

"Do you know this man's name, Mrs. Cummings?"

"Yes." Her gaze hardened as she said flatly, "But not so well as you, from what I've read in the papers."

Max.

Noreen Cummings lifted a heavy antique locket that she wore on the fine gold chain about her neck. She opened it to display two beautiful, youthful faces. "Take a good look, detective. These are the two most precious things in my life. And he took one of them away from me. What are you going to do about that, detective? You think about these faces the next time you're in bed with him."

BABINEAU DROVE HER back to her car in silence, then kept the motor idling as he turned to her.

"Did she give up any names?"

"Who?" Cee Cee glanced at her partner, startled from her somber thoughts.

"The Mrs."

"Nothing specific or recent. How about Cummings? He give any specifics?"

"Not in so many words."

Oh, how carefully he chose that remark. "Just say it, Babs. Say what's on your mind."

"You know where this is leading, Ceece."

She said nothing.

"The minute he connected you and Savoie, he shut down tight. How are we going to run an investigation when they're as suspicious of us as they are of the criminals?"

Her temper flared and cold anxiety clawed at her insides. Her tone was brittle ice. "Are you telling me to walk away, Alain? Is that what you're suggesting?"

"No. You're a good cop, Cee Cee. I wouldn't want to work with anyone else." He was so earnest, some of her fear fell away—but not all. "All I'm saying is, be prepared for that suggestion to come from another direction."

"Cummings is going to request I be pulled from the case?"

"I wouldn't be surprised."

She cursed passionately. "Then we'll have to

nail this down quick before it gets pulled out from under us."

Babineau sighed and ran fingers through his wavy blond hair, a rare sign of agitation. "I thought we'd seen our last of this . . . this obscenity. When we locked down Spratt for doing Vantour, I thought we'd gotten our monster off the streets. What's going on? A copy cat, you think?"

"Maybe. If someone is trying to get a lot of media real fast, this will do it. We'll be up to our asses in press alligators."

"I'd hoped we wouldn't have to go up against all that late-night-creature-feature bullshit again. It scares folks. Even sensible folks." Babineau was silent for another long minute then asked, uncomfortably, "Will Savoie give you anything?"

Cee Cee recoiled, not because she resented the suggestion but because she was already considering it. She liked hearing it spoken out loud even less. "I'm not sure I should ask. I'm not sure I'll have the chance to ask. We didn't part on very good terms this morning, at his office."

"He'll get over it a lot faster than he'll get over you."

"I wish I could be so sure."

"Then what have you got to lose by asking?"

Everything. Only everything.

THE FEAR THAT maybe she already had was enough to darken her mood for the rest of the day. She canvassed the university area, speaking to roommates in the fancy sorority house, study group partners, and teachers, and all said essentially what the parents had. Everyone liked Sandra Cummings. That was the same conclusion Babineau came to, after speaking to her employer and the patrons at the club where Sandra had had her last drink.

So why did Cee Cee feel so certain this attack on the attractive young coed was purposeful, not random? And that it was a lot closer to her own home than she cared to admit?

She studied her notes over a fried oyster po' boy at the House of Blues. Then she indulged herself in a leisurely smoke in that dark, noisy atmosphere, along with some icy mugs of beer at the ornately carved bar.

It all came back to Max. Max and the way their relationship balanced so precariously on that narrow line of the law that was her career.

In the not-so-distant past, she wouldn't have been moping over a pint and an ashtray. She would have zealously pursued what was logically laid out for her with single-minded blinders on. She recognized the cause of that young woman's death. While others could only speculate based on rumor and whispered folktales, she knew, she'd *seen,* the kind of creature capable of inflicting such brutal damage. She was sharing a bed with one.

When fortuitous evidence had linked Benjamin Spratt, the janitor at St. Bart's church, to a history of mental illness and murder, she'd breathed a grateful sigh that suspicion was turned away from Max. The gruesome method Spratt used to kill as part of his supposed psychosis made him for several unsolved killings in the Quarter. And everyone from the police to the press was satisfied. Cee Cee hadn't made waves, but she knew the truth—or part of it.

Spratt had been a convenient scapegoat at a convenient time, taking the heat off Max for things he'd done to save an abused young mother and a cocky female police detective. Cee Cee had been showered with glory for putting together the gift-wrapped pieces to close the case, but the case still stuck in her throat. Because she knew it covered a lie. She knew it protected Max Savoie.

And now, by her failure to act aggressively, she was doing the same thing.

She didn't want to believe Max had killed Sandra Cummings. But she knew he could have. And that had her knocking back another logic-numbing brew. Her heart insisted it wasn't Max; it had to be another of his kind. But her head refused to not consider him a suspect. And now those parts of her were at war again over this new crime, the part that accepted who and what he was when she'd embraced her love for him and the part of her that swore to see justice to its most unpleasant end regardless of personal cost. She was violating her oath by not going after him. But she'd be violating her vow to Max if she failed to trust him.

Do nothing and be a bad cop. Follow procedure and ruin the best thing she'd ever had. Neither choice led to a happy ending. Well, it was time to deal with it—no matter how much it sucked.

Cee Cee stubbed out her last cigarette and headed out into thick evening air. She sat behind the wheel of her car, fighting back the heavy melancholy stirred up by too much drink and too little sleep. And by a fact she'd been trying to ignore: Sandra Cummings reminded her of Mary Kate Malone.

By the time she climbed the outside stairs to her second-floor apartment, she was feeling the beer and the heart-crushing wretchedness of her lot. Especially when she unlocked her door and found the place empty of all but her hungry guinea pigs. She hadn't known until that instant which she dreaded more: finding Max there waiting and not knowing what to say to him or having him not there at all with so much left unsaid.

She fed the animals, dropped her holster on the coffee table, then plopped onto her sofa in a boneless sprawl. Her head resting against its back, she closed her eyes, feeling the prickle of sorrow burn behind them as a frightened voice cried out through her memories.

"Make them stop. Lottie, please make them stop."

Though there'd been nothing she could do, she'd still tried. She'd forced down her own panic, her own pain, and done her best to distract the worst of it away from her battered friend.

"Does it make you feel like a man to hurt little girls?" she'd sneered. *"Can't get it up unless you're using your fists? Do you have to tie them up before they'll let you touch them? Is that because you're ugly or because you're impotent?"*

Oh, she'd had his full attention then. And the violence in his face was born of a murderous rage.

He hadn't used his fists. She would have preferred that. Instead, he'd gotten creative. And she would never again underestimate the imagination of a monster in men's clothing as a horrible new agony backed with death had ripped into her.

"Charlotte?"

Her eyes flew open as she pulled herself from that long-ago scene now, as then, due to the timely arrival of Max Savoie. He stood in her living room regarding her with concern.

"I knocked but you didn't answer. Are you all right?"

She came off the cushions with a quick, denying move, her arms locking around herself to restrain the tight clutch of panic. She paced, her movements agitated. He watched, saying nothing, waiting for her to share what had made her mood so raw and restless.

"Sorry. I got lost in thought for a minute."

He didn't have to ask where. He could tell by the sweat dotting her brow, by the snag of her respirations. He could smell the remnants of terror on her. And it took all his will power not to act upon it. Instead, he spoke her name softly.

"Charlotte."

"Give me a minute, okay, so I can pull myself together."

He could see she was on the verge of coming apart, so he stepped into the hasty path she walked while trying to outdistance her pain. She attempted to sidestep him and he moved to counter. She looked up at him then, her eyes angry, shadowed, afraid.

"Back off, Savoie," she growled with warning.

"No."

The touch of his hand on her cheek was all it took for her to cave. He waited for her to lean into him before anchoring her there within the wrap of his arms.

Her voice was muffled against his shoulder. "I'm sorry. I'm a mess."

"You're beautiful."

She gave a cynical snort. "I'm all soggy and stink of smoke and beer."

"True, but I'd still do you."

The sound of his voice, all rumbly with tender humor, the warmth of his body, the scent of his skin provided rescue on the turbulent sea of her emotions. She laughed raggedly and held on for dear life, her fingers clenching in his hair and his collar. Her damp face pressed against the side of his neck, where she whispered, "Max. Max, hold me. Don't let go."

"I won't, *sha*. I won't ever let you go."

Safe in the wrap of his solid familiarity, Cee Cee

released the fear and pain, those dreadful scars on the psyche of a seventeen-year-old girl, in cautious increments. She couldn't speak again until she gathered up a degree of control. "I don't want to remember anymore, Max."

He made a soft sound, his embrace tightening. "I know, darlin'. I know. I'm sorry."

"I was afraid they were going to kill us. And then I was afraid they wouldn't. I had to stay alive for Mary Kate. She was so scared."

He pressed a kiss to her brow, his voice a hoarse whisper. "I'm sorry, Charlotte. No one will ever hurt you again. I won't allow it."

"I tried so hard not to let her know I was scared, too."

"You are the bravest, strongest person I know. I love you so much."

"I should have been able to save her from all that pain."

"I should have saved you both. Forgive me." He waited, held her, surrounding her, protecting her from the worst of the remembered misery simply by being there, as he'd been there twelve years before. When she didn't answer, he said again, with a deep, forceful urgency. "Please say you forgive me, Charlotte."

"I miss her so much," she went on as if she hadn't heard his plea. "Some days I wake up and I start to call her, and then I remember that she's not there. I don't know if she'll ever be there for me again."

"I'm here. I'm here for you."

"I just feel so alone. So empty inside."

Max closed his eyes and buried his face in her hair, suffering for the fact that he would never be enough to fill that spot within her guarded heart. If there was any permanent place there for him at all.

She was steady again, breathing deeply, heart rate almost normal. He marveled at her courage, knowing what it took to overcome those terrors from the past, having done so himself. Having witnessed her nightmare firsthand humbled him all the more. And made him that much more culpable.

She stayed in his arms, comfortable in their protective strength. She rubbed the dampness from her cheek against his shoulder as she continued, "I don't know if I can work this case. I see the Cummings girl, and I see Mary Kate. I can't do my job properly when I'm so torn up. Maybe Babineau is right. Maybe I should step back from this one."

Because she didn't ask him what he thought, he didn't offer an opinion, saying instead what he knew she needed to hear. "You and the job are a coin. You can't separate one side from the other. It's not a random toss, detective. Sandra Cummings couldn't be in better hands than yours. And neither could Mary Kate. You know that. You know that even though it hurts you. You'd give anything to find justice for them both because you still suffer for those wrongs done to them. They know you won't let them down."

"It's all I can do for them now. I can take up their cause. I can't let this girl's death go unpunished."

Her voice grew stronger as the inner determination that powered her through her often-ugly days clicked into place. Her hold on him loosened, secondary to the spinning of her thoughts. And a deep, dark worry began to gnaw at Max as he remembered where Mary Kate Malone's cause had led her.

"Help me, Max."

His breath stopped for a moment. "How?"

"Help me find out who scared and hurt and killed this girl, and help me punish him. Will you do that for me?"

"I would do anything for you, Charlotte. Not for your badge. For you."

"Then promise me. Promise you will."

He was hearing the bargaining voice of Mary Kate Malone, weighing his guilt against her grievances. He should heed the wariness whispering that he needed to have Charlotte spell out more specifically what she wanted him to do. Instead, he said, "I will. I promise. I love you, Charlotte."

No reply in kind. Just a quietly relieved "Thank you, Max." Her arms relaxed about his neck and she nuzzled his throat with a sleepy sensuality.

"Let's get you to bed."

"Yes," she murmured. "Take me to bed, Savoie."

He lifted her easily, carrying her through the dark apartment, heading for the bedroom. He freed one hand to pull down her carelessly arranged covers, then sat her on the mattress edge. Her arms went up agreeably so he could skim off her T-shirt. He was grateful to see plain ivory cotton beneath it instead of the naughty confections she sometimes wore to shock his libido into reckless overdrive. She flopped onto her back and obligingly canted her hips up so he could peel down her snug jeans. He was very, very careful not to let his hands graze her soft skin. He was rolling off her socks when she sat up. As his head lifted in question, her palms scooped beneath his jaw, holding him in place for a rather sloppy kiss.

Because his willpower turned to melted wax the second she touched him, he quickly leaned back out of her reach.

"You taste like cigarette butts floating in stale beer, detective."

She was too groggy to whip up more than a mild grumble of irritation. "Considering what you've been known to dine on, I had no idea your taste buds were so discriminating." She crawled up to her pillow, dragging the sheet to her chin. As she burrowed in with a weary sigh, she murmured, "Would you lock up for me?"

"Sure."

"Thanks."

Even as she spoke, Cee Cee's eyes were closing beneath the pull of exhaustion. The rips of emotion were finally at a manageable ebb. She would sleep, deep and dreamlessly now, and when she awoke, a new sense of purpose would be waiting.

She never heard him leave the room. And when she opened her eyes, it was morning.

She was immediately aware of two things. Her mouth tasted like her socks had been lying in it, and the sheets beside her were empty. She rimmed her teeth with her tongue and grimaced. Her breath had probably driven him out of the room. She lay on her back and listened for him, hearing no movement in the apartment. But that wasn't unusual. Max Savoie moved like a ghost.

Thinking of which, she let her gratitude toward him for chasing her ghosts away deepen into a feeling that still surprised her at times. And because it made her a bit uncomfortable, she focused on a simpler, safer emotion. Lust.

"Max?"

A glance at the clock told her there was time for what she had in mind. Perhaps even twice. She smiled as her mind began to clear—and then she became more aware of the silence.

"Max?"

There was no sign of his clothes—just hers where he'd laid them after putting her to bed. The covers beside her were undisturbed because he hadn't shared them with her.

Damn.

When she'd asked him to lock up, she hadn't meant behind him.

Three

MAX WALKED THROUGH the French Quarter, half listening to the sounds of the city that woke only after sunset. The other half of him ruefully considered the warning he'd never thought to heed: that Charlotte Caissie would only hurt him.

He'd been in love with her for almost half of his life, though he'd barely spoken a handful of words to her for eight of those twelve years. Since the first fateful time they'd crossed paths, she'd become one of only three people he'd ever trusted.

She'd hit him like a locomotive while he stood frozen on the tracks, unable to move out of the way even as the whistle shrieked in warning. His emotions had been a train wreck ever since. He'd simply not been prepared for her. He'd been startled, then amused when she got in his face, that sassy, sexy mouth ripping into him as if he was some small-time pickpocket rather than the power behind the most powerful criminal in New Orleans. And he could think of nothing else but how those lips would taste.

She was a cop, the antithesis of everything he'd been since Jimmy Legere took him out of the swamps.

Legere had groomed him from the time he was led away from the decomposing body of his mother to be the perfect weapon to wield against his enemies. A fierce, emotionless killer, he'd been feared since he was a teen. He'd heard them say he murdered without conscience, but that wasn't true. He hadn't measured the right or wrong of what he did against the tremendous need to repay the man who'd rescued him. Doing whatever was asked of him. Without question, without pause. Until Charlotte Caissie.

She and her friend Mary Kate Malone had been held hostage in a dockside warehouse by a couple of Legere's goons as leverage to keep Charlotte's cop father from testifying. They'd been little more than children in the hands of cruel, amoral men, and Jimmy swore to him that the plan was never to harm them. But harm them they had, in ways that still sickened him to the soul. So he'd stepped in to free them, but not until he'd debated for long hours over doing so without Jimmy's permission. A delay that cost the two girls unforgivable suffering.

To make amends, he'd acted as an avenger for the adult Mary Kate's crusade to protect the weak and vulnerable—beginning a chain reaction of conflicting loyalties that ended with Mary Kate lying in a California hospital in a coma from which she might never awaken, and with Jimmy Legere in a vault in St. Louis No. 1, where he would remain forever. And still it wasn't enough.

What did he have to do to be worthy of her?

He paused to toss some bills into the open case of a sax player on the corner of Chartres and St. Ann. He didn't notice how much it was, but the young black man in his top hat and colorful patchwork jacket sputtered with gratitude and demanded he name a song. "Play something foolishly sentimental," Max said.

He walked along the edge the square to the melancholy tones of the horn, thinking how perfectly they echoed the dark brooding of his soul.

How could Cee Cee have doubted him that morning?

He understood the needs of her job. Considering the circumstances, he'd expected her and her partner to come calling. But not to have her look at him through those flat, sharklike cop eyes when it was just the two of them alone and demand he prove his alibi.

He'd been angry, insulted. He was still pissed about it now. So he'd gone to her apartment to force a confrontation. Was it too much to expect her to believe him, to believe *in* him, when he'd surrender everything for her? *Everything*.

The pain of her distrust cut him in two.

But he hadn't gotten the chance to vent his irritation. Instead, she'd wound him up by the heartstrings and spun him like a top.

Help me, Max.

Didn't she know what she was asking? Wasn't it enough he'd sacrificed the man he'd thought of as a father? Did she expect him to turn upon his own kind, too?

He growled in self-disgust. He was pathetic. He'd had to force himself to walk away from her, from the temptation of lying beside her, for fear she'd have him rolling over like a dog begging favor with his feet waving in the air.

I promise.

What the hell had he just given away over a few tears and the press of feminine curves?

Anything. Everything.

Was that what being in love did to the male of the species? Even if he was a male of another species?

Suddenly he stopped in midstride, in midthought, and went completely still.

His breath caught.

Awareness of something unexpected crept over him, a faint prickling, and suddenly he was all icy gooseflesh.

He continued walking, his senses all turned outward now, sweeping like psychic radar. What was it? *Who* was it? He'd felt this strange quiver of energy once before, but its source was a mystery then, just as it was now. He casually skimmed the sidewalk and business fronts with his gaze, not sure what he was looking for. But he could feel it. Power. Focused. Nearby. Unmistakably from one of his own kind.

Then, it was gone. As quick as it had come over him, the feeling disappeared. Just like that. A stranger had reached out to ring his doorbell, then run away before he answered.

Disturbed and restless out in the open, Max moved with swift purpose. Dodging down mist-draped backstreets, away from the pulse of the city nightlife, into shadows lying dark and faintly menacing, he sought out an unmarked back door. He tapped in a distinct pattern, and it opened to a newly discovered world.

Cheveux du Chien. Hair of the Dog. The name amused him with its appropriateness. The moment he stepped inside its unique patrons welcomed him, touching his psyche lightly on a preternatural level like the warm embrace of family. The experience was still new enough to make him shiver at the strangeness of it.

"Mr. Savoie," the darkly lovely female at the door crooned with more invitation than necessary, "your table is ready."

He followed the twitch of her skirt down the long hall that opened into a multitiered night-club, all nonreflective black paint, ductwork, and pulley-systemed warehouse chic. Tonight heavy metal music assaulted the eardrums, and from the shadows, eyes gleamed red and gold.

His kind.

Charlotte Caissie had given them, and him, a name. Shape-shifters.

Jacques LaRoche stood at the bar. A huge, bald mountain, he ran the dockworkers who'd once been under the hand of Victor Vantour. The owner of the exclusive club with its unnatural clientele, LaRoche was a conduit through which all information flowed. Max had sought him out down on the wharf earlier that day, but he'd been unavailable. Their relationship was tenuous. It wasn't quite friendship—not without a little more trust. But there was a foundation of respect. And underlying it, fear. Because of what Max was, and what he could do that no other in the room could match.

He was a pureblood.

Up until a month ago, he hadn't known what that meant. He hadn't known there were any others even remotely like him. He hadn't known what *he* was, except that he was different.

"Savoie," LaRoche called out, his voice booming. Big, bold, aggressive, he never spoke quietly, never moved cautiously. Only to Max Savoie was he subservient. He pulled out a chair and dropped down at Max's table. "Where's your scrappy little girl tonight? She doesn't hold a grudge, does she?"

"If she did, you'd certainly know about it by now."

LaRoche chuckled. He harbored an instinctive dislike for most humans, but Charlotte Caissie had earned his reluctant admiration. She was a fighter. And she held Max's heart in a fierce, greedy fist.

"Who killed Sandra Cummings?"

LaRoche's smile faded. "No foreplay first? Won't even buy me a drink?"

"I need to know. My girl recognized the way she died as by one of us. She came to me for answers."

His eyes narrowed warily. "Are you going to give them to her?"

"Depends on what I hear. What have you heard?"

"No one here is any fan of Cummings. He interferes in our means of making a living, crowding us out with his condos and his resorts. We can't get work there because we have no papers. Many have expressed a wish to run him down in a dark alley. But murder his child? No. That's not our way. That's the human way. It was your way, Savoie. Look to them, not among us."

Max considered that. So if not one of them, then who? Who recognized him for what he was, enough to orchestrate a killing that would point to him and his? Who would benefit from laying the blame at his door? *Everyone.* The rival bosses, Cummings's people, the police, even factions within his own cadre of followers. And he needed to know why. Quickly. Not just to satisfy his promise to Charlotte, but for his own survival.

"Has anyone you don't know been hanging around lately?"

A laugh. "Do you think I recognize every shifter in New Orleans?"

"Probably, if there's work to be done or money to be spent."

Another loud chuckle. "Two things that rarely escape me." He thought a minute. "No one comes to mind. We're a pretty tight clan. We can sense outsiders."

Knowledge, Jimmy always told him, was power. And he had so much to learn.

"Jacques," he began casually, "why is it that you never sensed what I was, or I who you were, until the first night I came in here?"

LaRoche leaned back, getting comfortable. "We call it a glimmer, that sense we get of one another. It's not quite smell, not touch, not sight. In some, it's just a whisper. With the stronger ones, it's a signature. The cleaner the bloodline, the less diluted by mingling with humans, the stronger the glimmer. I can recognize most of those here tonight by the vibration of their glimmer."

"And me?"

"Sometimes."

"Only sometimes?"

"In here, yes. You're unmistakable. But out there, no. There's no feel of you at all. But you must know that."

He didn't, but he had to be careful. He couldn't afford to let LaRoche discover how little he knew about what he was. He'd had no one to teach him the finer points, only the broad, brutal aspects of his powers.

He tested the surroundings, able, if he concentrated, to separate out the subtle impressions. Vibrations. Like variations on the same note, similar yet distinct. Interesting.

"So it's not something everyone can control?"

LaRoche was looking at him strangely. "No. We're on all the time, like high- or low-watt bulbs. But you can switch it on and off. That's why we feared you. Because we couldn't sense you as one of us. What a gift that must be—that control that comes with being of pure blood."

A gift.

"You're special. You're blessed."

He could hear his mother's voice telling him those things over and over. Was this what she'd meant?

"Any others like that around here?" Perhaps out on the streets, casting off an unrecognizable signature? Killing young women with careless or perhaps very purposeful indiscretion?

"Around here, no." LaRoche's manner wasn't so relaxed now.

"But you know of others," Max pressed.

"Yes."

"Where are they?"

"Up north. They come down here now and again."

"For what?"

"Whatever they want," LaRoche snapped with an aggravated sharpness. "Why the interest? This isn't something we talk of. It's something that we try to forget exists. I suggest you try that."

Their waitress stepped between them to refresh their drinks. LaRoche had water with a greater part of Jim Beam. As the waitress leaned in over Max's shoulder to refill his water, her other hand rested lightly on his back.

"Can I get you anything else, Mr. Savoie?"

Her voice was a velvet ripple. He turned toward her, only to get a face full of voluptuous bosom bared by the low V of her shirt.

His gaze jumped awkwardly away. "I'm fine. Thank you."

When she straightened, her nose brushed his hair and he heard her inhale his scent. He held his breath until she stood away.

"If you think of anything, my name is Amber."

LaRoche laughed at Max's anxious expression. "Amber, you've an eye for the fellas." As she started to scowl, Jacques patted her fanny. "You seen any strangers around lately? Someone not of our clan?"

She removed his hand from her hip, then smiled at Max. "There is one who comes to mind. Older fella, keeps to the shadows. I heard he asked after you, Mr. Savoie, like he knew who you were but had never seen you before."

Max's insides tensed. He heard the whisper of his mother's warning. *"They'll find you. They'll hurt you. They'll take you away."*

LaRoche was studying him carefully, maybe seeing more than Max would like. He gave Amber's rump a squeeze. "You tell me if you see him in here again, will you? Think you can remember, sugar?"

She shrugged. "Sure, boss. That's easy. He left about ten minutes ago, after a couple a shots and a beer." Her gaze slid over Max. "Be happy to be on the lookout for you, Mr. Savoie." She slapped at Jacques's hand, ignoring his grin.

LaRoche followed the swivel of the waitress's hips appreciatively. "You lucky dog. Ah, to be you for just one night."

Max frowned. What a novel idea. He'd always wished to be anyone else. Anyone human. "Why?"

"Look around. You could have any one of them."

Max scanned the smoky room. Every female gaze was either blatantly or covertly fixed on him, he realized with an uncomfortable start. And the glimmers they gave off pulsed with heat. More alarmed than aroused by the interest, he shut himself off so he wouldn't feel the caress of their roving desire.

"I already have all the woman I want."

LaRoche shrugged. "But she's not of us. What she doesn't know won't hurt her. A shame to waste such a delightful perk of being what you are."

"What I'd be is dead meat."

"She keeps you on a short chain, my friend."

Max admitted the truth without shame. "It's one I have no desire to escape."

LaRoche's big hand slapped down on his shoulder. "I don't know if I should envy you or pity you for that." His stare skipped back to Amber. "Tonight I think I'll simply be grateful that you prefer captivity to the chase. If you'll excuse me, I think I'll go see if she'll settle for second best. Be careful, Savoie."

"What do you mean?"

"There isn't a one of them who wouldn't kill to mate with you."

Surely he meant that figuratively.

"Why? Because of what I am?"

"No. Because of what you can give them." He walked away, muttering, "Lucky dog."

CEE CEE STOOD over Devlin Dovion's shoulder as he weighed what was left of Sandra Cummings's internal organs. The sound track from *Guys and Dolls* played in the background. Dovion was nuts about Broadway, traveling with his wife and daughters to New York once a year just to sit in a narrow seat at the Majestic or Lycium and lose himself in song. He was humming "Sit Down, You're Rockin' the Boat" as he scooped up half the usual length of small intestine in gloved hands.

"So, how are things going with you and your fella?" he asked.

"What?"

"Don't look so shocked. Gossip eventually travels downstream far enough to reach me here in my little pond. What's his name? Savoie?"

"Max Savoie."

"Seems to be a decent-enough sort."

"Max?" she blurted in surprise. Who would have told him that? "Most would characterize him as a mobster and a murderer."

"I seem to recall hearing he was involved in the messy business with Legere. Could you pass me that bowl, darlin'?" He spilled the entrails into it as if they were pasta. "Does he treat you good?"

"Yes. Yes, he does."

"Has he killed anyone we like?"

"Not that I know of."

"Then why should I have a problem with him? It's the opinion of some that the police are mobsters and murderers. I don't always put stock in what folks are saying. It's those upstanding citizens you have to worry about—them and their secrets. Professional criminals are usually the most level folks. They raise good families, pay their parking fines, give generously to charities, love their wives, children, and dogs. They're scrupulously honest and cry at sad movies. It's not personal, what they do. It's business. When it's not business, when it's not up front, that's when it gets ugly."

Cee Cee had never considered it quite that way.

"When do I get to meet him?"

She gave a start. "You want to meet Max?"

"Of course. Why wouldn't I? You're as close to me as my own daughters. If you're serious about him, I want to give him the once-over to see if I need to kick his ass to set his thinking straight where you're concerned." When Cee Cee simply stared at him, he began to frown. "What? Has he got something against your friends? I mean, other than the obvious." He paused. "Are you serious about him, Lottie?"

"Yes."

Dovion grinned. "Miserably said, like a woman in love."

She didn't argue.

"Bring him on down with you next time you visit. He's not queasy, is he?"

She snorted a laugh. "Not hardly." A moment's thought. "You'd probably like each other. You both have that rather twisted sense of the macabre."

"Wonderful. I'll let him put on gloves and get his hands dirty." He made it sound as though they were going to play in modeling clay instead of chest cavities.

Cee Cee scowled a bit jealously. Dovion hadn't let her touch anything until she'd made First Grade. "It's probably just the kind of date activity he'd enjoy."

"Good. I like him already. Now, what is it you need to know about this poor little lady?"

"The basics. Causation, for starters."

Dovion half closed his eyes, viewing the scene through the science, as if her death was a play unfolding before him. "She was at her car, her keys in her hand. Her assailant approached her there from behind. The keys were found beneath the vehicle. Signs of a brief struggle. She fell, scraping her knees, but was able to get to her feet and run. There are no signs of any offensive wounds, so I'm a bit puzzled as to why she was able to just run away from him. Maybe he got distracted by something or someone. Anyway, she'd gotten three blocks when he hit her from behind, tackled her, and brought her down, face-first on the sidewalk with him on top of her."

Cee Cee tensed, her stomach clenching, her breath coming soft and quick as she imagined the panic, the pain, the terror.

"Do you want me to go on?" There was an expected kindness in Dovion's voice. He'd been the one to pick her up at the hospital when she was the same age as his eldest girl. He'd been there because her father was out on the Gulf somewhere following a lead. There were no secrets between them. He knew how difficult it was for her to stand there and speak of this atrocity with a degree of distance.

"Yes, of course," she told him. "Go ahead."

"He raped her. And then he killed her."

"Come on, Dev. Don't be shy with the details. It's nothing I haven't heard before." It was nothing she hadn't experienced before.

"It was a particularly vicious assault, lots of tearing and internal bleeding. But at least it was quick. He bit her shoulder and her neck, severed her jugular. She bled out in minutes. I don't think she was aware of the rest of what he did to her."

"Thank God for that."

He nodded, looking sadly at the still face of the victim that he'd never seen flushed with life.

"You mentioned bites. Human bites?"

Dovion studied the dead girl, his features looking perplexed. "No. Not exactly. No."

"Are they the same type of wounds you found on those two down in the Quarter?"

"Gautreaux and Surette? Yes, same type."

"Can you tell if it's the same perp?" Her breath froze as she waited for his reply.

"I haven't finished all the testing, but it looks like a different bite radius. My guess: not the same attacker. I'll have to do some casts to be sure."

Her eyes closed. *Not Max. Thank you, thank you, thank you.*

Real proof of what she'd already known in her heart.

Dovion was watching her. "What's going on, Charlotte? What do you know that you're not telling me? What's killing these people? Spratt wasn't the only one, was he? I'd say who, but I think it's more a what, isn't it?"

"I don't know what or who killed this girl. That's what I was hoping you could tell me."

He scrutinized her for an uncomfortably long moment then sighed. He clearly knew there was more to it, and someday soon, she knew, he would press harder for that truth. But not today.

"Well," he said at last, "I will tell you one thing. If you bring in any suspects and you do a line up, you'll want to do it from the waist down, too."

She blinked. "Why's that?"

"Because your boy here is, shall we say, endowed beyond a porn star's wildest dreams. He literally ripped that poor girl apart."

DOVION'S WORDS STAYED with her, a cold residue she couldn't wash away. On mental autopilot, she sat in on a meeting with the investigating team, compared notes with Babineau, checked the too-long list of sex offenders for any similarities. By the time she headed for her car, she was knotted up tight from the effort of keeping it all safely contained inside.

It was late, past nine, so she went to her apartment. No messages on her phone. Nothing in her rooms but shadows. She paced those rooms, arms about herself to control her shivering. Finally she pulled an exquisitely expensive men's suit jacket from her closet and put it on. The weight, the feel, and the scent provided an immediate comfort. But still, it wasn't enough to hold the mounting worry at bay.

Not Max, but like Max.

In asking for his help, she was asking him to turn in one of his own. If she couldn't come up with a believable suspect, how was she ever going to clear Max of suspicion? By having him volunteer a bite impression? How could she exonerate him without revealing what he was? She had to convince him that this was about far more than what she believed. It was about what she could prove to others.

She drove out to River Road, and as her car approached the opening in the stone wall surrounding Legere's estate, the wrought-iron gates swung wide to let her in.

"He's not here, Detective Caissie," she was told by the poker-faced woman who met her at the door. Helen was her name.

"Where is he? When do you expect him back?"

"He didn't say. Of course, you are welcome to wait."

There was an uneasiness in that invitation. Jimmy Legere's former staff wasn't certain how to treat their new boss's relationship with the law. He'd told them to open all doors for her, but that didn't make them happy about it.

"Can I get you something, detective?"

Yes. Max. Get me Max.

"No, thank you," Cee Cee told her with cool civility, well aware of the woman's dislike of her. And unwilling to suffer it until Max's return. "I'll wait upstairs."

Helen opened her mouth, then snapped it closed to grit out, "Very good, detective. I'll tell Mr. Savoie you invited yourself up when he arrives."

"You do that." *Bitch.*

She jogged up the wide curve of the stairs, her starched manner lasting only until she closed the door to Max's bedroom behind her. Then the need for pretense was gone.

She shed her clothes and slipped under the fine sheets covering Max's bed, burrowing, huddling, waiting anxiously. Afraid to sleep until she'd had the chance to explain herself to him. Afraid to close her eyes lest the dreams be crouched and ready to spring.

Please, Max. Hurry. I need you.

HE WAS SURPRISED to see her car blocking the front steps. She didn't know how to park in an accommodating manner. There was little she did do that was accommodating. He slipped inside the house. All was darkness at 3 a.m. He stood at the foot of the stairs, eyes closed, reaching up to her with his highly developed senses.

She was sleeping fitfully, warm and naked in his bed, tears long since dried on her cheeks. The need to go up to her rose in an inevitable tide, one he resisted on this lonely, unhappy night.

Had she come for answers or reassurances?

Probably both.

Or just with more veiled accusations?

He wasn't in the mood to face any of them.

Soundlessly, while everyone slept but the men paid to watch the surveillance cameras, Max went inside the big, empty room Jimmy Legere had used as his office. He rarely went there. Too many ghosts, too many memories; some bittersweet, some monstrous. Tonight it was a sanctuary, a place to escape the expectations of others.

Months ago he'd stood at Jimmy's back, content to be in his shadow. He'd enjoyed a spirited flirtation with a certain police detective and he'd pretty much lived his life under the radar. He was avoided, ignored, and had no problem with that. Things were so uncomplicated then. He understood his role. He had no great conflicts of heart and soul. But all that had changed.

He went down to his knees slowly, then wearily onto all fours.

"Jimmy, why did you give me all this without teaching me what to do with it?"

He took a shaky breath, exhausted, uncertain, alone. There was a woman upstairs he loved more than his life, who was about to use and discard him. There was a bloodstain on the floor where he'd lost the only guiding force in his life. He'd been pushed from the shadows into the glare of attention—from the media, from the police, from the various corners of the huge empire he now controlled so blindly, and he felt paralyzed with inadequacy. And a wary alarm.

Someone was stalking him, unseen, for reasons unknown. Someone from his mother's past, from that mysterious "up north" LaRoche had mentioned? A body lay in the morgue, the nature of death pointing to him in neon. There was no one to trust, no one to confide in. And tonight he could no longer pretend it didn't matter to him.

He lay down on the cool parquet flooring the way he would if he was in his lowest, most basic form. His hand touched the stain that no amount of scrubbing of wood or conscience could remove. He closed his eyes tightly and whispered, "Jimmy, please. Jimmy, please tell me what to do."

Four

CEE CEE WOKE to the inviting scent of chicory coffee. It was an effort to drag her eyes open, even more so to recognize where she was. Unrelieved white walls lifting to a twelve-foot ceiling. Cotton sheets as smooth as satin. No roar of road traffic. The sweet tang of mock orange instead of Iberia hot sauce from the crab shack down the street.

"Good morning."

And a sound like no other: the low seismic rumble of Max Savoie's voice.

He leaned with his back against the jamb of the French doors that led out onto the balcony. He was dressed in the easy drape of a black suit, his white shirt open at the neck. Short black hair was still damp from the shower and the hard angles of his face were smoothly shaven. With pure morning light reflecting off the green of his eyes, he looked like hot sex in shiny shoes.

She was suddenly wide-awake.

"Why are you already dressed?"

"I've got an early meeting in the city and I didn't want to disturb you."

Disturb wasn't exactly the verb that came to mind. "When did you get in?"

"Late. I didn't know you were going to be here. I'm sorry."

He didn't sound it. He sounded . . . wary.

Her confidence jerked to a shuddering halt. "I should have called first. I shouldn't have assumed I'd be welcome."

"You can come here anytime. I've told you that."

So why didn't she feel like it was true this morning? She sat up, keeping the sheet trapped under her armpits. She needn't have bothered. There was no spark of anything in his steady stare.

"I wanted to see you," she began carefully. "I wanted to talk to you about the words we had in your office."

"What words were those?"

He was angry. Or was it something else? Sometimes he was so hard to read. Hell, most of the time she felt like she was stuck with only the foreign language directions that accompanied their relationship. And there weren't even any pictures to help.

"I know you didn't kill that girl. I only asked about you being gone because I wanted to be able to eliminate you completely as a possible suspect. I was just doing my job. It wasn't personal. I'm sorry if it felt that way."

He didn't blink. Finally some of the stiffness eased from his expression. "I apologize for feeling offended."

She smiled. Crisis averted. "Besides, Dovion will be able to confirm that the bite marks on the girl weren't the same as those on Gautreaux and Surette."

Max didn't move. "Was this before or after you decided to have faith in me? Nothing like belief when it's backed by fact first."

"Why are you so angry with me?"

That surprised him. "I'm not angry. I never get angry."

She arched a brow. "Really? Then that must have been someone else threatening to eat that redheaded guy's face if he didn't take his hands off me."

"That wasn't anger."

"What was it? Small talk?"

The stern set of his lips twitched.

"If you're not angry, come over here."

Caution crept into his gaze.

"Come here. Coward."

That brought a flash into his stare. He came away from the doorframe and strode to the bed with his strangely graceful yet powerful stride. He stopped just out of reach.

"Closer."

He took another step and she stood, catching the lapels of his jacket as the sheet dropped away. She touched her mouth to his, then leaned back. His eyes were closed. He never closed his eyes when they kissed.

"Max, what's wrong? What is it? Please tell me."

He rested his head on her shoulder, the breath sighing from him wearily. "It's nothing. I'm sorry I'm being . . . how do you put it? Pissy? I'm just tired and overwhelmed. I'm not used to having to be everything to everyone, with all of them pulling in different directions."

"What can I do?"

"Stop pulling."

She touched the back of his head, letting her fingers trickle through his silky hair. She knew from listening to Babineau that in a relationship, each partner was supposed to be the other's port in emotional storms. She was at a loss there. Hers wasn't a quiet, comforting nature; she preferred to wade right in swinging.

Where had Max learned to be so damned perfect at it? All she had to do was hint at an approaching meltdown and he had her wrapped up tight in a cocoon of care. She wanted to do that for him, to be there for him, but she had no nurturing role models to turn to for advice. Babineau's dewy-eyed wife? No thank you. She'd rather muddle through on her own.

"I'm sorry," she told him with a cut-to-the-chase candor that wasn't particularly sensitive, but at least was honest. "I get so caught up in my job that I sometimes forget that you're in the middle."

His hands came around her, one sliding between her shoulder blades, one following the curve of her spine down to the small of her back, both making restless, soothing circles. Her body went liquid. Oh, yes. He was damned near perfect.

"It's okay."

"If I'm pushing and pulling, it's because this case is so personal," she confessed softly. "Everything about it takes me back, makes me feel helpless and scared and angry. I want to nail the man who did this to that poor girl, who made her face all the awful things I had to. Until I have him, I can't concentrate on anything else, I don't have time for anything else, I'm no good for anything else. I know that's not fair, but I'll make it up to you. I will."

Her tone had grown hard and fierce, vibrating with the passion that made her job more than just that. She hadn't meant it to take over; she'd wanted to concentrate on him—and here she was shoving him out of the way.

It was a vendetta she had against those who harmed the innocent. She and Mary Kate Malone had gone after their demons in different ways. She became a cop. Mary Kate became Sister Catherine. And both used Max as a tool toward that personal and spiritual vengeance. And what a fierce, avenging tool he was.

Max stepped away from the temptation of Charlotte Caissie. He held her gaze with a flat stare, giving her what she wanted.

"I went to the club last night after I left your apartment. I went to see to my promise." He told her the gist of his conversation with Jacques LaRoche, perhaps unintentionally confining the information to the dock clan—not including the spooky unknowns of the North. Nor did he share the disturbing contacts he'd had from that unidentified source. He wasn't sure he wanted her exploring those areas, for the protection of all involved.

Her expression grew thoughtful, her attention focused beyond the room where she stood naked beside his bed. She might as well have been wearing a uniform.

"Do you believe him? Did you get the sense he was trying to cover up for someone?"

Max shrugged. "Yes and no. I don't think he was lying to me, but I've no reason to think he'd be entirely truthful if it wasn't to his advantage." He quickly skimmed her sleek nudity. "You should get dressed, detective, since you're already on the clock."

She eyed her rumpled clothes. "Can I borrow a shirt?" Then she added a bit shyly, "Maybe I should start leaving a few things here."

"If you like," he murmured with an astonishing lack of enthusiasm, after he'd campaigned so ardently for her to claim a small portion of his closet. "I have to go."

"I can give you a lift in, if you can wait for me to grab a shower."

"Thanks, but I'm in a hurry."

Piqued by his gruff rejection, she jerked a T-shirt out of his dresser, grumbling, "I don't remember Jimmy Legere running into the city every day."

"Jimmy had people there that he trusted. I don't. I have to be on top of things or they'll get pulled out from under me. I'll let you know if I find out anything else that might interest you."

She slipped his shirt over her head. For a moment, he couldn't take his eyes off her.

"Good-bye, detective." His words were soft and tight-throated.

As he started to turn away, she said, "Max? When will I see you?"

"I don't know. It seems like we're both too busy to find time for each other."

Something anxious swelled within her heart and filled her uplifted gaze. "Find time."

He smiled faintly. "I'll try if you will."

She waited until she heard the front door close before going out onto the balcony, leaning against the railing. He emerged from the shadow of the house to stride across the lawn toward the carriage house where Legere's marvelous collection of cars was kept. Cars Max didn't know how to drive. One of which he'd given to her as a gift.

She loved watching him. He moved differently when he thought he was alone. Quicker. So quick, sometimes he seemed to blur. The irony of him going off to work at LE International troubled her. Jimmy Legere's teasing, relentlessly lovelorn leg breaker was now a somber executive in his designer suit and Italian leather. Something gave way in her chest, like a lynchpin holding the gate to her emotions closed.

Gripping the rail, she leaned out and said softly, "I love you, Savoie."

He stopped.

For a moment he just stood there in the damp grass, the slant of early sunrise gleaming off his dark head. Then he turned, gaze lifting. Nothing changed in his expression as he touched his fingertips to his mouth and waved the kiss her way.

His image shimmered, forcing her to blink rapidly. "Wait!" she called.

She darted back into his room, returning in seconds.

"You forgot your shoes."

He caught the red high-tops she tossed down, holding them to his chest in bemusement.

"You're mine, Max. I'm not going to let them have *all* of you."

He levered off the shiny shoes that had become a frightening symbol of the changes demanded from him. Then he slipped into the Converses—the footwear of her savior of twelve years ago, of the man who'd courted her with unflagging determination and simmering innuendo, of the lover who'd stolen her affections and filled her dreams with a sense of safety. He laced them quickly, then straightened.

Her desire for him began to simmer. "You are *so* hot."

He smiled. "Get some clothes on before I'm tempted to come back inside."

Boldly she gripped the hem of the T-shirt and pulled it up to her chin.

He blinked, then his sober expression split with a wide, wicked grin.

"See you soon," she called down to him, restoring her modesty and his ability to breathe.

"Yes, you will."

He strode away, leaving the shiny shoes in the grass. She could hear his low chuckle, and was able to let him go.

MAX ENTERED THE garage, still smiling foolishly, to find Giles St. Clair, his quasi bodyguard, lounging on the hood of a BMW, slurping up a bowl of grits with red-eye gravy.

The big thug grinned and nodded toward the house. "Nice way to start the morning, with breakfast and a show."

Max drew up short, a dangerous glitter in his eyes. At one time, that look would have reduced the larger man to quivering. Now he simply set his bowl aside with a good-natured laugh.

"Yeah, yeah, I know. You'll eat my eyes on toast. Might be worth it, if that's the last picture stuck on my brain." He opened the car door. "You're a lucky man, Max."

He considered that with some surprise, then answered quietly, "Yes. Yes, I am," as he got in the car.

WITHOUT MAX IN it, the huge house held no appeal. Cee Cee pulled on her stale clothes and snatched up her keys. Cup of coffee in hand, she went downstairs, slowing when faced with the austere glare of the housekeeper.

She hoisted her cup. "Great coffee. Thanks, Helen."

"Is there anything else I can get you, detective? I was just about to straighten up Mr. Legere's office after Mr. Savoie slept there last night."

Oh, what a not-so-subtle jab to the kidney *that* was. Cee Cee regarded Helen with reassessing eyes. "I think I'd like some eggs hussarde. You can bring them to me in the study. Thank you, Helen. You've made me feel right at home."

She stepped inside Jimmy Legere's office, hesitating just inside the door because she could feel the old bastard's disapproval of her presence vibrating through the room. The gloating sense of victory she allowed herself faded when she saw Max's coat on the red leather couch, where he must have slept beneath its drape instead of coming upstairs to share the sheets with her.

Why hadn't he come up? Why hadn't he stayed with her in her apartment? Things had been going so wonderfully well, in her inexperienced estimation. Why all the tension and mixed messages now? It wasn't her fault the city had pulled the plug on their idyllic vacation week. It made her head ache, trying to decipher his almost invisible signals and to second-guess how he might interpret her every word. He was pissed off about her questioning him—that much she got. And, okay, she didn't blame him. But he knew that was her job, so what was the big deal?

She needed to get him back into bed. They never had any trouble understanding each other there.

She made a wide circle around the rusty stains on the floorboards, remembering the harsh pang of horror she'd felt when she'd expected that gruesome splatter of blood and brain to be Max's instead of Jimmy's.

"You've lost, Jimmy. Let him go. Let him the fuck go."

"Excuse me, detective. Did you want one egg or two?"

Cee Cee gave a guilty start, then faced the scowling housekeeper. "One."

Helen began to turn, then confronted Cee Cee with a level stare. "Mr. Legere doted on him, you know."

"I know."

"And Mr. Max loved Mr. Legere like a father. You're the reason he's dead. Max may care for you, but he's never going to forget that. Not ever."

"I know that, too."

"Show some respect when you're in this house."

"It's Max's house now."

"You think so? Then you're a fool. Did you still want your egg?"

"Yes. Please. On second thought, make it two. I find myself wanting to tear into something substantial."

Her combative manner fell away when the older woman left. Because Helen was right. Jimmy Legere, living or dead, would always stand between any complete happiness she might have with Max. As long as he lived in this house, he would belong to the man who had raised him on that short leash. And by letting her job drive an even bigger wedge between them, she was playing right into Jimmy's selfish hands.

She picked up Max's coat, bringing the battered brown leather up to her nose. She slipped her arms into the sleeves and wrapped its generous bulk around her, enjoying its weight and warmth. Comforted, strengthened by the feel of him about her, she crossed to Jimmy's antique desk, plopping into the chair from which the old bandit had played puppeteer with the strings tying him to the interests he controlled throughout New Orleans. Interests on both sides of the law. Interests Max and Jimmy's vile cousin, Francis Petitjohn, who'd killed Legere in hopes of gaining his power, now managed in a precarious truce. She glanced at the blank computer screen, let her fingertips run over the silent keys. What secrets were held on its hard drive? What answers to the mysteries plaguing her life?

Would she find the truth behind her father's death?

The computer was probably passworded.

Her forefinger tapped restlessly on the space bar. Who would know it?

Max had told his household staff to grant her access to anything and everything in it. All she had to do was ask. Open sesame. She moved the mouse around, imagining Jimmy directing the rise and fall of companies, of lives, with the same movement.

Would she find a connection between Legere and the death of Sandra Cummings in some innocuous file with a simple double click?

And if she executed that double click, would she be irreparably damaging the fragile trust that bound her and Max together?

Yes. She pushed the mouse away, and pushed away from the temptation.

She stalked out into the hallway, nearly colliding with Jasmine, the pretty young servant whose duties she hadn't yet determined.

"Would you tell Helen I've changed my mind about breakfast? I have to go. Thank her for her trouble."

"Yes, detective. Is that Mr. Savoie's coat?"

"Yes, it is. Tell him I'll take good care of it. He knows where to find it. And me."

MAX WOULD NEVER have guessed her destination. If he'd suspected, he would have put a stop to it.

It was late afternoon, happy hour in most Big Easy establishments. *Cheveux du Chien* was no exception; alternative species were apparently equally eager to shake off the dust of labor with a cold one. She'd parked her car at a discreet distance to watch the comings and goings, while sipping coffee and taking pictures. It still amazed her. Here was a totally unknown race living, working, and breeding right in the heart of the city, under the very noses of its citizens and law enforcement officials. A race with its own culture, its own community, its own rules. And its own predators.

She was all about "live and let live," but one of them had ended that right to live for one of hers, and that could not be ignored. She had a plan in mind. Not a great one, but it was a start. She'd show the pictures to Sandra Cummings's friends and see if any of the images looked familiar. Maybe she'd get lucky. Maybe it was as simple as an imagined slight on the sidewalk, a discouraged advance at the bar that had triggered the attack.

She glanced down to put her empty cup into its holder, and turned back with the camera's viewfinder to her eye. But instead of the group of laborers on the opposite sidewalk, her screen was filled with a row of sharp canine teeth.

"Oh, fuck me!"

She lunged backward, trying to scramble over the gearshift column as hands reached through the open window to grip Max's jacket and drag her toward the door. Three of them stood next to her car, and none of them looked like they were there to ask her to join them for a drink. With her elbows pinned between the seat and the wheel, and her holster at the small of her back, there was no room to grab for her gun. She went for the automatic window. Before it had whirred halfway up, one of them smashed it off the track.

Writhing and cursing, she was pulled against the window frame with enough force to split the skin on her forehead. The feel of blood beginning to ooze sparked her temper and determination. She popped the door handle and threw herself against it, knocking the one who'd had a hold of her off balance. She came out low, in a roll, slipping between them to come up to her feet, her pistol quickly wedged up beneath one's chin.

"I'm a detective with the NOPD. Back off," she snarled at the other two. When they didn't heed the warning, she nudged the barrel more meaningfully. "Whaddaya say, sport? Wanna take one for the team, or do you tell them to stand down?"

The one she held on to dropped and feinted to the side. A jarring blow to her forearms from another numbed her fingers and her pistol clattered to the ground. Blood dripping into her eyes, she'd assumed an aggressive stance, ready to take on the three of them, when her elbows were suddenly clamped from behind.

"Here now, what's this? Easy, Detective Pretty. Nobody's gonna hurt you." She recognized the drawling voice of Jacques LaRoche's second in command, the redheaded Philo Tibideaux.

Contrarily she kicked out at the creature closest to her, the toe of her boot in his kneecap sending him stumbling back with a howl.

Tibideaux gave her an eyeball-rattling shake. "Stop it now." To the others he said brusquely, "What's going on?"

Her camera was recovered from the car, a damning bit of evidence quickly crushed between heel and pavement.

Cee Cee demanded, "I want to see LaRoche. Take me to him."

"Do you now? Does Savoie know you're here?"

She said nothing.

"I thought not." Tibideaux pushed her to one of the others, then bent to pick up her gun. "Hang onto her. Careful, she bites. And be careful you don't go bruising her, or Savoie might just bite off your head."

With Tibideaux leading the way, they dragged her down the alleyway to the entrance of the Shifter club. Once inside, she realized her mistake. She had no advantage here. She was in an alien world where her badge meant nothing. The only way she was going to get out alive was on sheer bravado and Max Savoie's name.

LaRoche was tending bar for the first-shift crew, who still wore their work clothes and smelled like the docks. They were immediately aware of her, picking up her human scent and turning almost as one to stare in hostile challenge. The low lighting glinted off ruby flickers in their eyes.

Only LaRoche offered a welcoming smile, a feral showing of teeth.

"Detective, what a surprise. If you're looking for Savoie, he's not here."

"She ain't here to socialize," Philo told him. With a lithe move, he vaulted the bar and leaned in close to whisper something to his boss. Though there was no change in his expression, Cee Cee could feel LaRoche tense.

"Take over for me here, Tib, whilst I make some talk with the detective." He handed Tibideaux the rag he was using to swab out glasses in exchange for the police-issue weapon and circled out from behind the bar. He was huge, easily six foot six or better, and all of it bulky muscle. He took Cee Cee's elbow, his dinner-plate-sized hand gentle but firm. "Let's you and me sit down a spell, detective. You want something from the bar? On the house."

"No. Thank you."

"Suit yourself."

He steered her through the crowd, up into the top tier of tables that were empty this early in the day. From there they could oversee the room and not be overheard, since the sound system was pounding decibels down like a heavy rain. LaRoche held out a chair for her, then turned the opposite one around so he could straddle the seat and lean meaty forearms upon its back as he studied her.

"Are you stupid?" he asked mildly. "You don't have the look of stupid about you, detective, but I could be wrong. Look down there. That's no petting zoo, darlin'. With half a reason, they'll turn you into a bar snack."

"Is that what one of them did to Sandra Cummings?"

He said nothing for a long minute. When he finally spoke, his tone was rough with impatience. "How you think it is that you knew nothing of us? How you think we live here, right in the middle of all you Uprights, like we was invisible? Because we work to stay that way, *cher*. You think you can clickety-click your pictures and show them to the world? I don't think so. What are we gonna do about you, detective?"

"Help me do my job, so others won't figure out what I know. Others who have no reason to keep quiet about it."

He frowned at that. "You think if I knew who did this careless, dangerous thing it wouldn't have been dealt with by now? And believe you me, detective, our ways of dealing with them who threaten our secret are a lot more final than yours. That'd be true even if it was Savoie's doing, now that he's one of ours."

That set her back in surprise, then had her bristling up. "It wasn't Max."

"I didn't say it was, darlin'. I'm just saying that what he done in the past, him and that other fella, brought a lot of attention to things we don't want considered. You done a right fine job of tidying up after Ben Spratt, hiding what he was behind a bunch of smoke and mirrors. We appreciated that, but know you done it for Max, not us. But if we go down, he goes down. There's no way to separate him from us anymore."

"I need to find this killer. If I don't, someone else will. And that someone else won't be playing kissy face with Savoie or give a damn about any of you."

LaRoche chuckled at her gruff tone and gritty logic. "Does he know you're here?"

"I don't run my investigation through him."

A bigger laugh. "You're not stupid, *cher*—you're dangerous. And I like that about you." Then he sobered. "If one of our kind is killing yours, it's our problem as much as yours, detective. If we find out before you do, we'll take care of it our way. Now go back to your world and forget about ours, lest you become the next statistic."

"MR. SAVOIE, CAN I be of some help to you?"

Max smiled up at the man standing on the opposite side of the rail. He was a big man, built like a boxer. His nose bore the breaks of it, angling in several different directions before mashing flat upon his face. His hands were huge, calloused, and scarred like those of a heavy laborer. Only the quiet confidence of his voice told of his current calling. That and the collar he wore.

"Father Furness. Just stopped in to see how the

repairs are going. And to ask after Sister Catherine."

"They're going very well, and we have you to thank for much of that. Your donation of immediate funds and manpower while we were waiting for the insurance to come through were a tremendous help. As for the sister"—his voice lowered regretfully—"no change."

Max looked away, awkward with the praise, unhappy with the news. "I owe Sister Catherine a great deal." He paused, then added, "She was my friend."

"She was a selfless crusader for the church and for the community. She is missed."

"Yes."

"How is Charlotte? I haven't seen her since Benjamin's funeral. It meant a lot to her to have you there."

"Did it?"

"Of course. Charlotte isn't one for forming close bonds with people, even as a child. The fact that she would reach out to you says a lot for you, Mr. Savoie."

"She misses Mary Kate. She worries about her. She dreams about the past. She won't let me help her get over that pain. I don't know what to do, and I'm afraid for her." He hadn't meant to say that, to say anything. Maybe it was the memory of the talks he'd had with Charlotte's best friend. Maybe it was the sense of peace he'd always found within this place. Or the kindness he saw in Father Furness's eyes.

"Charlotte doesn't think she needs any help to deal with anything. She's amazingly strong, but don't let her convince you that she's self-sufficient. It's that same strength that makes her so alone. If you stay close, she'll let you share that burden when she's ready. Have patience."

Max smiled. "I've been waiting for her for a long time. I can wait a while longer."

"Good. And what about you?"

"Me?"

"Who do you share your burdens with, now that Sister Catherine is gone? I'd be happy to take some of that load, if you'd let me."

Max laughed softly. "Father, mine isn't a burden I'd willingly wish upon another. But thank you for asking."

"Anytime, Max. I'm on call twenty-four/seven."

"You work Charlotte's hours."

"The gladly shouldered burden of those who serve. The door's always open."

"I'll remember that. Thank you, Father."

As he started down the aisle, the priest called out his name. He looked back.

"You're not beyond redemption, Max."

Max stared at him for a long moment, then smiled again, slowly, sadly. "You wouldn't say that if you knew what my burdens were."

"Maybe I understand more than you think. I have connections, you know. Come talk to me sometime."

"Perhaps I will."

Max stepped out into the hazy late afternoon and was in the middle of a big cleansing breath when awareness hit him like a knee to the groin. He gasped and grabbed the opening bar of the church's big door. Wave after wave of intense sensation hit him—not as a nudge, the way he'd experience at the club or on the street, but with the full force of a 12-gauge blasting through his psyche. He put up an instinctive defense against that invasive probing of self.

Then it was gone.

When he lowered his head to shake off the dizzying sickness, he was surprised to see bright spots of crimson dotting his shirtfront. His nose was bleeding? Pinching off the sudden flow, he looked about the street, gathering his inner control to throw out his own inquiry with the accuracy of a heat-seeking missile. He staggered when it hit, following the direction to a figure standing between two parked cars on the other side of the road. The man's smile goaded him.

Max came down the stairs with a fiercely controlled step. All his preternatural senses were shaking—not from danger, not from fear. From something bigger. Something huge.

The man waited for him to cross the street, that smug grin never changing until they were eye-to-eye.

"Hello, Max. I thought it was time I introduced myself."

"Who are you?" *What are you?*

"My name is Rollo. You can call me Daddy."

Five

THE SHOCK OF it blanked his mind. "Liar."

"Max—"

He took a rigid step back. "I have no father. Who are you, and why would you say such a thing to me?"

"You remind me of her. The same eyes. Those big green eyes, so full of life and mystery."

Max said nothing as he studied the other man. Rollo. The pureblood who'd walked behind Jimmy Legere's father. Whose reputation for viciousness far exceeded his own. He was tall, still lean and hard at fifty-some. Hair and brows thick and black, like his own. Face built of strong sharp angles, like his own. Smile slick, wide and white, like his own. While his mind rebelled against what he saw, his heart started beating faster.

"How is she? How is Marie?" Rollo asked.

"She's dead. Don't bother with condolences. They're almost thirty years late."

The stranger took a shallow breath and let out a regretful sigh. "So long ago, yet I can still remember the scent of lilac on her skin."

Max shut down tight behind the expressionless mask he wore so well. He refused to let this intrusive stranger twist his memories into painful knots.

"How did she die?"

"She was shot. Murdered." He kept his answers quick and clean as surgical cuts.

"Was she alone? Was she afraid?"

"I was with her. What we were or weren't is none of your concern. Just as it was none of your concern then."

"You would have been . . . just a child. Who raised you?"

"If you cared so much about how we lived and she died, you wouldn't have waited thirty years to ask. We have nothing to discuss. Stay away from me."

Max turned and started walking. His head was pounding, his stomach roiling with thick waves of sickness. For his whole life he'd dreamed of this moment, of this meeting. And now all he wanted to do was run, to get away, as far and as fast as possible, from the crippling shock of discovery. Away from this creature with his own face who'd deserted them, who'd let his mother die and only now thought to ask about her.

"She didn't tell me, Max."

He paused, but didn't turn. "Tell you what?"

"About you."

His eyes squeezed shut. His breath constricted. And up through the burning sorrow and panicked surprise rose the anger that would get him through this. "How convenient for you."

"If I had known, I would have never let her go." Rollo's voice lowered to a hard fierceness. "I would never have let her take you away."

He didn't respond. He couldn't.

"Max, talk to me. You must have questions. About your mother and me. About what you are."

There was nothing he wanted to know about this rough, brutal stranger and his mother. But that last lingered, seductively taunting. *About what you are.*

"You have nothing I want," he said curtly, and strode down the sidewalk.

"You know that's not true, Max, and so do I," Rollo called after him. "When you're ready, come find me. Max, you're my only son."

The glimmer Rollo cast was warm as an embrace, wrapping around him like an enveloping hug. Max mentally flung it off, hurling back a disembodied shove that made Rollo stumble. Then laugh with delight.

"Who taught you to be so strong? Think of what you could learn from me. Max, you are the best of both our lines. You have no idea what that means." His voice lowered reflectively. "No idea what that means."

No, he didn't. And that scared him to death.

THE SETTING SUN drenched rows of white vaults in gossamer tints of pink and orange and crimson.

Silence settled deep as the shadows between them as Max let his fingertips outline his mother's name, chiseled into warm stone. It seemed like forever ago and yet like yesterday when he'd stood at Jimmy Legere's side, shaking with internal sobs, as they sealed her inside for eternal rest. He remembered the weight of Jimmy's hand on his shoulder, how the firm squeeze of it helped him push the panic and terror away. At least until the nightmares came.

I saw to my promise, Max. She's safe now. And I'll take care of you for her.

And he had. Jimmy was the only father he knew. He'd sat up long nights to keep a child's night fears at bay. He'd seen to Max's needs, because his wants were so few and never named. To not be hungry, to be warm and dry, to not wake in darkness with the stench of death in his nose. To not let the awful things that prowled in bayou fog reach him. And because Jimmy saw to those things, he claimed Max's unwavering devotion. Though Jimmy had an appreciation for all the ways in which Max was different, he shared his mother's insistence on secrecy.

Never let them see you for what you are. You'll frighten them. They hunt and kill the things that frighten them.

The glimmer: he had a name for it now. As a child, he thought it was as natural as his mother's voice, her scent, her touch. That light, tender caress he'd feel on the inside when she was a room away. A sense of reassurance when he was upset or afraid, knowing he could reach out to her and not be alone anymore. He tried connecting with others the same way, but it was like tossing coins down a bottomless well. Until one day, when a response came back with the startling force of a blow. And he'd come to their door, the man with red shoes. It was the only time his mother had ever taken a harsh hand to him. Usually punishment involved an isolation that he feared more than any threat of pain.

Never, never, never do that again. They will find us. They will kill me. They will take you and hurt you.

Had she been hiding from Rollo? But it wasn't *he*, it was always *they* when she spoke of what scared her.

She couldn't tell him now.

Perhaps Rollo did have the answers. If he could be believed. If he could be trusted.

Max could still feel the sting of her hand on his face. But it wasn't those fierce slaps that left an enduring impression on his young mind; it was the terrible fright in her voice. And he had never done it again. Not until the night Charlotte Caissie took him to *Cheveux du Chien.*

Still, he hadn't understood until just this moment. Marie Savoie hadn't been afraid her son would alarm humans by his differences. She'd been terrified that he'd alert one of his own kind as to who and what he was.

WEARY, HEAD ACHING, looking forward to something unhealthy to eat and a few bouts of sweaty sex, Cee Cee climbed into her car and cranked over the big-block V-8. The locker room shower hadn't perked her up. She'd lingered only long enough to stick a Band-Aid over the cut on her brow and comb some hair down to hide it. Tomorrow was soon enough to worry about repairing her window and replacing her camera. As she reached for the gear shift, her system lurched in surprise. She wasn't alone in the car.

"Geez, Max. I'm going to have to put plastic down to protect my seats," she growled to cover up her fright. He sat on the passenger side, staring straight ahead. He didn't speak. He didn't look at her. Her instincts quivered. "Baby, are you all right?"

"Just drive."

She popped the car into gear and spun out of the police lot. After several blocks, she asked, "Where to?"

"It doesn't matter. Your place is fine."

She negotiated the early-evening traffic while keeping a cautious eye on him. Something wasn't right. But unless Max chose to tell her, she couldn't guess at it. She wouldn't ask him again. A new unwritten law: don't pester him for his secrets. Sometimes it was better not to know, for both their sakes. If it was something she needed to know, he'd tell her. If it was something she could help him with, he'd ask. Otherwise it was hands off. She didn't like it, but that was the way it had to be.

She reached out to touch his hand. The fingers twining between hers were cold and clutched tight. She locked her jaw against the urge to ask again, to demand to know what had him so anxious that he was strung tight and trembling. He didn't release her hand, not even when she had to downshift. The tension was contagious.

It wasn't until they reached her home and she turned the light on in her living room that she got a good look at him.

"Oh, my God. Are you hurt?"

He followed her alarmed gaze to his stained shirtfront, staring at the blood in a moment of perplexity. Then he shook his head.

"It's nothing. I had a nosebleed."

Her palm pressed to his cheek. "Are you okay?" She examined him for bruises before she realized she wouldn't find any evidence of injury on him. "Were you in a fight?"

"Just an unexpected go-around. I'm fine. Just a headache. I need to close my eyes for a bit."

"Stretch out on the couch while I make something to eat." Did she have any food in the place? She could run out for some takeout while he rested. "What are you hungry for?"

His head bent. His mouth fit softly against hers. Her lips parted on a sigh, inviting a deeper intimacy as her hand shifted to cup the back of his head.

Finally, after a slow, leisurely sampling, she whispered, "I think I'll have what you're having."

He stood motionless as she started to unbutton his ruined shirt. She could feel something building in his silence, and unfortunately she didn't think it was lust.

"How did you and your father get on?" he asked.

That was the last topic she expected.

"Good. There was no one I admired more." She eased his shirttails free of his trouser band. "Why do you ask?"

"I met him a couple of times. Not socially, of course. Usually our conversations were limited to 'You have the right to remain silent.'"

"Yeah, he was great at small talk."

"A quality I believe you inherited, detective."

"Where are you going with this, Savoie?" She parted his shirt, pushing it and his jacket off his shoulders.

"To the couch. I need to sit down."

She settled beside him on the cushions, her head on his shoulder, her fingers threading through the crisp mat on his chest. Waiting for him to get where he was going.

"I'm probably not the first pick he'd make for your boyfriend."

She chuckled. "Not even the last, I'm afraid. He thought you were an extremely dangerous, extremely well-trained attack dog for Jimmy Legere. I'm sure he would rather I had followed Mary Kate into the nunnery."

He winced at that. "He was a good judge of character."

Sorry she had hurt him, she kissed the warm pulse of his throat. "Not always. He missed the mark by a mile with my mom."

"Why didn't she take you with her when she left?"

Cee Cee squirmed but answered honestly. "I think she knew he wouldn't let her take me. It was easier just to let me go."

How could that be? he wondered. How could anyone who loved her just walk away? "Do you miss her?"

"I can't even remember her without a drink in her hand and a mean word coming out of her mouth. No, I don't miss that. My dad and St. Bart's were my family."

"I remember your father as stern and inflexible, always playing by the rules. Was that how he treated you?"

"He wasn't usually putting handcuffs on me while quoting the Miranda. Of course, there were times when he'd catch me and Mary Kate sneaking in late. Boy, did he know how to interrogate." She smiled, affection filling her heart with a bittersweet ache. "I loved my dad. He was everything good that I wanted to be."

"And what if you found out that your father wasn't what you thought he was, that he wasn't a good man? Would you still love him?"

She moved away, bristling like a threatened cat. "What are you saying? Are you saying my dad was a bad cop?"

He caught the back of her head, compelling her back to his shoulder, his fingers massaging firmly. "No. That's not what I'm saying at all. Hypothetically."

"I don't know how to answer that, Max." She frowned as she settled back beneath his chin. "If you're wondering if I think of you as a father figure, the answer is no. It would be way too creepy, considering how I'm thinking about you right now."

Her hand trailed down to a rock-hard middle that had never needed a gym membership to attain its contours. She was about to go to work on his belt when he captured her hand. He lifted it to kiss her knuckles, then pressed her palm to his heart. It wasn't passion kicking up its tempo. What, then?

"Is this about Jimmy?" she asked quietly. "Is that what has you so sad and far away?" A sliver of guilt twisted. "I never told you how sorry I was that you lost someone so close to you. He thought the world of you, and I will always be grateful to him for that."

"It's not Jimmy. Well, it is and it isn't. It's about secrets. It's about all the things Jimmy and my mother kept from me. Things I need to know, but I have no way to find the answers."

"What kinds of things?"

"Things like what my mother was so afraid of, who my father was, and what's so damned special about me that I'd be worth killing and dying for."

"You are."

"What?"

"Worth it, to me. No question about it."

He stared down at her, eyes huge. "Don't say that, Charlotte. Don't say it, and don't think it."

"Would I step in front of a bullet for you? Yes. Would I stand off a room full of angry were-creatures to protect you? Been there, done that. Would I tear down the walls of this city with my bare hands to keep you safe? Without blinking an eye. Does that frighten you, Savoie? To know you mean that much to me?"

"Yes." His fingertips charted the smooth curve of her cheek. "Yes, it does. It scares me and it humbles me and it excites me. It makes me feel like the most powerful man on earth. And lucky. So lucky."

His hand scooped the back of her head, pulling her up to meet the hard, hungry slant of his mouth. She straddled his lap, holding his face between her palms so she could return the urgency, the longing, the desperate need that always flickered like a pilot light waiting to take flame. It ignited as their kiss grew open mouthed, breaths and tongues shared in hurried plunder. Just as that pyre of want was about to consume her, he fisted his hand in her hair to pull her back slightly so he could study her passion-flushed features, and she could delve into the glittery heat of this stare.

"Would you break your precious laws for me?" he asked with fierce intensity. "Would you look the other way while I broke them?"

Her mood cooled slightly, as did her tone. "I've bent them plenty already."

"That's not what I asked." His voice lowered to a silky rumble. "The truth, Charlotte."

"It depends on—"

"Nothing. Don't hedge your bet. Just answer."

She scowled at him, furious because she'd been tiptoeing around their contrary careers and now he was shoving it in her face, demanding she make a choice. And he would know if she wasn't being honest, *damn him*.

"Yes," she growled. "For you, if you asked, yes, I would."

A satisfying amount of surprise registered in his eyes. Which irritated her enough to elaborate.

"I would hate it, but I would do it. It would destroy everything I built my life on. It would strip me of every ounce of dignity and self-respect. But I would do it, without hesitation, without regret, if you asked me to. That's how much you mean to me. And if you care for me even half that much, you would never ask."

A slow smile spread. "Clever girl. But weren't you the one who said I had no conscience, no morals? If that's the case, why would using you cause me any remorse if it got me what I wanted?"

When she didn't speak for a long moment, he began to regret his goading, wondering if she believed those things of him still.

She finally answered with heart-twisting bluntness. "No matter what else he might have been, Jimmy loved you enough to raise you to be faithful and trustworthy. Tenacious and possessive, too. You would never harm me, or allow me to come to any harm. I know that. I believe that in every beat of my heart. And that's why I can't stand not having you touch me. That's why I would surrender up so much to have you."

He leaned into her, tucking his head beneath her chin, breathing her in with deep, shaky draws. She simply held him, uncertain of his mood. Until his fingers hooked on the hem of her T-shirt, and began to slowly pull it up. She gripped handfuls of it and yanked it over her head.

His palms cradled the undersides of her breasts, lifting them, mounding them into inviting swells. He buried his nose in the valley between them, inhaling her fragrant heat and unique scent. The tip of his tongue traced the edge of the inexpensive bra she'd purchased for utility rather than sex appeal, making her feel sexy in it as his thumbs dragged across white nylon, revolving purposefully until he'd provoked the desired hard pucker of response. A moan shuddered from her as his mouth fastened hot and hungry over one hard peak, then the other. Raw, fierce sensation rippled all the way to her toes and back.

He unsnapped her jeans. She lifted off his lap so he could pull the zipper down and slip the denim and her nylon panties off her hips. Then he cupped her with his palm, priming her with pressure from the heel of his hand, with the slow glide of his fingers, over her, into her. A riot of tense, bunchy shivers possessed her as she panted out his name; her hips began to rock.

Ringing.

She blinked to clear the glaze from her mind. Her phone?

Max snatched it from her side clip with his free hand and flicked it open. His voice was smoothly professional.

"You've reached Detective Charlotte Caissie. I'm sorry but she's unavailable to take your call. She'll be with you in just a moment. Please hold."

They could hear Alain Babineau. "Savoie, I need to talk to her. Max, it's important."

Tossing the phone to the other end of the couch, he grabbed her by the hair and yanked her mouth down to his, not giving her time to think as his tongue and his fingers plunged hard and deep. Not giving her a chance to breathe or resist her sudden explosive reaction as he demanded more and more of her. Driving into her, forcing her to surrender all control until at last she gave that soft, plaintive little whimper of abandon that never failed to rock his world.

When she slumped with deliciously boneless satisfaction upon him, he passed her the phone.

"Your call, detective."

She took the cell, then hesitated in a moment of thought-blanking eroticism as he sucked the taste of her from his fingers and thumb.

"Caissie," she all but purred.

Babineau's taut voice cut through her lethargy. "Ceece, I'll be there in two."

She was all business as she jerked up her jeans. "What's happened?"

"I'll explain when I get there."

Max said nothing as she scrambled off his lap. He watched her through expressionless eyes as she geared up for battle, tugging on her clothes, restoring her phone, checking her weapon. Her tone was brusque.

"I've got to—"

"Go. I know. Don't apologize."

His quiet acceptance knocked the wind from her for a moment. Then she fixed upon his lips, kissing him with hurried longing.

"Stay here," she urged between needy nibbles. "Wait for me. Wait here for me, Max."

"Okay."

She straightened just enough to devour him with her gaze. "Take a nap. You'll need all your strength. When I get back, I'm going to ride you like a Grand Canyon pack mule."

He blinked, then smiled faintly. "That sounds delightful."

Her resolve melted down into a ridiculous puddle of tenderness. She kissed him again, softly, slowly, with all the grateful, mushy sentimentality he stirred within her usually practical soul.

A horn sounded.

"To be continued," she murmured against his

mouth, while she still had the willpower to leave him.

MAX PUT ON his blood-stained shirt and his jacket, smoothing out the wrinkles from unconscious habit. Then he sat quietly, motionlessly on the sofa, closing his mind to all the conflicts of his day. Waiting for her return some hours later.

With Babineau.

One glimpse at her stern expression told him everything.

There'd be no Grand Canyon ride for the two of them tonight.

He asked no questions as she reached down for his hands; he could smell violent death all over her. As she ratcheted on the cuffs, she told him with a level gravity reminiscent of her father, "You have the right to remain silent. . . ."

Six

BY THE TIME he was fingerprinted and photographed and processed and led to interrogation, Max's attorney, Antoine D'Marco, was tapping his briefcase impatiently. He gave his client a quick once-over, checking for signs of mistreatment.

"Always nice to hear from you, Max, but I prefer more pleasant circumstances and a more civilized hour. Are you all right?"

"Fine. I've been Mirandized." He settled into the seat beside D'Marco and looked across the table to meet Alain Babineau's steely glare. Charlotte stood a few steps behind her partner but he didn't glance at her. All he would have seen was her somber game face.

"Would you like some time to confer with your attorney?"

Max regarded Babineau with a mild disinterest. "No. Let's just get this over with."

"What are the charges, detective?" D'Marco demanded as he flipped open a yellow legal pad. "How soon can I arrange bail, if necessary?"

"Suspicion of murder, premeditated. You can assume that means not anytime soon. We've got forty-eight to hold him before an arraignment and we're gonna hang onto him for every minute of it."

"And the victim would be?"

"Vivian Goodman, forty-two, married, mother of three. Stalked, raped, and mutilated between seven and eight thirty this evening." He slapped a line of color photos down on the table, from a smiling, attractive, dark-haired woman to progressively grisly depictions of her body sprawled nearly naked and close to dismembered on some playground.

Max studied the pictures without a betraying flicker of response. "Who is she?" he asked at last.

"She owned a public relations firm recently hired by Simon Cummings. She was in charge of the PR campaign for his run at the mayor's seat. See a pattern, Mr. Savoie? Other than the one detailed in blood and internal organs?"

Max made no comment.

"All right. Let's get this show started. Mind if I put this on record, counselor?" When D'Marco gave the go-ahead, Babineau prefaced their discussion on tape, then began with the obvious. "Give me a rundown on your movements leading up to your arrest."

"I was at my office for most of the day. I had meetings in the morning and contracts to review in the afternoon. Mr. D'Marco was with me until about three, while we worked on the legal language of a proposal to present to, ironically enough, Mr. Cummings."

"What kind of a proposal?"

"A marriage of convenience, detective. I have some property he wants to develop. He was doing a mating dance with Jimmy—"

"Legere."

"Yes. But Jimmy didn't trust him, didn't like the numbers or the players, and was planning to go courting elsewhere."

"So what made you want to sleep with him?"

"There was a lot of baggage between Jimmy and Cummings. I don't know the particulars. If Jimmy didn't like someone, it didn't matter how sweet the deal was, he wouldn't bite. That's just the way he was."

"And you're not as discriminating about who you get under the covers with, is that it?"

Max's eyes narrowed slightly but there was no change in his voice or posture. "Oh, I wouldn't say that at all. It's a trust issue with me. I insist on loyalty. I refuse to invest anything without assurances of a mutual degree of commitment to the end result. I don't care about the details. If it's all one-sided, you might as well save yourself the aggravation and just jack off."

Babineau's jaw tightened. "Are we still talking about business here?"

"I was. Were you speaking about something else, detective?" His tone was mild, his eyes glittered. "We were discussing my day, I believe."

"Yes. Go on."

"After we prepared the rough drafts of some contracts, I met with Francis Petitjohn until four thirty to go over some labor issues on the docks, then I dictated some correspondence to my secretary, Marissa Oliver, until five fifteen. I ate the other half of the muffuletta that was delivered at noon that I hadn't had time to finish. Undressed with extra hot sauce, detective, in case you were wondering how I like it. I walked to St. Bartholomew's and spoke with Father Furness for a few minutes. Then I went to visit my mother."

"And where was that?"

"At her permanent address. St. Louis No. 1."

Babineau had the decency to look disconcerted. "I'm sorry. I didn't know." When Max had no reaction, he cleared his throat and continued. "How long were you there?"

"I don't know exactly. Until dark. The police warn you not to loiter there after sunset because it's dangerous."

Babineau crooked a smile at him. "Yeah, I'm sure you feared for your safety."

"As any unarmed, law-abiding citizen would."

"Can anyone verify your presence there or what time you left?"

"I didn't see anyone. It's very quiet, very peaceful. That's why I like it."

"And after you spent this indeterminate and unverified amount of time there, where did you go?"

"Since I was in the neighborhood, I stopped to say good night to Jimmy Legere. He let my mama have a corner in his family's plot because I . . . I was just a boy when she died and didn't have any way to take care of her." He took a slow breath, then continued in the same easy tone. "I didn't stay because a couple of teenagers were necking on the step. Since they weren't bothering him, I didn't bother them."

"Did they see you? Could they recognize you?"

"I think they were too preoccupied to even notice the second line of a marching band, detective."

"Too bad for you."

Max shrugged. "I didn't know I was going to need an alibi, or I might have intruded. Maybe I should hire Karen Crawford and her news crew full-time to follow me around to document where I am . . . and where I'm not. She seems to enjoy making my private life very public."

No reaction from Babineau. "So you left the cemetery and then what?"

"I waited at Charlotte's car for her to go off duty. We went to her apartment. We were in the middle of discussing dinner options when you called."

"That's Detective Charlotte Caissie?"

"You know it is."

"And it's Detective Caissie who can also vouch for your whereabouts on the night that Sandra Cummings was killed?"

"Not entirely."

Cee Cee struggled not to respond to that calm admission. *Max, what are you doing?*

"I left her for a period of about an hour and a half."

"What time would that be?"

"From about one a.m. to two thirty."

Dammit, Max. Don't do this!

"And where were you during that time period, when Sandra Cummings was being raped and murdered?"

"It was a nice night. I went out for some air."

"Did you go into the city?"

"On foot? That's a twenty-minute drive, detective, and I don't drive. I can provide you with the security tapes from that evening that will show no vehicles left the property."

"Do that. And why are you sharing the news of your little unwitnessed *fais-dodo* now, and not at the time you were originally questioned?"

"A memory lapse, I guess. Once I was reminded of it, I wanted to make sure I said nothing contrary to Detective Caissie's potential testimony." He did look up at her then, his gaze cool and emotionless. "Because I love her that much."

She clenched her teeth to keep her jaw from trembling. Why did he have to pick the absolute worst times to make his declarations?

Babineau was clenching his teeth, too. He gritted out, "Witnesses said you spoke with a man outside St. Bart's, that that's where you got the blood on your shirt. Care to tell me about that, Max?"

"There's not much to tell. He was a stranger.

He called me over to ask a couple of questions. He thought he knew me, but he was mistaken. The blood on my shirt is mine. I had a nosebleed."

"We'll want to test that."

"Of course."

"What did you think to accomplish by this brutal attack on Vivian Goodman?"

Max interrupted D'Marco's objection, saying evenly, "I didn't know the woman. I've never met her, seen her, or even heard her name before you showed me these photographs."

"You didn't know she was working for Simon Cummings?"

"Why would I?"

"Because the leverage of having killed his daughter and his PR director might encourage that fidelity you're so keen on. Is that part of the business proposal you were putting together for him? Did threats entice him to listen to what you had to say?"

"I've never even spoken to the man. I have no personal interest in him, in his family, his employees, or his campaign."

"Then why," Cee Cee asked abruptly, "did you approach his wife some months back and threaten her?"

Both Max and Alain looked to her in surprise. Max recovered first.

"I never made any threats toward Mrs. Cummings."

"Do you deny speaking to her at a charity event you were attending with Jimmy Legere?"

"No, detective, I don't deny it." D'Marco started to lean in but Max waved him back. "I complimented her on her daughters. They'd both given speeches at the fund-raiser and they impressed me. I just made a comment to her about the danger of putting children into a controversial situation."

"You threatened her children."

"No. I did not. I just thought she and her husband should be more careful. Cummings was making a lot of dangerous enemies."

"One of them being your boss."

"Yes."

"Did Jimmy tell you to scare her by hinting that her daughters might be targets of some kind of violence?"

His voice became slightly colder. "No. He didn't. I don't terrorize women and I don't endanger children. But I thought it was naive of her not to realize there were others who might not be as honorable."

"Why would you feel it necessary to warn her? Were you aware of any such plot to harm Cummings or his family?"

"I was not involved in any such plot."

"That's not what I asked, Mr. Savoie."

"I'm sorry. I thought it was."

"Why did you warn Mrs. Cummings that her daughters might be in danger?"

"Because, as you well know, that's the kind of

business I'm in, detective. That's the kind of thing people do."

"People like Jimmy Legere?"

"Yes."

"And Francis Petitjohn."

"You'll have to ask him. I have no personal knowledge of his activities at that time."

"And you? You're a Boy Scout, Mr. Savoie?"

"I was never a Boy Scout any more than you were a Girl Scout, detective. I'm just answering your question."

D'Marco looked between them impatiently. "Are there any other relevant questions for my client?"

"Just one." Babineau tapped one of the gruesome photographs. "In looking at these pictures, Mr. Savoie, how do you think a man managed to inflict such a horrendous amount of damage?"

Without blinking, Max said, "By growing fangs and claws, detective. That would be my guess."

"We're done," D'Marco announced, standing up and placing a reassuring hand on Max's shoulder. "I'll get you arraigned as quickly as possible and out of here."

"Thank you, Tony."

Babineau started for the door behind the attorney, but Cee Cee hung back.

"I'd like to speak to Max alone for a minute."

"Ceece," her partner warned quietly. "That's not a good idea." When she didn't back down, he sighed. "Make it quick and keep your distance."

She waited until the two of them were alone to turn to Max. She kept her back to the camera and her voice low.

"What the hell are you doing? Why did you open up your alibi for Sandra Cummings?"

"I didn't want to make things awkward for you, detective. Honesty being the best policy and all."

His calm annoyed her, because she felt helpless to protect him. That worry made it hard to hold to her impassive face even when he seemed determined to provoke her with his attitude.

He assessed her with a far-from-flattering look that had the hair on her neck bristling, then drawled, "You were quite a bulldog with your questions about Mrs. Cummings. I wasn't aware you were only interested in a pen pal relationship, care of the state."

"If she said something to me, it was only a matter of time before she pointed the finger of blame at you in front of someone else. I thought it would be smart to get it out in the open so it wouldn't look like you were trying to hide anything."

"I'm not, detective. And that sharp little slap on my wrist made you look pretty good, too." His voice lowered to the gravelly rumble that always stroked her nerve endings into a quiver. It made her think of rough-and-tumble sex in the dark. "You look pretty good to me right now, all starched up and sassy. I'm afraid we'll have to make a rain check for tonight.

I would have preferred your Grand Canyon tour to the lockup."

What did he want from her? He had to know his sudden burst of candor had cut the legs out from under her plan to insulate him from suspicion. Did he *want* to go to jail? Something was going on with him, something reckless and distressing, and she was just too damned dense in the sensitivity department to figure it out.

He was trying to tell her something with all his cryptic talk about fathers and secrets, but what was he getting at? How did he expect her to finesse his meaning when she had all the subtlety of an urban assault vehicle? How could someone so direct and intense suddenly dance a light-footed two-step around what was close to his heart, when she was clogging away to a different rhythm?

He'd had something to say to her, had been trying to get to it the last two times they were together. But the sex kept getting in the way. And she just wasn't noble enough to force her hormones to take a backseat, when the backseat she desired involved rolling around in it naked with him. Whenever she was around him, the need to touch him, to hold him tightly, even here, even now, was almost overwhelming. But she clung to her control.

"Are you going to be all right? Dammit, Max, I can't do anything to help you now."

"I know. I know the drill, Charlotte. D'Marco

will take care of me. And I'm fairly capable when it comes to handling myself."

"Max, who were you talking to outside of St. Bart's?"

His expression locked down tight.

"Cee Cee," Babineau called in. "They've got to take him now."

She swore softly. Then, without considering the repercussions, she ducked down to fix a swift, hard kiss on his mouth, whispering, "Be careful. I'll see you soon," before she strode out the door.

"YOU WANTED TO see me, chief?"

Cee Cee didn't quail beneath Chief Byron Atcliff's pale glower, the way the most seasoned veterans of the force would have. But she didn't underestimate the seriousness of this call to his office.

"Shut the door, detective." When she complied, he gestured to the straight-backed chair in front of his desk. The hot seat. "Sit." She sat. "You're too smart not to know why you're here."

"Max Savoie."

"What's the story?"

"My partner and I were told to bring him in as a suspect in a murder investigation."

"I can read that in the report. What's going on between the lines? Cummings is screaming in the commissioner's ear about unethical behavior on the part of one of my team. Would he be correct?"

"Absolutely not, sir."

"Then your relationship with Savoie is . . . ?"

"He is . . ." She searched for a word then settled for "my boyfriend. We're dating when I'm off duty, sir."

"Dating." There was a long, suspenseful silence, the kind that followed the sudden loud crack of thin ice before a frigid plunge. "You know, don't you, detective, that the public doesn't believe those who serve them are ever off duty *or* have the right to a private life, especially if it involves playing suck face in the interrogation room with a suspect."

"Would you let Mrs. Atcliff go off to jail without some expression of support, chief?"

"Mrs. Atcliff would not be going off to jail, and that was a very private display on the public's time."

"I apologize, sir."

"I'm afraid that's not going to be enough, detective."

She sat straight and still, waiting to hear the worst.

Atcliff sighed in aggravation. "He's a criminal, Lottie. The kind of lowlife your daddy and I dragged in off the streets every day and night on the streets together."

"I know. I can't help it. I'm crazy about him, Uncle Byron."

Byron Atcliff was tall and stringy and tough as bullets. He'd taken one, in fact, to save her father's life. And he was also no fool. He could see in his goddaughter's eyes that it was more than a casual thing with Savoie. *Savoie.*

For a responsibility he'd shouldered willingly, for a girl who'd never given him reason for grief, he was abruptly floundering. There wasn't a step she'd taken in her career that didn't puff him up with pride. He couldn't help but see this one as a disastrous detour off that path. "*Crazy* would be the word. Your daddy's most likely rolling in his grave," he mourned.

Cee Cee gave a small smile. "I don't know. I think he and Max might have liked each other. They're both stubborn and loyal and dedicated. And they both love me."

"So do I. That's why I can't let this go. Hell, you practically grew up in the squad car between me and your daddy. And as much as he loved you, he hated Jimmy Legere. You know Legere put the hit on him."

She said nothing. Her eyes glimmered damply.

"And yet you go and fall right into the arms of his top enforcer, his successor."

"I didn't mean to." Her tiny apology chiseled none of the granite from the stern expression.

"Do you think you could have picked someone a little lower on the illegal food chain?"

"I didn't pick him, Uncle Byron. It just sort of . . . happened. I can't explain it."

"Kidney stones just sort of happen without explanation, and look at the hell you have to go through to pass one of them. Do you have any idea what you're going to have to deal with once he's out of your system? The kind of damage control it's going to take?"

Her smile was bittersweet. "I don't think he's something I'm going to get over."

"Thirty to life might be one helluva cure."

The dewy-eyed vulnerability was gone in a blink, and he found himself looking at the hard-edged female version of Tommy Caissie. Tommy hadn't listened when it came to romance, either, and he nearly hadn't survived that mistake. His daughter wouldn't suffer equally if Byron could do anything about it.

But what *could* he do about it? There was nothing more stubborn than a Caissie once they'd dug in their heels and attached their heartstrings.

"He's not guilty, chief. He didn't do this."

Atcliff's expression hardened. "You know that for a fact? Even though facts tie him in with a hangman's noose."

"Any number of people could have set him up for the fall. The MO is right out of the horror stories Legere built around him. My gut tells me he's not involved."

"Your gut, your heart—I don't care if it's your damned pancreas. You know what he is."

"He's not Jimmy Legere. He's a good man in a bad spot. He didn't have the chance to grow up any differently, to make any other choices."

"And I'm supposed to feel sorry for him, is that it? That's a weak excuse and you know it, detective. Prison is full of those victims of society. He doesn't need a social worker, Lottie. He needs a jailer. He needs to be behind bars. If not for this, then for any number of other things he's involved in."

"He's pulling Legere's interests away from the other side of the law," she argued doggedly. "He's making them legit. Give him a chance."

His jaw set. "We don't give chances here, detective. Once they get to us, they are out of them."

"Yes, sir."

"Don't be a fool, Lottie. Don't let him take you down with him. His type will grab anything to keep from going under. You know that."

"He's innocent, sir."

"Prove it, detective. Prove it first, then talk to me about chances."

"I will."

"You've put me in a bad spot, Charlotte. Your off hours are yours to do with as you choose, with whomever you choose. But I can't have you compromising the integrity of an investigation by playing house with one of the main suspects."

"So where does that leave me?"

"You know where. Either you put distance between yourself and Savoie for the duration of the case or you take yourself off it. I don't have any other choices for you. Not with Cummings demanding you be disciplined."

"So that's my punishment?" Her tone was cool and flat, betraying none of the temper cooking up a spicy hot roux on the inside.

"I don't let civilians tell me how to handle my people," he snarled, letting his anger slip out for a moment. "But politics is politics, and the higher-ups want us to play the game. Help me out here, Lottie. I don't want this to mark your career. Your daddy was the best cop I ever knew and you're just as good. Don't throw it away. I want my best and brightest on the team. I need this wrapped in a hurry with a pretty bow, and you and Babineau can make that happen. You can give these families closure for the ugly way their loved ones died."

That hit her hard and low, just as he knew it would. "I want that, too."

"Then talk to Savoie. D'Marco will earn his fee and have him sprung before he has a chance to wear the creases out of his jail issue. I don't want Cummings and his people mucking up our inquiry with hints of impropriety. If Savoie's the stand-up guy you want to think he is, he'll understand and give you room to work."

"It's not fair, sir."

"I'm well aware of that, detective. Little about our work involves fairness. We're lucky if we can squeeze an ounce of justice out of it once in a while. If you want fair, ask yourself how fair it would be to pull your partner off a high-profile case that will look impressive on his résumé. Ask yourself how fair it would be to tell the Cummings and Goodman families that you put your love life above the arrest of the one responsible for victimizing their daughter, wife, and mother. The department doesn't need any more sensational press like the garbage cranked out after Legere was killed. Don't start that feeding frenzy up again just because you have a jones for this guy."

"I'll do my job, sir, and I'll do it under Cummings's microscope. But I don't like it." And Max wasn't going to like it, either.

Not one damned bit.

"Bring me proof, detective, and I'll give him his chance."

"I will."

Seven

SHE SIGHED INTO the slow, reacquainting kiss that coaxed her from slumber.

Even before her eyes opened, her arms were around him, holding to the tough, rangy build, tugging him over her to enjoy the way their contours fit, hard to soft, so perfectly together.

"Heya," he whispered against her lips.

She looked up at him as if surprised. "Oh, it's you."

"Expecting someone else, were you?"

She shrugged. "What can I say? My lover's in lockup, leaving me so very, very lonely. You didn't think I'd wait forever, did you?"

"I've been gone two days, not two years. And, yes, I did."

Because he sounded disagreeable, she lifted up to lick the scowl from his mouth, confessing, "I've missed you, Savoie. It felt like years."

He sucked in the teasing tip of her tongue, stroking over and around it. Her legs parted and he settled between them as her heels rubbed the backs of his thighs. He was fully dressed. She was wearing his

T-shirt. His hands slipped under its hem, his palms moving slowly and seducingly on warm skin.

A soft sound of pleasure purred from her. "Did you miss me?"

His scowl returned. "I was in jail. There wasn't a lot else to do."

"You could have made new friends."

"You know me, detective. I don't play well with others."

She smiled up at him, adoring the angles of his face with her fingertips. Her darkly dangerous, preternatural lover. "You didn't escape, did you?"

"D'Marco sprung me. There wasn't a scrap of evidence. Cummings must have pulled some pretty fancy strings for them to hang onto me for the full forty-eight." He flopped over onto his back, his mood cooling with displeasure. She rolled onto her side, propping her head in one hand while the other roved the tempting, if clothed, manscape of chest and abs.

"He thinks you killed his daughter."

His gaze fixed on hers, intent and unblinking. "Do you?"

Her reply was satisfyingly simple. "No."

He closed his eyes and for a moment, the effects of worry and sleeplessness scored his features.

"Did they treat you all right, baby?"

He slanted a look her way, amused. "It was jail, *cher*, not the Marriott. I prefer the Marriott. The room service is better."

Her fingertips ran down his shirt buttons in a quick stroke, then up again more slowly, working each one free. "This is the same suit you were wearing when you went in. Haven't you been home yet?"

"I came straight here. To see you."

Her heart gave a funny little shudder. Her voice grew gruff. "I think you need to take it off."

His lowered to the same husky register. "Take it off me."

As the last button gave way, she pushed his shirt aside so her palm could ease across his chest, so her fingers could comb through the mat of hair covering it. She lifted up, taking a moment to revel at the harsh beauty of his face, softened by the long slant of his closed eyes and slight curve of his lips, before lowering to taste the jut of his collarbone, the warm hollow of his throat where his pulse kicked up into an aggressive thunder. Moving lower to tongue his nipple into a hard point. His breathing became quick and shallow. He gripped her hand and jerked it downward, moving it over the hard ridge of his erection in fierce strokes.

"Unzip me," he told her, his deep voice rough, not like Max.

She opened his trousers with oddly hesitant motions, her hand withdrawing as he freed himself.

His breath panting out in fast, harsh bursts, he clasped the back of her neck, forcing her head down as he growled, "Take me in your mouth."

The instant her chin brushed over his coarse hairs

and a hot male scent seared her memories, something broke inside her. She reared back against the press of his palm, struggling as if he was holding her underwater, drowning in panic and desperate to escape it.

He let go of her immediately, then watched with surprise as she lunged up against the headboard, her posture stiff, her gaze wild. When it finally met his, for a moment there was no recognition in those dark turbulent depths.

He didn't move. He didn't dare.

Then she blinked rapidly. Confusion melded into an awkward need to apologize as she stammered, "I'm sorry. I don't know what—"

"It's all right," he soothed with the caress of his voice, with the touch of his fingertip light upon her damp cheek. "I shouldn't have tried to push you into something you were uncomfortable with. I'm sorry. I didn't think . . . I shouldn't have expected . . ." A deep flush of crimson crept up into his face. Because she looked mortified and anxious and he wasn't sure what to do, he kept rambling on. "The fellas in lockup got to talking in that disgustingly colorful way fellas do, and they got to boasting about the women they'd had and what they liked them to do."

"You were discussing me with your cell mates?"

"What?" He blinked. Then he laughed at her brittle tone, the sound sudden and loud, startling her. "No. Of course not. When you've got yourself a secret recipe that other folk would kill for, you tend to keep it to yourself."

A smile trembled weakly on her lips. "No wonder you didn't make any new friends."

He flashed a quick grin, then drew her gently to him, cradling her close with his chin atop her head so she couldn't see the horrible guilt and anguish flooding his eyes. "They were talking about their women. I was pretending not to listen. I was daydreaming about you, and the stuff they were saying just kinda spilled over into what I was thinking. Stuff I'd never even imagined doing got me all riled up, when I thought about doing it with you."

"Pretty hot stuff, huh?" she ventured carefully.

"No. Pretty disgusting stuff, but when you're stuck behind bars with a bunch of rude and horny fellas, it starts sounding pretty hot."

"And you want to do these things with me?"

"No! No. Well, yeah. Yes, I do. I'm sorry. I guess I'm just a rude, horny beast after all."

"You and the rest of the male gender.

"I love you, Charlotte," he told her tenderly. "You're safe with me." He rubbed his cheek over her hair. "You're safe with me."

She burrowed in tight, breathing in his familiar scent, soaking up his comforting heat, calmed by the careful way he handled her until her pulse slowed from its frantic gallop. The denying tension drained from her body. He was so perfect, so tender. So why had she been so afraid?

She wasn't sure what had happened. Something in the forcefulness of his touch and tone set off a chain reaction of remembered distress. It took her under so quick and so deep, she'd no time to prepare for it, no way to battle out of it. And now he was being so solicitous, she could weep in grateful misery.

The fact that she didn't have to explain only wound those emotions up into more complicated knots. Because she knew he would never ask for more than she was willing to give. That knowledge came with a humbling sense of security and a frustrating impatience with her own inconvenient frailty.

"I don't deserve you, Max."

He was silent for a moment, then, as she braced for his scare-the-crap-out-of-you laugh, a quiet chuckle vibrated beneath her cheek. "Now, there's a ridiculous statement if ever I heard one." His lips brushed along her brow. "I love you, Charlotte."

She expelled a shaky breath. Her arms slipped around him, curling tight. He held her easily until she began to nuzzle his neck, igniting a renewed desire in him that he thought best suppressed for the moment. And nothing quelled passion like bringing work into the picture.

"Have you found out anything? Any ideas on who killed these women?"

"Nothing yet. I'm sorry."

The fear bred into him, that terror of being discovered for what he was, kinked up in his belly. Without Jimmy's protection, he felt vulnerable, exposed, unable to hide. His voice was flat beneath that weight. "Like I needed more attention turned my way. I don't have time for this now. I'm trying to quiet the situation on the docks, and I've got the press swarming me like fire ants."

"Did they follow you here?"

"No. Of course not." But he'd caught her anxious tone. He lifted his head to look at her. "Why?"

Her hand clutched the fabric of his shirt, kneading restlessly.

"What? Charlotte, tell me."

"The department is under a lot of heat to get this case resolved quickly."

"Good." He noted her discomfort. "It isn't good?"

"Cummings has a lot of pull in the force. Particularly with the commissioner."

"And?"

"The chief called me in after you were arrested."

"Is he giving you grief over not having this solved already? You're the best they have, Charlotte. No one can do the job better."

"He knows that."

"So?"

"He gave me grief about you."

He went very still. "Oh."

"He said our relationship was—"

A hot spark of frustration flared. "You don't need to tell me what he said. I get the picture. He didn't officially reprimand you, did he?"

"No. Not exactly." Her eyes clouded with upset and anger.

Max reared back in alarm. "What?"

"He told me to either take myself off the case or break it off with you for the duration."

Max took a long moment to process the enormity of that. And he said what she needed to hear, not the protest that beat wildly in his heart. "You can't leave the case."

"No, I can't."

"Then that's what you need to concentrate on."

She met his unblinking stare and found the strength to say, "Yes, it is.

Without another word, he rolled off the bed and headed for the door, not looking at her. If he did, he'd never find the strength to go.

She bit back the need to tell him to stop, to call him back. The effort had her shaking.

He stopped at the threshold of her room to ask softly, "Is this what you want, too, Charlotte?" He waited a beat, two, then he started forward again.

"No."

He paused but didn't turn.

"No, it's not what I want, Max."

The stiffness ebbed out of his posture and he leaned his head against the doorjamb. His words were low and rough. "I need you, Charlotte. I need you like air, like light. Without you there's only darkness. There's just emptiness. Tell me what you want me to do. I'd wait forever for you. Just don't tell me you don't want me back."

She crossed to him quickly, encircling him with

her arms, resting her cheek against his shoulder. "Of course I want you back. I've always wanted you. I will always want you. It's just until this case is closed. I need to finish this for you, for the families, for Mary Kate. Please say you understand."

Instead of answering, he surrounded her hands with his, squeezing tightly.

"It will only be for a little while." Was she trying to convince him or herself?

He straightened suddenly, releasing her hands. "There are reporters outside."

She swore fiercely and went to the window. Sure enough, there were several unfamiliar cars out front. She saw a cameraman darting furtively through her neighbor's flower bed. "We've got to get you out of here without them seeing you."

"Walk me right out the front door."

She turned toward him, then drew up, stunned.

Max stood naked in a pool of his clothing. He smiled faintly at her astonishment, and at the hot way her gaze ran over him. He pointed to his discarded suit. "Could you get that cleaned for me?"

And then, while she watched in amazement, his form compressed with the speed and ease of a computer graphic morph, then dropped down onto all fours. Within seconds she was regarding a large, lean, wolflike creature, sleek and black with startling green eyes.

"Max?" she said cautiously. "Can you still understand me?"

The big creature trotted forward, nudging his warm nose into her palm, then beneath the hem of her T-shirt into her crotch. With a laugh, she shoved his head away. "Behave, you beast. Sit."

He sat, watching her with those unnervingly human eyes while she pulled on a pair of jeans.

"Right out the front door, huh?"

She crouched down in front of the still animal and warily touched the soft, thick ruff of fur, running her fingers through it.

"You're magnificent, Max," she told him with hushed awe. Without hesitation, she slowly put her arms around the powerful shoulders and buried her face in his dark pelt. Soft and ermine sleek, just like Max's. He sat motionlessly, his chin resting on her shoulder, eyes closed.

Finally Cee Cee stood, her hand still atop his head. "Walk nicely. No biting the nasty reporters, even though they deserve it."

He got up and trotted into her living room, where an immediate ruckus started in the guinea pig cage. He went to stand with snuffing nose against the bars and her furry pets huddled in terror in the far corner.

"Max, leave them alone." Before she could catch herself, she'd snapped her fingers to bring him to heel. "What do you know? You mind better this way." She grinned, then bent to kiss the top of his head, and was startled by the wet slap of his tongue across the side of her face. She pushed him away, smiling. "No tongue. I'm not going to French you while you're wearing your dog suit. Come on. Let's get you out of here."

He gave her a quick wolfish grin that was pure, mocking Max, then walked tamely at her side.

The reporters who'd camped out on her steps jumped up.

"Oh," she said in feigned surprise. "I thought I heard prowlers and was about to sic my dog on them."

"Karen Crawford, Detective Caissie."

Cee Cee eyeballed the reporter with malice. Crawford had once been a top-notch journalist, but as the inevitability of age started to nudge her out of her lucrative career, she'd begun to resort to less savory means of grabbing a story. Her favorite was sensationalism, manufactured or truthful, it didn't much matter to her anymore, as long as it got her ratings points and kept her lifted and tucked self in front of the public. She dogged Cee Cee's steps because eventually there'd be a payoff. The two women hardly bothered to hide their animosity.

"I know who you are. What are you doing invading my privacy in the middle of the night?"

The chic newswoman came up a few steps with her microphone, but a sudden rumbling growl had her quickly backtracking. To her credit, she didn't alarm easily. "What a beautiful animal. Is he yours?"

"We belong to each other. He's not fond of strangers."

"Is he vicious?"

"He can be when he's provoked. Uninvited guests provoke him a great deal. He doesn't play well with others. He's very protective."

"What's his name?"

She couldn't very well say "Max." "Baby."

Crawford came up the few steps more cautiously. "Will he let me pet him?"

"I don't know. You can try. I have liability insurance."

Trying to ingratiate herself, the newswoman reached out to fondle one of his ears. When he allowed it, she grew bolder, coming closer to croon, "Why, you *are* just a big baby, aren't you?" She jumped when his nose went up under her short skirt.

"Stop that," Cee Cee hissed, smacking the back of his head. "Get, you ill-mannered beast." She gave him a boot in the hind quarters to send him trotting down the stairs. The other newspeople scattered at the sound of his throaty snarl. Then he was gone, slipping between their parked vehicles and into the shadows.

"You let him run loose?"

"He knows where he belongs. Now, what can I do for you, Ms. Crawford?"

"Were you aware that Max Savoie was released this evening?"

"I just put them there. It's not my job to keep them there. He has a very good attorney." She noticed the way the woman was glancing around her toward her open door. "Did you think I had him stashed inside?"

"Is he?"

"One, if he was, it would be none of your business. Two, no, he's not, because I'm working on a case that involves him at the moment as a suspect. You and I are both professionals, Ms. Crawford. We know better than to mix business with pleasure when it can damage our approval ratings. If I see Mr. Savoie, it will be on a strictly professional basis. I have too much sympathy and respect for the families involved for them to think I would care so little for their pain. Can you say the same, Ms. Crawford? Any of you? I thought not. Good night, then. You're welcome to camp out here in hopes of catching a shot of someone jumping out of my window. Far be it from me to interfere with the freedom of the press."

And she went inside, closing the door on them.

MAX SHOWERED IN water as hot as he could stand it, remaining under the spray until the film of captivity was washed away. Then, dressed in loose jeans and a sleeveless sweatshirt, his feet bare because his shoes were still at Charlotte's, he began to pace. Even the big rooms of Jimmy's house seemed too confining. Too uninviting with no one he loved inside them.

Frustration and fear knotted. Frustration because all the attention from the police, from the press, from his own people, still caged him and made him helpless. He preferred the shadows to the glare of media lights, but there was no way to escape them now.

Fear knotted because he knew that it *wouldn't* be just for a short while. If Charlotte allowed her superiors to push her job between them this time, they would again the next. And the next. Until they had no time for each other at all.

He remembered her earlier warning about all her energies going toward the job. Having only leftovers after enjoying the feast left him unsettled and discontent.

He could pace and fret, or he could do something about it.

After all, he'd made a promise.

And there was one place the press couldn't follow.

The noise and smoke welcomed him like a bad habit.

Because he'd had enough invasion of his personal space, Max strode through the crowded club with his presence cloaked, psychically invisible. He could see their surprise when he was upon them without their notice, see their awe, their uncertainty as they parted to let him pass. And their fear. Just enough to remind him that even here, among his own kind, he was alone.

As he eased into his chair at the table reserved for him alone, the voluptuous Amber was immediately at his elbow.

"Good evening, Mr. Savoie. Your usual?"

"I've got it, my lovely."

They both looked in surprise at the lean, dark figure who'd approached undetected. Rollo grinned and placed a bottled beer on the table in front of Max. He sat without being invited, not bothered by Max's glittered stare of objection.

"I've been expecting you, boy. Bit of trouble, I hear. Bad business, jail. Our kind wasn't meant to be caged."

"What do you want?"

The cold greeting didn't lessen the other's cheer. "To chat. To get to know my only son."

"It's several decades too late for that, don't you think?"

"For father and son, perhaps. For two of a kind, I don't think so. I've been asking around about you, just in case you are stingy with the details."

Uneasiness rippled. "And what did you discover?"

"Not much. You are an enigma, my boy. I like that. You've kept yourself hidden. Your mother's influence, no doubt."

"Why would you say that?"

"'Rollo, don't make a spectacle of yourself. You'll draw attention. They'll see that you're different.'"

His imitation of Marie Savoie was so dead-on it took Max aback. And for the first time, he could see them together, his mother and this man he didn't know. He sat frozen in his seat.

His father . . .

Mocking his mother.

His eyes narrowed slightly, their inner light growing cold and clear.

Oblivious to the insult he'd delivered, Rollo chuckled. "Such a strong, vibrant woman, but a little too conservative. Always seeing worries that weren't there. Always putting boundaries around any kind of fun. I wished she'd learned to just relax and enjoy life."

"Perhaps she didn't have the luxury."

"She deserved better," the older man mused, suddenly somber. "Better than me, certainly. I was young and wild and irresponsible. The thought of trusting me to take care of her and a child must have terrified her. She was right to run from me when she did, before I knew about you. I would never have let her leave and take my son from me." He frowned at the tabletop for a long moment, then his gaze lifted to study the impenetrable features opposite him. "How did you get on, just the two of you?"

"We got by. She saw I had everything I needed."

Rollo let it pass for the moment, asking instead, "Who killed her, boy?"

"I didn't know them. But I took care of them for her. And then I took care of her for as long as I was able."

Rollo stared curiously at the calm face, into the unblinking eyes. "You killed them." When Max didn't answer, he sat back in his chair. "You were four, maybe five years old?"

"I don't know. I don't know how old I am now."

"Your first kill. So young."

"No. Not my first."

"My, you are full of surprises," Rollo murmured, impressed and something more. Something Max couldn't identify as Rollo leaned forward to clink his bottle against Max's.

Behind his blank facade, Max pushed down the horror of what he was, of what he'd done. His hand was steady when he picked up the bottle and drank the contents in several quick swallows.

Rollo grinned at him and gestured to the waitress. "A couple more here." After he thanked her, he turned back to Max with renewed interest. "So Jimmy Legere took you in and raised you. He knew what you were, of course, and was more than happy to exploit you. Just like his father before him."

"Yes."

"And Legere was the one who taught you about what you are?"

"Yes."

Rollo chuckled. "I'll bet he did. Just enough to keep you under his control. Jimmy was more clever than his old man. But he left everything to you. Why, do you suppose?"

Max didn't answer.

"You think it was because he cared for you?" A loud scoffing laugh. "They don't care for us, Max. They tolerate us when it suits them. They use us when it's to their advantage. We are a wonderful, unstoppable weapon when clenched in their greedy fists. But like us, care for us? Never. They fear us like they fear the shadows, like they dread the corners of the night. They would destroy us all if they could. Because we're stronger, we're smarter, and they're just beginning to figure out the one thing that terrifies them more than anything else."

"What's that?"

"We don't need them."

Max emptied the second bottle as strange, unsettling emotions prowled through him. He'd never considered what Rollo said. Would never have believed it to be true.

Until Charlotte Caissie.

"I think," Max drawled, "that it's you who's afraid of them."

Rollo's eyes gleamed hot gold. "For now, but not for much longer." He shoved his chair back but found it stopped by the solid bulk of Jacques LaRoche.

"Who's your friend, Savoie?"

Before Max could answer, Rollo twisted to glare up at the intruder. "No one who is interested in becoming yours, so back away, mongrel, and mind your business."

LaRoche's eyes narrowed, but his voice remained pleasant. "This is my business and if you're bringing trouble to it, you'd best think again."

Rollo came up out of the chair like a rocket fueled by rage. He had the bigger man by the throat, and with a roar threw him like a stunt dummy over a half dozen tables and through the last of them. Before Jacques could gain his feet, Rollo was on him, crouched upon his chest, head flung back to transform into a snarling, shaggy beast, red of eye and long of fang.

As he readied to tear into the lesser form below him, while those around them shrank back in shock and dread, a hand took a tight, twisting grip in the ruff of long hair at his nape and propelled him, headfirst, into the oak bar.

Dazed but still wild with fury, Rollo rolled to his hands and knees. His assailant caught him by the lupine face, thumb hooking beneath his ravening jaw and fingers clamping hard about the jowls and pressing into his eye sockets. Unable to attack and mad with frustration and pain, Rollo heard a single word spoken low, pounding like blunt force trauma.

"Think."

He blinked. Max stood over him, eyes hot as molten gold, but otherwise unchanged. His powerful grip didn't ease until Rollo's tense pose relaxed. Then he was released, and Max stepped back to offer a hand up to LaRoche.

Rollo gained his feet slowly, aware that the others kept their distance but that Max held without a flinch. He laughed, letting his features reform, ignoring LaRoche to focus upon his son. "Forgive me. I didn't realize this group of runts was yours."

"Now you know," Max told him.

"You waste your time with them, boy. You are so far above them and their petty, groveling lives."

"It's where I belong."

Another loud, mocking laugh. "You need to decide where you will stand, Max. Will it be with those Uprights who pretend to accept you? Or among your own kind, your peers, where you could be royalty? Think about that. We'll talk again."

No one moved to challenge him as Rollo strode out boldly through the crowd. They were seeing something new, something both terrifying and wonderful. Two purebloods in their midst with unimaginable power. The power to protect them . . . or destroy them.

"Who is that?" LaRoche growled, recovering from his defeat with a surly humor.

"No one you want to know," Max said.

Someone I may have to kill.

MAX TRIED NOT to think about it as he stood in the shadows across the street from Charlotte's apartment. The beers had him slightly off balance—his first experience with alcohol—but it was the scent of the woman asleep upstairs that had him reeling.

One ring, two, then her husky voice.

"Caissie."

He closed his eyes. He was trembling.

The silence made her tone sharpen. "Who is this?"

"Heya."

"Hey, yourself." The tough edges melted into a soft murmur.

"Can I come up?"

A telling hesitation. "It's three o'clock, Max. I have to be up in less than two hours, and the reporters just stopped rummaging through my trash like raccoons about an hour ago."

"Is that a no?"

"I wish it didn't have to be."

"Okay."

"Where are you?"

"Across the street."

The curtains were pulled back from the window in her bedroom. Ordinary eyes would have seen just a silhouette, but Max could see the expectation brightening her features. His system clenched at the sight of her sleep-tousled hair and the rumpled shirt that looked so much better shaped to her curves than his hard lines. He could breathe in the heat of her from her sheets. Her head turned, tilting. He could almost taste her pursed lips.

"I don't see you."

He didn't move into the light. "Oh, *sha,* but you look good to me. I couldn't convince you to pull up that shirt, could I?"

She smiled against the cell phone. "For the edification of my neighbors? I don't think so."

"I'm so hungry for you, I could devour you in one bite."

"Hmmm. More ideas gleaned from your behind-bars buddies?"

"I don't need any help coming up with ideas where you're concerned. My mouth is watering for the taste of you."

"Yeah? What kind of ideas?"

"I want to pour syrup on you and have you for breakfast."

A pause, then a low purr. "Think of the mess."

"I'm thinking." More softly, more seductively. "I'm thinking it would be worth it."

"Ummm. What else are you thinking?"

"How it would pool all warm and thick on your skin. Sweet. Sticky sweet trickling down your belly. Me chasing those drips with my tongue."

The sound of her breath growing light and fast made him hesitate, giving her a minute to let her imagination work before continuing. "I'd have you naked on the dining-room table. Ready for me. Hot and ready."

"I'm burning up for you, baby. Don't hurry. Make me wait."

"I don't know if I can. I want to taste you. Can I taste you, Charlotte?"

"Not yet. Not yet. Touch me, Savoie. Tell me how you'd touch me." Her head was thrown back, resting against the window sash, offering her arched neck, the thrust of her torso.

"Slowly. Like torture. Gliding over that thick, sweet syrup. Spreading it over your skin with my palms. Rubbing it over your breasts. Warmed by my hands. Can you feel it? Close your eyes, Charlotte. Can you feel me?"

"Yes." A whisper.

"Your body burning. Wanting me. My mouth on you. My breath on your throat. Soft. Light."

"Soft," she sighed.

"On your lips. Open for me, Charlotte. How do I taste?"

"Sweet." Her voice was a rough moan. "God, you're sweet."

"Can I come up?"

He heard her take a quick, gulping breath. "Geez, Savoie, I don't think I need you to, now. Whew." Her laugh was low and rich. "I'm out of syrup and now I'm a mess. Go home, Max." Silence, then a tender confession. "It's good to hear your voice."

"Dream of me, Charlotte."

She closed the phone, touched her fingertips to her mouth, then pressed them to the window screen.

Eight

"Francis, come in here a moment."

Francis Petitjohn hesitated outside the open door, telling himself it wasn't because he was afraid of Savoie. Wiping his palms on his pressed trousers, he stepped inside what used to be his office, smiling.

Savoie turned to him, that rich, glossy exterior hiding the monster within, the monster no longer under anyone's control. In that confident stance, T-John saw no trace of the frightened, silent kid Jimmy had brought back from the swamps. The one he used to tease and belittle out of boredom and jealousy because he knew Max would never strike without Jimmy's say-so. That reassurance was gone now, and he wondered how much resentment simmered behind the cool green stare. The fact that he'd tried to kill Max might also have something to do with his uneasiness.

"What can I do for you, Max?" The humble tone, like the smile, pained him, but he knew how to play the game. He knew how to be patient and wait for the right moment.

"Rollo. Tell me everything you know about him."

T-John's surprise was genuine. Rollo? What had brought him up? "He worked for Jimmy's father, Etienne. Dangerous and unpredictable, he was. Never took to the leash, like you did."

No reaction to the swift sharp barb. "Where did Etienne find him?"

"Doing illegal fighting down at the docks at night. He was the odds-on favorite when it came to ripping apart an opponent. They said he couldn't be hurt. That no matter how much damage was inflicted on him, the next day, he'd be on the job without even a scratch. Something you'd know about. Even his own kind was afraid of him. Which is, of course, why Etienne went looking for him. He was a crude, brutal creature. What little power Etienne gave him was enough to send him out of control."

"Tell me."

"Oh, he was good at taking care of any problems Etienne gave him. Took care of them in an unmistakably messy way. He didn't have your . . . discretion or delicacy. And he also lacked your dislike of notoriety. He loved the attention. Liked to boast and shock and swagger. He enjoyed all the vices Etienne's money would provide, too much so.

"My father went to his brother, told him Rollo was bringing too much notice to their business, with his sloppy habit of bragging about what he'd done at the bar with his booze and whores. He told Etienne to take care of it, to take care of him.

"But Etienne wouldn't listen. I don't know if it

was because he hated to give up the power or if he was afraid of his own creation. Like father, like son, I guess. Kind of an ironic pattern, eh, Max? Kind of a 'bit the hand that fed them.'"

The glitter in Savoie's eyes told T-John he might have gone too far, so he quickly soothed over the insult.

"Rollo was a savage animal. He didn't have the advantages you had. Jimmy gave you polish and self-restraint. And he made you smart enough to see consequences. To know how to weigh the value of those around you instead of slaughtering indiscriminately."

"Which is probably why you're still alive."

T-John's smile thinned. "Exactly." He moved restlessly to one of the walls, studying the odd collection of masks Max had displayed. Not the elaborately decorated and elegantly detailed porcelain Mardi Gras masks sold for a small fortune in the Quarter to grace a stylish parlor, but crude, feral depictions roughly carved into animalistic demons with jeweled eyes and wicked fangs. Reminding him of the reality that lay behind the mask of humanity Max wore all too easily these days. Frowning slightly, he turned his back on them.

"Was my mother one of his . . . women?"

"I don't know, Max. I didn't know your mother. Jimmy, like his daddy, kept those details to himself."

He couldn't tell if he was believed or not.

"You said there was a falling-out between your

father and Jimmy's and that Charlotte's father was involved. What was that about?"

"Caissie set up some sort of sting operation using a project of Cummings's to draw Etienne in. When the trap slammed on him, Etienne blamed my father for the betrayal and killed him. Another irony. That death was the reason he went to prison."

"And who do you blame for your father's death?" Max asked softly. "Jimmy, because of his father's greed? Charlotte, because of her father's ambition? Cummings, because he was in the middle? Or me, because of what I am?"

A trick question.

"I blame my father for being a mean, selfish bastard in a long line of mean, selfish bastards. Why all the interest in Rollo?"

"Just trying to fit some things together."

"What things, Max?"

"Nothing important." Max withdrew into his own thoughts, his expression unreachable.

"What is important to you, Max? I'm wondering if it's Jimmy's business or yours with those creatures from the docks."

"You mean, my people."

T-John ignored Max's smooth comment, refusing to be drawn into that dicey area. "You spend more time cultivating their favor than those who control them."

"They control themselves now, Francis. And they look to me. Jimmy never understood the strength that powers a leader. It's loyalty in numbers. He took that for granted."

"Like he took you for granted."

Max had no reply to that. It was still a fairly raw subject, one he'd yet to address in relationship to his own guilt and regret. "Jimmy taught me to make the most of what was at hand, to seize an advantage even from an unlikely source. The way he did with me. The way I will with them."

"The way you're losing thousands upon thousands by turning away from the way my family's done business for generations?"

"Illegally, you mean? Times change, T-John. A fella doesn't have to be dishonest to make a dollar. He just has to be smart. I have my reasons."

"A long-legged, hard-nosed reason by the name of Caissie?"

But Max had already dismissed Petitjohn from his mind.

Caissie, Cummings, and Rollo. He now had a link, a place to start, with Petitjohn tossed in on the periphery. What he needed was motive. And proof would be nice. Something he could present to Charlotte to earn his way back into her arms, and her trust.

Rollo was the key, and getting close to him was the only way to find out the truth. The truth of what happened to Sandra Cummings and Vivian Goodman. The truth of why his mother ran away with him.

The secrets of what it meant to be pure of blood.

CUMMINGS WAS THE key. Cee Cee dug through the public records, sitting at her computer screen hours after Babineau had gone home to his wife. Until she broke this case, she had nothing to go home to.

The floor was quiet. Apparently everyone else had lives to go home to, too. The night shift was out on some drug-related shooting where the Quarter spilled over into Faubourg Marigny. She leaned back in her chair, trying to rub the grit of fatigue from her eyes and find some still-functioning brain cells to continue her search.

There had to be something she was missing. Some connection she wasn't making. With her eyes closed, with the silence surrounding her, she could see Sandra Cummings's lifeless stare pleading for justice for a life not yet lived. Could see the dull despair in the eyes of Vivian Goodman's husband as he gathered his children to him, seeking to protect them from a loss of love that tore through his soul.

These people needed someone to care about their pain, their loss. Someone who would understand their fear and be strong enough to strike back, hard. Without the mercy that they never received. Knowing she was letting them down with every day she delayed brought a fist of frustration to clench her heart. An ache that just kept getting bigger until it was difficult to work around it.

Because behind the expectant, needy stares of the

Cummings and Goodman families were the desperate, trusting blue eyes of Mary Kate Malone begging for rescue.

"*Make them stop. Lottie, make them stop.*"

"*I can't, Mary Kate. I couldn't then, and I can't now.*"

Her cell rang. She snapped it open, snarling, "Caissie."

A pause, then a deep, caressing voice.

"What are you wearing?"

All the tension ebbed from her on a shakily grateful expulsion of breath. Desire and longing flushed heat to all the cold niches of her spirit. She leaned back in her chair, smiling.

"I'm dressed to meet my lover. How do you think?"

"Tell me."

"Where shall I start?"

"With your feet."

She looked at the stubby toes of her Doc Martens as she lifted them to the corner of her desk. She'd gone for comfort today—boots, jeans. And one of Max's silky shirts rolled up to the elbows.

"I've got on heels. Three-inch, with open toes. Black. My nails are hot pink."

"Hot. I'm taking them off you. I'm rubbing your feet. Your sexy feet."

"Ummmm. Nice."

"Are you wearing stockings or are your legs bare?"

"Stockings. The kind that only go up to midthigh. Black and sheer."

"Ooo. Put your hands on them. Tell me how they feel."

"Smooth and silky."

"And your legs?"

"Hard. I've been working out."

"Hard. Yes. I'm ready to give you a workout." His tone roughened. "Higher."

"I'm wearing a skirt. Short, leather. The one you like."

"And under it?" His breathing quickened.

"Just the bare necessities. Silky and black."

"And damp?"

"For you. I want you, Savoie."

"Where are you?" A husky growl.

"At work."

A shocked pause. "Dressed like that?"

She grinned, imagining his expression. "I'm on loan to the hooker detail."

"Yeah?" Hopefully. "I have money."

"Yeah? I like 'em rich. Maybe we can work something out that's mutually beneficial."

"I don't suppose you take American Express. I'm trying to build up some bonus points."

"Strictly cash, and get carried away. Unless you want to just go at it with this luscious lonely lady over the phone. Then you can just whip it out and start reading me the numbers and expiration date."

"Sounds delightful, but I'm in the mood for hands-on. How much should I bring?"

"Depends on what you want me to do for you, and for how long. You might want to consider asking for some of that disgusting stuff. High-ticket items, but I'm *so* worth it."

"Yes, you are. I want it all. Everything. All night."

"Could you be more specific there, sexy guy?"

"Whoa, detective. Moonlighting?"

At Babineau's amused tone, Cee Cee's eyes popped open and her feet dropped off her desk. "Gotta go," she whispered into the phone.

"I miss you, Charlotte."

"Same here." She snapped the cell shut and glared at her partner, her face flaming. "You could have knocked."

He spread his hands wide, gesturing to the big open squad room. "I thought I was being discreet in announcing myself before you started running a per-item cost analysis on your desk calculator. Then I would have had to run out and find a quarter movie in a beater booth somewhere."

"Ha, ha, ha."

"Ha, ha, hot. Shame on you for misusing office communications. Maybe you should call it a night. Savoie is probably already camped on your doorstep, counting out twenties."

Cee Cee turned back to her computer. Her tone was flat. "We're not seeing each other."

He perched on the corner of her desk, his pose

casual, his attitude that of a confidant. "That's news. Since when?"

"Since Atcliff told me to cut him loose or take myself off the case." She started entering in data to look busy.

"And Savoie's okay with that?"

"Why wouldn't he be? He knows how important my job is. After all, it's his bacon I'm trying to keep out of the frying pan."

"Then he's a better man than I would be," Babineau muttered under his breath.

She wheeled her chair back to glare at him. She didn't want to hear his lecture on Max, nor did she want to bare her broken heart by discussing him. "What are you doing here? I thought you clocked out for some domestic bliss?"

"The mother-in-law stopped over." He made a face. "Tina suggested I bring some of her leftover lasagna down to you."

"She did?" Cee Cee's eyebrows flew up in genuine surprise. "That was nice."

"She *is* nice." His tone betrayed the annoyance he rarely displayed regarding his partner's unreasonable prejudice against his wife. He didn't argue the point because it didn't really make a difference. It wouldn't change Charlotte's mind and it would only tick him off about it even more. He sighed in resignation and explained as if to a stubborn child, "She's a nice person. That's why I married her."

"How nice for you both. Now, go home and let me get back to work. Leave the food."

He put the plastic dish down on her desk, then hesitated.

"What?"

"Ceece, there are some things more important than the job."

"Name one."

He could have mentioned the circles under her eyes, the downward turn to her mouth, the unhappiness that radiated from her. But if he told her, she'd just deny it. He shrugged. "That's for you to figure out."

"Great. Another mystery of the universe to solve. I'm out of time and tolerance."

"Any leads?" He craned his neck to get a look at her screen. Archived press clippings on Cummings and the waterfront. Again.

"No. I think I need to have a heart-to-heart with Cummings. He knows more than he's telling us, and I'm running out of patience with secrets."

And she was running out of patience where Max Savoie was concerned. As enjoyable as it was, she was tired of having a $2.99-a-minute type of relationship with him.

She didn't want anything coming between them except a good, healthy sheen of sweat.

So she chased Babineau home, brought up another screen on the computer, and began to read.

———

HE STOOD AT the bar, surrounded by eager women drawn by his dark good looks, rough charm, and blatant desire to bed one or all of them. And by his power. He was never without a drink or a smile, yet Max detected a subtle disgust for those who fawned over him. He remembered Petitjohn's summation. Rollo loved the adoration, the sense of superiority. The vain, boisterous top dog who wouldn't like being challenged or pushed or pressured. And that's what Max would have to do if he wanted to discover what was behind Rollo's reappearance in New Orleans.

The instant Max let down his guard, Rollo was immediately aware of him, as were the others. He watched Rollo's expression tighten as attention shifted from his raucous storytelling to the new lord of the Crescent City underworld.

Max paid no notice to those who rushed to greet him, or to LaRoche, who stood silent and glowering behind the bar. Max's focus was on the man leaning against the bar on his elbows, waiting for his approach.

"Hello, Max. Buy you a drink?"

"No. Let's take a walk."

Suspicion narrowed his eyes. "I'm comfortable here."

"We can't talk here." And with the arrogant assumption that he'd be followed, Max started for the door.

Rollo hesitated, debating, then fell in step.

The hole-pocked street was puddled with water

from a late afternoon shower. Steam rose from its glossy surface, creating a curtain of mystery before the sidewalk's end. Noise and music from the tourist traps on the next block dimmed and faded as they moved in silent accord into deeper shadows. Going where no casual fun seekers would dare venture without a wish to lose their wallet. Or worse.

"What do you want?" Max asked without preamble.

"To finish my drink and pick from among those hot little beauties at the bar."

"Why are you here?" Max clarified, his voice clipped and impatient. "What brought you back here? To my city?"

A pause. Max could sense Rollo's irritation at the demand to know his business, and at the possessive way he lay claim to all around them.

"I wanted to meet you."

"You've met me. Why are you still here?"

"Not a man of many words, are you, Max?"

"No. I prefer actions."

Rollo chuckled. "A silent, deadly assassin. When you come up on them, they don't even know you're there. Not me. I like them to know. I like them to see me coming. The anticipation is half the fun."

"You like it, then? The killing?"

"There's no drink, no drug, no woman that can come close to matching that kind of rush. The excitement. The danger. The power. You know exactly what I mean."

"Do I?"

Again the soft, mocking laugh. "It's instinct. It's what we are. Or did your mother and Jimmy civilize that out of you?"

"No."

"What about your woman? Your policewoman?"

A prickle of alarm. "What about her?"

"Do you wear the Upright role to impress her? Do you pretend to be less than you are so you won't scare her into squeezing her knees together?"

Max bit down on his reaction to defend Charlotte Caissie; he didn't want Rollo to know the depth of his feelings for her. So he shrugged off the crudity. "She's not that important. It's hard to carry a torch for someone who would happily set fire to your windmill."

"What?"

"Never seen any of the Frankenstein movies? You know, where the frightened mob traps and burns the monster? To kill what they fear?"

"Ahh. You think those ignorant villagers are all you have to fear? If you do, you would be sadly mistaken, Max. Sometimes your greatest enemy is the one that knows you, the one that calls you friend."

"LaRoche?"

"Perhaps. But there's a bigger picture, Max. A much bigger picture, way beyond the borders of this little city you're trying to control."

"Explain."

"I'm not the only one interested in you. Were you

naive enough to think that all of our kind is concentrated here in your swamps, in your city?"

Max stopped. Was Rollo speaking of those mysterious others from the north? *"They will find you. They will hurt you and kill you,"* his mother had warned.

"Who's looking for me?"

"Let me worry about that. That's why I'm here. To protect you."

"Why should I believe that? Why should I trust you?"

"Because you are the last of my line, my son, the best of all that came before you. I don't want that to end. I don't want *you* to end."

"So you would save me from this danger you refuse to describe. That for all I know exists only in your mind."

"Yes. I need a job. A place to stay. Money. You have no idea how strong, how powerful I am. I can keep you safe."

"Like you kept Etienne Legere safe?"

Silence.

"If you are so strong, so powerful, why did you run away? Why didn't you protect him?"

"I don't risk my life for those not of my kind."

"You don't risk anything unless there's a profit to be made."

Rollo laughed. "I see you understand me well. Good. Make it worth my while, Max, and I'll protect you and I'll teach you the things Jimmy never would."

"What things?"

"You think this"—he gestured to their physical forms—"is all we are? Do you think it's just extra-sensory parlor tricks and the ability to transform ourselves like a child's cartoon character? No, Max. You and I are so much more. Capable of so much more."

A force burst inside Max's head like a bomb, dropping him to his knees. He struggled and was finally able to fling up a defense against it. A fierce growl rumbled from him as he crouched on the sidewalk, wiping at the blood streaming from his nose.

"I could have killed you, Max. Just like that. And you never knew it was coming. That was a pulse; pure sensory energy. Like a fist exploding on the inside, if you know how to do it. Easily detected, if you know how to feel it coming before it hits." He put down his hand. Max took it cautiously and allowed Rollo to pull him to his feet, where he assumed a stiff, offensive stance. "You have no idea what makes you vulnerable, what can cripple or control you, do you?"

"Silver."

Rollo made a dismissing gesture. "Not if you build up an immunity to it. I've been shot four times and I'm still standing."

"How?"

"I could tell you."

"So tell me now."

"So impatient."

"Don't play games with me. I don't like games."

"I do. Getting to know each other is the first we'll play. Humor me. Pretend to enjoy it."

"I'm not good at pretending."

Rollo laughed. "Then make it worth my while, boy. Make it worth my while."

GILES ST. CLAIR glanced into the rearview mirror to where Max sat still and straight. "Where to, boss man?"

"Home."

He'd almost said Charlotte's. But she didn't want him there, not while the bodies of Sandra Cummings and Vivian Goodman were laid out between them. She needed to focus on doing her job under a judgmental public microscope, and he needed to think of a way to keep her job from spilling over into his world. At least until he knew for certain what he was beginning to suspect. His suspicions wouldn't be confirmed until he knew why.

It was better that he keep his distance; he couldn't let Rollo discover his weakness for her. The only thing worse than living without her would be knowing he'd caused harm to come her way.

He was playing a dangerous game, trying to out-maneuver a master manipulator. How could he get what he needed from Rollo without becoming vulnerable to his treachery? Everything he said could be a lie. Or it could be a truth vital to his survival.

"They will find you and hurt you."

A shiver of dread started to uncoil inside him. He had no one to turn to, to trust. Not Jimmy. Not Charlotte. The panic just kept building, restrained only by his outer stillness.

He entered the quiet house, where he was alone with the darkness and troubled dreams that awaited. He stood at the bottom of the stairs for a long uncertain moment, looking up toward the old emptiness, unable to make himself move. He wanted to hide himself away, to howl in distress the way he had when he was a child.

"They will take you and hurt you."

"Some of the fellas and I are going to play a few hands. You can sit in if you like. They'd welcome someone who actually has some cash to lose."

Max glanced at Giles, startled by the offer. "I don't know how to play cards."

"It's easy. It's fun. If you're winning." He grinned, and Max felt a small degree of his terror let go. "Come on. Jasmine always serves up snacks that are almost as tasty as she is. You can watch for a while until you feel comfortable joining in. Or you can just kick back and let us make fools of ourselves."

"Are you sure they won't mind me being there?" That wasn't said by the man responsible for everything from the roof over their heads to the money they were placing on the table. It was from the shadowy figure at Jimmy Legere's back who was feared and ostracized from the time he made his killing bones as a teen.

"Naw. They won't care."

Max settled into one of the big club chairs set back away from the table. The men at play regarded him warily at first, then finally seemed to forget he was there. While not exactly embraced by their camaraderie, he was able to relax in the congenial atmosphere. He didn't intrude where he didn't think he'd be welcomed without an awkwardness he'd rather avoid. Better to just halfheartedly follow the plays, listening to their casual and often ribald conversation on the outer edge of their pack mentality of acceptance. Safe.

And finally, lulled by their laughter and the murmur of their voices, he fell asleep.

He never felt the housekeeper place a light hand on his head after wedging a pillow under it.

Giles turned to Helen with a nod. "Don't worry. We'll watch out for him."

And under that blanket of protection, Max slept without dreams.

Nine

THE SIGHT OF Max struck Charlotte like an unexpected punch to the midsection. Her breath faltered, then wedged in a huge knot of longing at the base of her throat, burning there until her eyes swam.

She hadn't seen him or spoken to him in seven days, yet he was rarely out of her thoughts. Her sleep suffered for it. Her work suffered for it. She was edgy, snapping at her coworkers, distracted and fatigued. Unable to focus on anything except how wretched she felt, she stumbled through that lonesome week wondering why the emptiness mattered so much. She'd been a loner all of her life, with the exception being her friendship with Mary Kate. She never went anywhere, did anything; she had no social life, nothing but the job. And she'd never faltered there. Not ever.

But now, what had been a pleasant distraction with an unsuitable male had become an all-consuming obsession, taking control of her life at the most inconvenient times.

Like now. When she was on her way to speak

to Simon Cummings about her unacceptable lack of progress.

She stopped abruptly in the busy lobby of the office building with its prestigious Canal Street address. And on the other side of the mezzanine, Max Savoie did the same. Her partner's restraining hand on her elbow was the only thing that kept her from tearing across the black and white marble squares to throw herself into his arms. That, and Babineau's quietly spoken words.

"Don't look now, but Karen Crawford and her camera crew just came in. You go over there, and you and Savoie will be all over the next edition. Then there'll be hell to pay all around."

"I don't care."

"Yes you do. Take a breath. Look away. You're jumping the man with your eyes."

That's not what she wanted to jump him with.

"Doesn't that woman ever follow up on real news?" Cee Cee grumbled. She started to walk, a fierce stride that paralleled Max's toward the elevator banks. He didn't look over at her again, but she could read his awareness of her in the way he moved. He was wearing his long dark raincoat in deference to the cloudbursts that had come and gone all morning, and impenetrable dark glasses that did nothing to disguise his identity. She'd never seen anyone control the attention of an entire room just by passing through. She could envision him striding in lethally sexy slow motion through a John Woo shoot-'em-up movie, his long coat swirling. The intensely dangerous aura surrounding him was unmistakable.

This morning he was traveling with an all-business entourage, starting with his attorney, Antoine. Giles and Teddy she knew, but the other man, the one she only caught glimpses of, was a stranger to her. It was for effect, she knew. Max Savoie didn't need anyone to protect him. Not when he was the most deadly force she'd ever encountered.

They reached the elevators at the same time, she and Babineau coming in from the left, Max and his party from the right. Crawford and crew charged down the center of the crowded lobby, trying to reach them before one of the doors opened. The car directly in front of Max came to a stop, its green Up arrow flashing on. A group of three businessmen slipped in ahead of him. By the time Max's trio of tough guys and his dapper lawyer joined them, Max took the last spot, facing front as the doors began to shut.

As Karen Crawford wheezed up behind Cee Cee on her nosebleed high heels, Cee Cee jumped forward between the closing doors before Babineau could stop her, wedging in at Max's side.

"What floor, detective?" Antoine D'Marco asked, much too polite to express his annoyance.

"Eleven."

"What a coincidence."

Max didn't glance at her as she settled in next to him. "Nice to see you, Detective Caissie."

How carefully neutral.

"With those dark glasses, I'm surprised you can see anything."

He reached up to take them off, and she could see immediately why he'd left them on. His eyes appeared bruised by fatigue when he slanted a look at her. But that wasn't what alarmed her. It was the awful regret dragging at the edges of his expression.

"You look good," he murmured quietly.

"You look like hell."

A faint smile, then his attention turned back to the closed door. Closing himself off from her. Leaving her so anxious and frustrated, she was about to push for the next floor just so she could shove him out into the hall and throw them both down on the tiles. Standing so close and yet a world away, the need to touch him, to lean into him, to reach up to turn his solemn face toward her, to kiss him with all the fierce, prowling passion that had been building for days and now seethed like a low-pressure system spinning out of control. She was shaking apart inside, while he was all cool and remote.

The edge of his hand nudged the side of hers. Then his little finger hooked around hers, and all the jittery panic racing through her system settled and calmed. She took a steadying breath, wishing for the ride to go on forever just so she could stand next to him, tethered by that fragile connection.

The doors parted on eleven. In order to let him go, she had to move fast and not look back. She was out of the elevator as if from starting blocks.

Simon Cummings's office took up one entire side of the building. His reception area was behind an expanse of etched glass, its interior cool in soothing pastels and plant life. Campaign posters were prominently featured on the walls. A staff of three elegant women handled the long counter of light wood, where stacks of political flyers were displayed. Two of the women were on the phone. The other offered Cee Cee a welcoming smile.

"Detectives Caissie and Babineau to see Mr. Cummings."

"He'll be just a moment, detective. Please have a seat." Then her professionally cheery expression froze.

"Max Savoie for Mr. Cummings."

"I'm sorry, Mr. Savoie, but I don't see that you have an appointment."

"I have what he wants. He'll spare a minute for that. Let him know I'm here, please."

"If you'll wait . . ."

"What the hell is *he* doing here?" Cummings's voice rose with fury. He crossed the reception area with angry purpose, shaking off restraining hands to demand, "What are you doing here?"

"You're avoiding my people's calls, so I thought

I'd take care of business personally. I'm Max Savoie." His cool facade was a glaring contrast to the red-faced rage of the other man. He didn't offer his hand.

"I know who you are, you son of a bitch. Get out of my office. If you think you can bully me—"

"I'm here to do business. I have the property and I have the money. And I have a condition. You can talk to me right here, right now, or I walk away and the matter is closed."

His inflexible chill finally reached through Cummings's anger. His seething breaths slowed. "What condition?"

"You can have your riverfront reclamation project. I have no objections to it. But I do insist on one thing. The housing has to provide a percentage of subsidized units."

"How many?"

"Half."

"Half? Are you insane? That will lose millions . . ."

"I already have all the money I need, and I have a place to live. I also have employees who can't find decent housing. Their families live in other parishes in poverty, while my employees stay in one-room dumps or trailers during the week to earn a wage. I don't like that. They are my responsibility. I want them taken care of so they will take care of me. Good business, Mr. Cummings. It's not all about money."

"With Legere, everything was about the bottom line."

"I'm not Jimmy. I want some of my people on the board that decides on eligibility for the units. I don't want to control it, I just want it to be fair. A fair shake is all some folks need."

"Since when is someone like you a champion of the people, Savoie?"

"Since I was forced to become someone like you." Max took a deep breath. "My attorney has the paperwork prepared. It's sound business and good PR."

"I don't want to get in bed with you, Savoie."

"Frankly I haven't been without a woman long enough to find you appealing, either."

Cummings's veneer of civility snapped. He took a quick step forward, pushing his face up into Max's. "You mean since you were with my daughter and my friend?"

"I never—"

Cummings's fist hitting Max's mouth ended whatever he meant to say.

Cee Cee was immediately between them, shoving Cummings back. "That's enough of that," she said sharply.

"Don't you mock my pain, you animal," Cummings shouted into Max's expressionless face. "You have no idea how it feels to lose something so precious. And now you stand there, hiding behind your whore with a badge, smug because you know she's going to let you walk without so much as a slap on your wrist. Where's the justice in that? Where's the justice for my little girl?"

The blinding glow of camera lights announced the arrival of a furiously scribbling Karen Crawford and a grim Alain Babineau. The detective gripped Cummings's arm and hauled him none-too-gently to a safer distance, out of Charlotte's striking range.

But it wasn't Cee Cee who retaliated.

"How can you stand there screaming about justice when *you're* the one who refuses to let it be done? You're a fool, Cummings."

"Max, stop." Cee Cee turned to press her palms against his chest. He swept her out of his way with his forearm without a glance.

"You disgust me," he told the other man with a deep volcanic rumble. But his fury didn't explode; it just kept building, venting steam that scalded. "Not because of your grief. I know how it feels to be gutted by the loss of someone you love. Not even because you're greedy enough to let your family suffer for your careless vanity. You were warned what might happen, but you chose to ignore it for the sake of earning more popularity as an underdog. That's politics, and I suppose acceptable. I despise you because you're stupid."

They all just stared. It was the last thing any of them expected to hear. But Max was far from finished.

"You cry about avenging your daughter's death,

and then you cut the investigation off at the knees by letting that woman"—he gestured at Karen Crawford—"smear the reputation of the only person who can help you uncover the truth.

"I don't need to hide, because I have nothing to be afraid of. I didn't harm your loved ones and I didn't order it done. If I wanted something from you, I wouldn't be that subtle. It would be you and me with no one in the way. That's the way I do things.

"Detective Caissie is just trying to do her job and you hamstring her by throwing scraps and bones of gossiping nonsense to that barracuda so you'll have more press. That's not going to get you a killer, you idiot. *You're* the one standing in the way of solving this crime."

His tone throbbed with intensity. "You had no cause to make this a personal attack on someone I hold in the very highest esteem. You are a coward, as well as a fool, to think you could damage me by ruining her. I don't give a damn about scandal. I'm not going to apologize for things that don't concern anyone else. I'm not ashamed of anything I've done or with whom."

His gaze met Cee Cee's, holding it, probing it, searching for something he didn't find in her wide, alarmed eyes. And then the moment was gone.

"But you"—he turned to the reporter with a withering contempt—"*you* would sacrifice truth and an impeccable career for the sake of a few more seconds on the air. Detective Caissie puts her job and her integrity above everything else, and she would never tarnish it with a personal compromise. I wouldn't let her. And I'm not going to let you, either. So I'm walking away from the best thing I'll ever have because our private life is suddenly the measure of her professionalism. So cut her some slack and let her do what she does best. You want a picture? Take one."

His hand forked under Cee Cee's chin, tipping her head up as he swung in to plant a swift, hard kiss that rocked her to the soles of her feet. Breath rasping fiercely against her shock-slackened lips, he said in a husky whisper, "I was never ashamed to tell the world I loved you, Charlotte."

He straightened and looked to his people. "We're done here. Tony, give those papers to Cummings. He can be smart and sign them or he can stick them up his ass and light them on fire. I don't care." He turned and his stare grew glacial. "Out of my way, Ms. Crawford, or I'll make sure there isn't a tabloid in the country that will touch your poisonous byline."

She jumped aside.

As Max left the office, Cee Cee started to go after him. Babineau grabbed her elbow.

"Let him go. He just gave you the opening you've been waiting for. Take it. *Take it,* detective."

Cee Cee sucked a quick breath, struggling to tear her frantic gaze from the sight of him disappearing into the elevator.

"Detective!" Babineau snapped.

Her head jerked up, her shoulders back. For a moment, her gaze was wild and despairing. Then that cool professionalism locked down tight. She nodded to her partner, then said in a clipped tone, "Mr. Cummings, let's talk."

Once they were behind his closed office doors, Charlotte rounded on him like a pit bull. "All right. Let's cut the crap. Why are you going out of your way to keep me from finding out the truth?"

To her surprise, Cummings's arrogance crumbled. In its place was the terrified expression of a haunted man. "I can't help you, detective."

"Why not?"

"Because Sarah isn't my only daughter."

That cracked her cold veneer. "Has she been threatened? Tell me who's doing this. I can protect you."

His eyes shimmered with fear. "You can't, detective."

"What's happened?"

"She was getting into her car, in broad daylight, in a crowded parking lot. And he was right behind her. He leaned over her shoulder and he told her that in the time it took her to scream she'd be dead. And then he was gone. He put his hands on her, on my other little girl. I *can't* lose them both. I can't."

Cee Cee bullied ahead, fierce and relentless, forcing him to surface from his shock. "Mr. Cummings, what did she say about the man? Anything specific? Anything that might help identify him?"

He stared at her, his expression numb beyond comprehension. Sitting in his posh office, in his trendy suit, surrounded by his efficient staff, with his well-oiled political machine primed for business, he floundered helplessly, a lost and frightened father. "She said he wasn't quite human. What does that mean, detective? What does that mean?"

Cee Cee didn't answer. What could she possibly tell him that he'd believe?

THEY GOT INTO the car, Giles behind the wheel with Teddy beside him, Rollo sliding into the back beside Max. D'Marco had left in his own car after dropping the contracts on the reception desk.

"So," Rollo drawled, "that was your girl."

Max didn't respond.

"I can't say that I was very impressed."

A ghost of a smile touched Max's lips. "You've never seen her in action."

"Where to, Max?" Giles called from the front.

"Take us to the club," Rollo ordered.

But Giles was looking in the rearview mirror, studying the tragic set of his boss's face in the brief instant before he put his dark glasses back on. "Max? What do you want to do? Do you want to wait for her?"

Rollo slapped his hand down on the back of the front seat. "The club," he insisted, voice rough because he wasn't used to having his commands questioned.

Again Giles ignored him. "Max? What do you want to do?"

"The club's fine."

Max settled back against the seat. It didn't really matter where they went. Not now.

He'd handled things badly. He'd let his frustration and worry and loneliness force out words that shouldn't have been spoken in front of the press, in front of Cummings. He'd gone with the intention of anchoring a business deal with Cummings, and in doing so maybe getting the chance to open up a tentative communication. Perhaps if he established a truce with the man, he'd be willing to ease off on his crusade against Charlotte. Noble intentions, until he'd seen her. Until he'd inhaled her scent. Until he'd touched her. Then nobility went out the window in a suicide dive.

He couldn't blame her. She was passionate about her work. Caught up in office politics, hamstrung by official orders, their separation wasn't her idea, and he could tell in that crowded elevator that she was just as miserable.

But beneath the understanding, behind the mask of nobility, rumbled a pure animal fury that something of his was being withheld from him. A possessiveness he didn't fully fathom, an anger he couldn't quite control. At circumstances, so unfair. At seeds being subtly sown that would tear her from him in the name of duty and public opinion.

And because of the irrational, inconsolable part

of him that hurt because she'd chosen pacifying the whining politician over him. After all he'd sacrificed for her.

Even though he'd given her the opportunity to say "To hell with all of you" and walk out the door with him, he was very, very glad she hadn't. Fragile emotions would mend. But cold, hard logic could not be ignored.

Cummings was only part of the problem, and the one he worried about least.

To keep her safe, he needed her away from him. If she got wind of what he was doing, of what he suspected, there'd be no dragging her out of it. She'd wade hip deep into his trouble, making it her own. And she'd make it impossible for him to both protect her and bring her the truth she needed.

So he'd keep her at a distance.

Then he'd stand back and have the pleasure of watching her work. That had always been a pleasure, even when she was chasing determinedly after him. He'd been chasing her, too, but not for the same reason. And catching her had led to his greatest reward. One he had no intention of losing.

Not impressive? He slanted a look at the man beside him. Underestimating Charlotte Caissie was going to be one of the biggest mistakes of Rollo's life.

Underestimating Marie Savoie's son was going to be the other.

———

ALAIN BABINEAU GLANCED at his partner. She hadn't spoken since they'd left Cummings's building. She accepted his choice of a dinner spot without comment, then ate next to nothing. She listened to him moan and complain about his mother-in-law without calling him a wussy whip. And she let him drive her car. *That* was the kicker.

"He talks a pretty good line, doesn't he?"

"Who?"

"Your fella."

"Savoie?"

"Have you ever had any other fella?"

She looked out the side window. "No. Just him." Her voice was low and flat.

"I've never seen anyone leave Karen Crawford speechless before. Even Jimmy never got in the last word, on or off film. I wonder what she'll run tomorrow."

"Probably something like 'Lead investigator indulges in hot sex with chief suspect in the office of grief-stricken father.' It wouldn't be so bad if we were actually enjoying the hot sex." She tried to laugh, but the sound was devoid of humor.

The fragile glimmer in her eyes kept his tone gentle. "What about a guy like Savoie did you think was going to be easy?"

She had no answer.

"Is the problem him or you?"

That was easy. Max had no problem with who she was. He'd announced her as his girlfriend in front of the entire crème de la crème of criminal society with a possessive pride that had shocked her as much as it did them. He hadn't asked for favors or excuses, hadn't demanded she make choices. He'd accepted her as she was, personal baggage, consuming career and all. And all he asked in return was that she love him and believe in him.

She'd never been one for public displays. She kept her emotions closer than her sidearm. That's why she and Max understood each other so well. They had both gone through life shut off from actual contact with others. She'd hidden behind her badge, and he'd stood in Jimmy Legere's shadow. Somehow passion had gotten them to drop their guards long enough for that first scorching kiss, and they'd let it carry them away, consequences be damned.

"Everything's different now."

She didn't know she'd said that out loud until Babineau asked, "What things?" trapping her into coming up with an acceptable answer that didn't involve criminal loyalties and a responsibility to a preternatural clan. Maybe a generality would suffice.

"I don't know how to reach him anymore, Alain. He's not the same person I fell in love with."

"Is that a reality or an excuse?"

"Max is . . . complicated."

"And you're an open book. Right."

"I don't know what he wants from me, and I'm afraid that when he tells me, I won't be able to give it to him." That truth was like a slide of her soul clipped beneath a microscope. It made her queasy to look at it that closely.

But the truth her partner spoke was even harder to take without flinching. "Charlotte, someday you're gonna have to draw a line—one that you'll never be able to cross again—and you're gonna have to be able to live with whichever side he picks for himself."

She was very afraid that that day was coming soon.

Ten

*T*HEY STOOD AT the marshy water's edge. The swollen moon's reflection dropped into the center of that smooth surface like the opening to another world. As if all one need do was jump in and have faith.

Night sounds filled the still humid air. Frogs, nutria, birds, insects, a symphony of mating calls and conversations hummed about them.

And Max stood with head back, eyes closed, his bare toes digging into the coarse damp grasses, breathing it in, tasting it all in every sense, that wildness of the night. He canted a glance at his father when he chuckled.

"A night like this was made for letting the hair down. But you wouldn't know about that, would you? Jimmy never let you run loose, did he?"

"I wasn't tied up in the yard." A prickly defensiveness sharpened Max's tone. "I could come and go as I pleased."

"But on your hind legs, like a good trustworthy imitation of a man. Am I right?"

Jaw tightening, Max stared back out over the water as Rollo laughed at him, at the tame limitations of his life. At his lack of freedom and his willingness to accept it.

"You don't know what you're missing, boy, if you've never been one with the night. If you've never shed the domestic lie we lead to fit in, to howl at the moon in your natural form."

Max inhaled slowly, and suddenly he was there again, in the putrid swamps, surrounded by the stench of death and danger. "You're wrong," he said tersely. "I do know." He clenched his shaking hands into fists, letting his nails grow until their sharpness pierced his palms. The pain shocked him from drowning in horror. "I do know," he repeated softly.

Watching him curiously, Rollo nudged his arm with the bottle of Jack Daniels.

In his oddly agitated mood, Max took it. He took a quick, burning swallow that somehow warmed the cold residue of terror left by his memories. And because it did, he drank deeply, desperate to escape that awful fear.

Rollo said nothing for a long while, taking back the bottle, taking another casual swig as Max wrestled his tie loose and stuffed it into his coat pocket. Holding to his smile as the younger man flung himself out of his jacket and tossed it carelessly to the ground.

"Bad day at the office?" Rollo asked mildly.

"Every day at the office is a bad day. I don't want to be there. I don't know what I'm doing there." Frustration growled through his words as he snatched the bottle back for another long pull. "Jimmy didn't teach me how to do those kinds of tricks, but everyone looks to me, expecting me to perform on cue."

"That's not what you were meant to do, boy."

Max turned to him, demanding, "What am I meant to do, then? I don't know. I don't know anything about who or what I am. Only what Jimmy's told me."

"And that, I'm sure, was only what was in his best interest." Rollo smiled easily, rubbing a calming hand across his son's tense shoulders. "Relax. Let me show you what you are." He noted Max's caution and chuckled. "You don't trust me at all, do you?"

"No."

He nodded in approval. "I don't blame you. Come with me, Max. Tonight's your night to howl."

The prospect enticed and terrified him. He'd been trained to repress that primitive side of his being, to deny those instincts, to bury them deep. By his mother, who frightened him; by Jimmy, who lied to him; by Charlotte, who was ashamed of him. He'd never been allowed to express his dark, wild side unless it was to protect or settle things for those he loved. He'd never dropped those cautious barriers just to see what he was capable of. He'd been forbidden. He'd been afraid. And he'd forgotten what beat at the heart of him.

Until this moment. Until this dangerous man

pushed the right buttons of pride and rebellious curiosity.

Who would know? His mother was dead. Jimmy was beyond caring. Charlotte had turned away from him. It was his chance to discover, to explore, to indulge in what he was. He could argue that it would bond him with this deadly creature who held tight to secrets he needed to know. But it was simpler than that.

He just needed to know.

"Close your eyes, Max."

At his sudden tension, Rollo laughed.

"I'm not going to steal your wallet. Just a few of your inhibitions. Close them. Now, listen."

"For what?"

"Listen. You'll know."

He sighed and closed his eyes. After a minute, he grew restless. "I don't—"

"Shh."

"But I—"

"Shh!"

Mentally muttering, he forced himself to relax, to forget about the man beside him as he reached out into the darkness of the night. Listening. Growing still. So still, he could hear his own heartbeat and that of Rollo beside him. Could feel the warmth of the blood in their veins, taste the salty sweat on their skin. And then, abruptly, expanding like a sensory explosion, there was more. So much more, he pulled back in alarm.

"No," Rollo told him softly. His hand caught Max's wrist, holding him in place, registering his hurried pulse beneath the press of his fingertips. "Don't fight it. Don't be afraid. Let it in. This is what you are."

It took a moment to get his breathing steady again, then he started to slowly seep out of himself, like liquid pouring out onto the ground, spreading into a wide, wider circle. He wasn't aware of clinging to his father's hand as a tether while he leaned out over the edge of his physical boundaries, wobbling there with a precarious balance, starting to fall. His fingers clutched tight.

"It's all right."

Was he hearing Rollo's voice or just reading a vibration of it in his mind?

"Don't be afraid. I've got you. Nothing can harm you. Relax. Breathe it in. That's it. Slow. Slow. Slow."

He could feel the enormity of it, just on the other side of his consciousness.

"Are you ready? Are you ready for it, Max? It's wonderful. Don't be afraid. Don't hold back. It's beautiful. It's what you are. Open your eyes and see."

Gradually he parted his lids and opened his eyes to a startling new reality. The wonder of it precluded fear. It wasn't sight or sense, the way he was familiar with it. Not even the eerie glimmer he'd learned to recognize. This was everywhere. Light, texture,

depth to everything. The air had weight and sub-
stance. The brightness of the moon brushed cool
upon his face. His extrasensory abilities blended
into an incredible new perception, not separated
into scent or sound or sight, but one fantastic awareness. He let go of Rollo and stretched his hands out
before him, feeling colors in the density of night air,
tasting fragrances as they teased along his fingertips.

"Can you hear me, Max?"

"Yes." But it wasn't sound, not like a speaking
voice. He wasn't cognizant of his physical form or of
the man beside him, and a stab of panic altered his
surroundings, making them into a cold, flat surface,
like a mirror, like the moon reflecting off water. He
reached again, fearlessly this time, to embrace the
strangeness, to let it slide over him, into him.

It was beautiful.

"Where am I?"

A soft chuckle. "Wherever you want to be. Focus.
You can control it. Let down the walls around your
mind so your spirit can fly."

"How far can I go?"

"Find out."

Focus.

One destination consumed him. The only place
he wanted to be. He concentrated on a familiar
scent, on a longed-for heat, let himself be drawn
across a distance that had no meaning.

And she was there.

He couldn't see her through his own eyes,

where she sat in the car he'd given her beside Alain Babineau. He envisioned colors, flavors, glaring infrared-like patterns of heat. Frustrated, he struggled to understand the input he was absorbing. She was speaking, but the sound was garbled as if stuck between two radio stations. He wanted to touch her but when he got close, he fell right through her image into pictures, feelings, voices. Hers.

"I don't know how to reach him anymore, Alain. He's not the same person I fell in love with."

Charlotte?

"Max? Max. Come on back, boy." Rollo's voice, taut and worried. Then sharp with a demand. "Take a breath."

He gasped. Air rushed into his lungs, and he choked as if he'd been suddenly pounded back to life with CPR.

He was lying on his back in the damp grass. He didn't remember falling. His muscles cramped with a hard bout of shivering as an icy chill like he'd never felt before chewed through him. A fierce, soul-emptying cold. He tried to speak, and grew agitated when words wouldn't come.

"It's all right, son. Give it a minute. Just relax. You'll be fine." Rollo pressed his shoulders to the ground, holding him still, forcing him to recover himself slowly. Then he smiled. "Now you know."

"What?" Max wheezed. "What do I know?"

"Why they fear us."

Rollo sat back as Max rolled awkwardly to his

hands and knees. The shaking wouldn't stop. His head spun. He was weak, so weak, completely helpless. Dangerously vulnerable at a time he couldn't afford to be. He swayed, elbows buckling, pitching him face-first. When Rollo's arm slipped around his neck, he knew a moment of perfect hindsight. What a fool he was, to place himself in the hands of this man who was about to kill him.

But instead of snapping his neck, that steely arm braced across his chest, holding him up, supporting him as he sagged, shaky and strengthless, senses whirling. Rollo's other big hand settled on the back of Max's head, still at first, then lightly rumpling his hair.

"The dizziness will pass. The first time's always a bit rocky. I've got you, son." His voice lowered to a husky whisper. "My son." Then his tone roughened. "You did well. How far did you go?"

"The Square."

"Into the city? My God. That's . . . that's amazing. You amaze me, Max. Such power with no training. My *son*." This time he spoke with fierce pride.

And suddenly the warming praise in words he'd longed to hear, the tenderness of an embrace never there to hold him when he'd needed to be held, that pleased assumption that this man, this stranger, had anything to do with what he'd become, ignited a deep, resentful fury.

You son of a bitch, where were you when I was desperate for my father's love?

Max backed out of the arms encircling him, coiling in a defensive crouch of suspicion and rage behind the practiced blankness of his expression. He felt steadier, but still too uncertain of his strength to try to stand.

"What was that?" he demanded.

"The closest I could come to a name would be astral projection."

"As in 'Out of body, be back in five minutes'?"

Rollo laughed. "Something like that."

"And we all can do it?"

A deeper timbre to his chuckle. "Oh, no. No, no, no. They have no idea. No fuckin' idea. LaRoche, the rest, they're herd animals. Clumsy instruments of destruction. Claymores to our elegant and lethal rapiers. I told you, we're the best of the best. We're capable of things that shouldn't be possible. Aren't *supposed* to be possible.

"The others are only capable of simple tricks: shifting, surface sensing. What we can do goes beyond that. So far beyond, it's another galaxy. We can shift, but we can also see and read and project. That's why we're a threat to them. That's what makes us so important."

A shiver of remembrance passed through Max. "Them. Who is them?"

Rollo smiled. "All in good time, boy. First, we need to feed. What you've just done requires an unbelievable amount of energy. You need to rebuild it with heat, blood and flesh."

Darkness flickered through Max's eyes, but his voice was even. "I know."

"Did Marie teach you that?" Rollo looked somewhat mystified.

Max pulled back even farther into himself. "She didn't have time. She didn't teach me anything except to hide what I was. To hide everything about me that was different."

"So how did you learn these things?"

When Max spoke, his tight reply invited no more questions. "Survival is a cruel and necessary teacher."

Rollo surprised him by reaching out, by gripping the sides of his face between his palms. The contact was warm, steady. His voice was intense, yearning. "Talk to me, Max. Tell me what you've seen, what you've endured, what you've done. Let me know you."

"No." He jerked away, then staggered to his feet. "You don't have the right to ask."

Rollo stared up at him, a bittersweet smile curving his lips. Then he nodded. "All right, boy. Your past is your own business. I'll respect that. But allow me just a piece of your future."

"Why?"

"So wary. Marie whelped a smart boy." When he saw the hard glitter in Max's eyes, he quickly moved on. "Curiosity, for one. That and the survival you just mentioned. Reasons enough?"

"For now."

"For now," Rollo agreed, rising to his feet in a powerful movement.

Could he take him? Max wondered. Could he overpower him and kill him if he had to?

Then the dank smell of the swamp stirred the curtain covering his memories.

Oh, yes. He could.

"Hunt the night with me, Max. Breathe in that freedom at my side." He reached into his coat and offered the bottle. Max took it, needing its stabilizing heat, because an uncomfortable anticipation growled through him, beckoned forth by the silky promise of his father's words.

Freedom. He'd never been free. Something had always chained him to this form, to this life, to these obligations. But tonight, on this moon-drenched evening when sorrow whispered through his soul on the words "*He's not the same person I fell in love with,*" he was ready to fling off those shackles and run.

And run they did.

Sleek, dark shapes skimming the shadows like clouds over the swollen moon. Silent, deadly predators seeking what they might devour. Eyes gleaming, nostrils damp and flaring wide at the scent of prey. Working together with a deadly pack instinct to flank and distract and to lunge. Facing off with hackles high and fangs bared, snarling to establish dominance. Then Rollo took a stiff-legged step back, watching his son claim the kill with a savage amusement.

Glorious madness. Tearing through warm hide, feeling the sudden hot spurt of blood on his face, tasting it, thick and potent in his mouth, letting its intoxicating heat rush down his throat.

Max sat back on his haunches, eyes closed, misshapen features lifting toward the stars to howl. The melancholy sound was filled with power and conquest, with the wild sense of freedom.

Crouched on the other side of the gutted animal, Rollo smiled. "This is what you are, Max."

The rest of the evening was a blur, a frenzy of drinking and reckless behavior. Foolish, dangerous animal behavior Max would never in a million years have considered had it been any other night. He followed Rollo along the river, chasing down and ripping apart any creature that frantically tried to outrun them. Tangling with a pack of gaunt, vicious dogs over territory consisting of back alleys and garbage bins. Frightening tourists into racing for their cars so they could root through their abandoned packages in search of anything interesting. Letting their eyes blaze like hellhounds to scare winos into dropping their paper sacks, then lapping up the sour spoils. When one produced a blade and managed to send Max yelping away with a few quick slashes, Rollo was on the derelict with malicious fury, gutting him while Max crouched in the shadows licking his wounds.

But killing the old rummy wasn't enough for Rollo.

Max was a firm believer in justice and retribution and he meted both out with swift, unflinching efficiency. It was something he had to do, not something he particularly enjoyed. And never something he relished with the unholy amusement he saw shining in his father's eyes. A terrible sense of sickness and horror cut through the fog of his conscience as he helplessly watched Rollo toying with the human as he was dying, clipping tendons as he tried to stagger down the alley, stalking him as he crawled, his insides trailing behind. Finally Rollo shifted into the huge man/beast form that had the poor drunkard shrieking as Rollo finally went for his throat.

Chuckling darkly, Rollo wiped the blood off his chin, turning to share the joke with Max—only to find him gone.

IT WAS LATE. Tina Babineau had called three times for an ETA, but Alain was still reluctant to head home. Which only made Cee Cee feel worse. He was feeling sorry for her in her miserable state of heartache.

She wasn't foolish enough to invite him up, nor he foolish enough to suggest it, so they sat on the steps outside her apartment and talked. About work, mostly, because it was the safest topic. She brought out a cold six-pack and they were just finishing it up. She was about to kick Babineau off her stairway and send him back to his wife when a deep rumbling growl made them both freeze.

From out of the thick shadows between parked cars, a huge animal emerged, wolflike in appearance. Its heavy black coat was matted with mud and burrs and blood, and rose in an aggressive bristling ridge from the back of its lowered head to the base of its stiffly held tail. Green eyes gleamed as its jowls curled back in a snarl.

"Don't move," Babineau whispered as his hand went instinctively for his gun.

Cee Cee was quick to curtail the move. "No. There's no need for that."

"Ceece, what are you doing?"

He grabbed for her arm but she was off the steps, approaching the threatening animal with palm outstretched. She advanced slowly, carefully, but without fear as Babineau eased out his piece, just in case the beast proved as vicious in action as in appearance.

"It's all right, baby. It's okay. Come here to me."

She crouched down and waited for the creature to start forward in a slightly altered gait. The crinkles eased from its muzzle and the menacing teeth disappeared. The badly scratched nose pushed into her hand. Her other immediately stroked over the filthy coat in search of obvious injury while she scolded softly.

"You are a mess. What have you been up to? Geez, you stink. What have you been rolling in? Let's hope it's what and not who."

The dark head nudged up against hers, chin resting on her shoulder, while the brilliant eyes closed on a heavy sigh.

"It's all right," she repeated gently as her arms circled the thick neck. "I'll take care of you."

Babineau resnapped his holster and came down off the steps. "Need any help?"

Hackles rose and lips curled back, but Cee Cee merely slapped one of the laid-back ears with a curt "Stop it," and the animal relaxed its offensive pose. "Thanks, but I've got him. He just needs to be cleaned up and fed."

"I didn't know you had a . . . dog."

"I don't actually own him. We kind of watch out for each other. You'd better take off. He can be temperamental."

Babineau hesitated. "Are you sure you'll be all right with him?"

"Oh, he wouldn't dare get ornery with me, would you, baby?" She pulled back his head by the ear and stared into the glittery eyes. There was a long stalemate, then the animal's tongue slapped wetly against the side of her face and he leaned into her wearily.

"Okay. I'll see you in the morning. And, Ceece, don't worry about Savoie. He can take care of himself."

"I know. I'm not worried."

As soon as Babineau's car pulled away from the curb, Cee Cee started up to her apartment. Max trotted up behind her and upon entering, immediately headed for her sofa. The guinea pigs started shrieking and raced about their cage, certain he was planning to snack on them.

"Oh, no you don't. Don't you dare get on my furniture until you get in the tub."

After a look of longing toward the soft cushions, he obediently walked to the bathroom, head and tail drooping. He nosed back the shower liner, then jumped in, claws scrabbling on the fiberglass bottom. Cee Cee regarded him for a long frowning moment, waiting for him to shift into human form. Instead he dropped onto his belly, chin on paws, eyes closed.

"If you think this gets you out of having to give any explanations, Big Dog, then you are sorely mistaken." Her chastising had no effect. Finally she relented and grabbed up a fine-tooth hair pick. "All right. Be that way. Let's get these burrs out of you."

He lay still, letting her pull out the nasty barbs, often with clumps of hair attached, twitching and occasionally yipping, but content to let her continue until his filthy coat was free of them. Then the sudden forceful spray of the shower had him scrambling for traction.

"Stand still, you idiot. I don't want to take a shower with you."

He stood quietly while the disgusting evidence of his night out began to swirl down the drain.

Cee Cee upended her shampoo bottle, pouring it along the tough, rangy frame, then gently worked up a lather that smelled a lot better than the creature that had followed her upstairs. As she scrubbed, her heart softened at the feel of his many scrapes and several ugly wounds.

"Out on the town, huh? Not frolicking in any wild doggy sex, were you? I wonder if that would be considered cheating?"

Unhappy because now she was wondering, she rinsed off the suds and briskly toweled him dry. Then she rose up, letting the towel drop.

"If you're not going to talk to me, I'm going to bed. You can sleep on the rug." She snapped off the light, and after a minute heard him skittering his way out of the tub onto the damp floor. After finding some leftover Chinese in the fridge and dropping the open carton on the floor, she went into the dark living room and flopped down onto the couch, irritated, angry, and hurt by his appearance at her door, wondering why he'd bothered to come at all. She could hear the cardboard scoot across her linoleum as he ate. She removed her gun and her shoes and socks and lay down on her back, her forearm braced across her eyes as tears began welling in them. She hated tears. They were so useless. So weak and unproductive.

Then a wet nose nudged under her hand, urging it to slide back over a glossy coat. Unconsciously she began to rub his ears and knead his ruff. He licked her other hand anxiously, quick, wet repetitions that abruptly became his human mouth sucking on her knuckles just as the fingers of her other hand slid into short black hair.

He fumbled impatiently with her jeans, managing to free one of her legs before he was over her, thrusting and thrusting and thrusting into her. Not stopping, not slowing until he heard her breath catch, then let go in a staggering release. A moment later, the hard punch of his own climax left him draped heavy and lax upon her. They didn't speak. They didn't kiss. They didn't look at one another as the sound of their ragged breathing filled the silence.

Don't let me go, Charlotte. Please don't let me become what he is.

Gradually he felt her palms move on his bare skin, charting the slope of his shoulders, the muscled striations and swells of his back and arms. He let his head rest on her shoulder, the tension and upset flooding out of him on a sigh, leaving him relaxed and at peace for the first time in weeks.

"He's not the same person I fell in love with."

Anguish tightened his chest, spoiling the moment. Worse, he couldn't argue the fact. So much had changed since she'd first spoken those treasured words to him. And while his feelings had never once faltered, hers, apparently, were more tenuous.

A sudden shrill whistle made him wince, and he lifted his head to find Cee Cee staring at him curiously. She hadn't heard it. He heard it again, piercing his head that still throbbed from the alcohol. He climbed to his feet, too distracted by the source of the sound from the street below to notice the flash of hurt on Cee Cee's face. By the time he glanced at her, there was only a tough veneer of pride.

"What was this all about?" she demanded with a low throb of insult. "Just thought you'd pop over for some quick TLC and wham-bam-thank-you-ma'am?"

Another stab of sound had him stumbling away from the couch. She was sitting up, jerking her jeans back on by then. He supposed he was lucky she wasn't grabbing for her gun.

"No time for small talk? Fine. Fuck off, Savoie. Who needs you?"

She did.

She needed him so bad it was like putting her heart in a blender and serving it up on the rocks to watch him back away without a word. She strode to the door, hurrying, because in a second she was going to be bawling like a baby. She held it open, her features stony, her jaw locked to keep it from trembling. Seeing him standing there in her living room, sleek, naked, and everything she'd dreamed of, she wanted to slam that door shut and barricade him inside with her until they hashed it out or died trying. But her damned pride wouldn't humble itself to make that first move.

In a blink, he was on all fours, once again the wild thing that had come to her door in search of comfort. He slipped past her to bound down the steps and into the dark car that was stopped at her curb with the door open. It shut behind him and pulled away. And only then did her features crumple.

Jacques LaRoche stood behind the bar, frowning as he toweled the water spots up. Something was very wrong, and he was wondering when he'd need to do something about it.

Max Savoie had come in an hour before with his new man, Rollo. They sat at Max's table and proceeded to drink like camels filling a hump. He'd never seen hard liquor touch Max's lips before, but he was matching the other one glass for glass, growing just as loud and troublesome.

LaRoche had no use for Rollo, finding him obnoxious and aggressive, a dangerous combination. And now Max was mirroring the kind of behavior he wouldn't tolerate from his clientele.

One of the clan women caught Rollo's roving eye. It didn't matter to him that she was mated to another. He stepped in to scoop her up for a dance, squeezing her close and groping her unforgivably. When her mate started from his seat, LaRoche held up a staying hand, then, sighing, put himself in the middle of it. He waded out onto the dance floor, twirled the indignant female back into her lover's arms, then put his own beefy one about Rollo's shoulders.

"Come sit down, my friend, and have a drink on the house."

"I'd rather have that little tasty piece under me."

"Wouldn't we all," Jacques agreed with a wide grin, steering him away from trouble. As Rollo dropped into his seat, scattering the careless stack of empty glasses, Jacques smiled amiably. "On second thought, why don't I bring you some coffee to clear your heads before you head for home."

Rollo sneered. "Are you saying there's something wrong with our thinking? I'm thinking you've got a helluva lot of nerve suggesting that, weakblood. Bring us a bottle and keep your fuckin' nose out of our business. Just do what you're told. That's all you're good for."

LaRoche gritted his teeth until they cracked, then said softly, "Max, are you gonna let him talk to me like that?"

"He can talk to you any way he pleases, as long as he's with me. And he's with me." Max said that quietly, with an icy smoothness. His gaze lifted slowly to fix on the big man's. His eyes were flat, still and deadly. "Now, bring us a bottle."

"Shit." He took a breath. "Don't make me have to ask you to leave, Savoie."

"No. You don't want to do that."

LaRoche wasn't a huge fan of diplomacy. But he was a huge fan of staying alive, and he knew Savoie could change that in an instant. The smart thing would be to back away and pray they didn't decide to tear his place to pieces. But Max's superior attitude was wedging like a chicken bone in his throat, and he was going to have to force it up or down.

"Max, I need to speak with you about something."

"Make an appointment at the office, puppy. We got no time for your kind."

LaRoche ignored Rollo's rudeness to smile rather grimly at Savoie. "Max, a minute."

Max rose up slowly, all distilled power and edgy silence, to follow LaRoche back to his office. The minute the door closed, LaRoche had him by the back of the neck, their faces inches apart.

"I don't care who he thinks he is or if you can rip me in half for saying it, but nobody talks to me like that in my place. *Nobody.* Not even you, Savoie." He waited, breath seething, for Max to tear his head off.

But Max placed a reassuring hand on his arm and said in a surprisingly sober voice, "I'm sorry, Jacques. I'm going to have to ask you to trust me on this. Things aren't what they seem."

The breath gushed from him. "I was about to kick your ass."

"You were about to try." A rather sloppy smile, then Max was all somber intensity once more. "Let it go, Jacques. Please. Trust me. I won't let him get out of hand. Give him some space."

"Why are you doing this? Why are you letting that loudmouth push you around?"

"There's a difference between being pushed and letting someone push you. I'd just as soon he not know that difference for a while yet."

"Why?"

"It's personal. It has to do with who I am and finding out where I come from."

"And what about your girl? What does she have to say about this?"

Max's expression and voice were suddenly murderously smooth. "Nothing. She doesn't know and I want to keep it that way. I'm doing it for her. For the both of us. I know what I'm doing."

"I hope so, Max. It's your game. I'm just on the sidelines."

But for all of his confident assurances, Max wasn't sure at all. All he knew was the dark joy he'd felt running the night, and the slick queasiness in his stomach from watching Rollo torture his victim in the alley. The game he was playing was life or death. He couldn't afford to get caught up. His only objective was to keep Charlotte out of it.

He'd been a fool to go to her. He'd risked everything just to see her, to feel her stabilizing touch, to lose himself within her. But she'd managed to do exactly what he needed done. She'd put his head and heart into perspective. And he'd almost given it all away at that glossy shimmer in her eyes.

He had to keep her away, to stay away even if he was hurting her. Even if it meant losing her.

Because her life was the one stake he wasn't willing to wager.

Eleven

CEE CEE POURED herself into the job, going over both crime scenes again and again. She immersed herself in the private lives of both victims, reaching beyond the obvious political connection to Cummings in hopes of finding some other angle. But nothing was there.

She returned to her apartment only long enough to feed her pets and grab a change of clothes. She didn't stay, because the suit she'd had cleaned for Max still hung on her bedroom door in plastic and his red high-tops were on the floor beneath. She couldn't look at them and keep it together. She knew she should return them to him, but part of her clung to the hope that he'd return for them.

He didn't. Nor did he call. Not even to apologize.

She wasn't making excuses for him, she told herself when she thought of that quick, hard ride on the couch. She was the one who'd told him to step back, to give her room to work the case. She was the one, when he disobeyed that command by coming to her door, who'd let him take her, then tossed him out with a brittle "Fuck off." And he'd gone. Without a word. Without a kiss.

She was so hungry for his kiss, her soul rumbled emptily. There was an intimacy to it that sex alone couldn't match. She'd risked her job for that quick taste of him after his arrest. But he hadn't kissed her.

To hide from the pain, she'd insulated her emotions in the job, blanketing them beneath exhaustion and a brutal self-imposed deadline. Because if she allowed herself even a second to mourn the loss of Max Savoie, she'd come apart at the seams.

What am I not seeing?

She needed to call California to see how Mary Kate was doing, but she was afraid to. Afraid she couldn't handle the news that she was no better.

She spent her nights in the station with a pot of coffee, raking through Cummings's causes and projects, smiling faintly when she came across the news of the riverfront reclamation effort that would provide substantial housing for low-income workers. Karen Crawford's video clip almost deified Cummings. But there was no mention of LE International's involvement or influence. Apparently Max had gotten the last word.

Rubbing her eyes, she switched off her computer. There was nothing in Cummings's business activities to suggest someone was leaning on him to the point of doing murder. And if it wasn't a why, it was a who. If not business, then personal. She didn't know who had killed the two women or why. But she knew *what* had. And she knew where to go to find out more.

After speaking to LaRoche, she'd pushed an entire section of her investigation aside that only she could pursue. The dark preternatural side went so much deeper than the surface connection to Savoie. She knew he hadn't committed the crimes, but that didn't mean he didn't know who did.

And that meant it was time to question him. Unofficially.

She called the house to be told curtly by Helen that he was not there and she didn't know when he was expected. She called his office, even though it was after hours. A recording. Finally she took a breath and dialed his cell phone.

"Savoie. Leave a message."

The sound of his voice shocked her into disconnecting. She studied her shaking hands, then cursed with irritation. Why was she stalling? She knew where he was.

CEE CEE PARKED several blocks down from the club, then stared at her reflection in the rear-view mirror until she had her best game face on. Though she could control her expression, her heart was racing like an Indy 500 car. Nervousness put extra aggression in her stride as she went down the uneven sidewalk. When she recognized a sleek Mercedes and the bulky figure leaning back against it, she stopped.

"Detective." A genuine smile.

"Giles. Is he inside?"

The pleasant expression faded. "Is he expecting you?"

Something in his tone quickened a quiver of ugly suspicion. "No. Why?" A spear of panic. "Is he with someone?"

Giles squirmed. "Don't jump to conclusions."

He was seeing someone else. He was with some-one else.

"He's not himself, detective. Hasn't been, since *he* showed up."

"He who?"

"Rollo. His new right-hand man. They're inseparable. He won't listen to anyone else. Not since you . . ."

Kicked him to the curb. She got it: whatever she was about to walk in on was her own fault. "Who is this guy? This Rollo?"

Giles possessed the fierce loyalty of a bull mastiff, along with the heavy features and brutal strength. Oscillating between his devotion to Max and his distrust of Rollo and the police, he spoke slowly, carefully. "I don't know. Bad news and bad habits. None of this is like Max. None of it. I don't know what's going on with him and I don't much like it. Not going in to work, leaving it to Petitjohn. Gone all night, spending all his time and money with booze and easy pieces." Remembering who he was talking to, he flushed unhappily.

Cee Cee had gone cold clear through. "Thanks for the heads-up." Her voice was as razor-edged as her mood.

Giles nodded miserably.

At the door, she was stopped by the icy female bouncer, who allowed a sneering smile.

"I'm sorry, detective. Mr. Savoie is otherwise occupied this evening. I can't let you in."

"He told you to tell me that?" Her tone crunched on the ground glass shredding her heart.

"He didn't have to."

"Get out of my way. This isn't a personal visit."

Smirking, the woman stepped aside.

Drawing upon years of grit and bravado in the worst possible situations to give her a "Don't mess with me" attitude, Cee Cee strode into the dark heartbeat of the nightclub.

His leather jacket was on the back of an empty chair. Four glasses, a butt-filled ashtray, and a host of empty bottles littered the tabletop.

Cee Cee scanned the dance floor. It was elbow to elbow with couples moving to a raspy-voiced Aretha Franklin crooning "Chain of Fools." And right in the middle of them, with his eyes closed, a cigarette drooping from the corner of his mouth and a longneck hanging from one of the hands curved about the waist of a phenomenally built beauty, was Max Savoie.

She was startled enough to stand there staring. At the way the woman's palms moved with a stunning familiarity along his shoulders, her fingers teasing up into his hair. She said something to him and Cee Cee watched a slow smile move his mouth. That wide, sensuous mouth that had said things to her that now wedged up hot and huge in her throat. She couldn't keep her gaze from scalding over the strong angles of his unshaven face, down the long leanly muscled body swaying with a lethally sexy grace to the music and to a deeper, more intimate beat with someone else. And the fury punching through her was almost as great as the pain. Almost.

His eyes came open slowly to do a quick scan of the crowd. Before he could spot her, Cee Cee stepped back and turned sharply—right into Jacques LaRoche. She jerked away from the big hands that instinctively caught her arms to steady her. LaRoche's sympathetic smile tore her heart and pride in two.

"Here to arrest him or shoot him?"

"I'm trying to decide."

LaRoche grinned at her fierce tone. But he'd also seen the hurt she was scrambling to suppress. His expression sobered. "Take him home. Get him out of here. He needs you, detective."

"It doesn't look like it to me. He appears to be enjoying the hands he's in."

"Looks can be deceiving. He's playing a dangerous game. I don't think he realizes how dangerous."

"I wouldn't waste a bullet on him and I'm not about to waste any more of my time."

His hand was firm on her elbow. "Charlotte, he's in trouble."

She shook him off. "It's not my problem."

His attitude suddenly cooled, as if she'd plunged in his estimation. "Can I give him a message?"

"Tell him—" She swallowed hard. "No. No, I got the message already. Good night, Jacques."

"Take care, detective."

She was pushing her way toward the exit when Max was suddenly in her path.

"Looking for me?"

She didn't dare meet his eyes.

"Not anymore. Move."

His feet planted, forcing her to look up at him. "I smelled your perfume."

"That's not all I smell on *you*. Step back, Savoie."

His voice lowered to a seductive rumble. "You look so good."

"You don't." That was a lie. Her gaze did a quick assessment of his features, loving, wanting what she saw. "You look like you've slept in those clothes and with that—" She broke off, lips pressing tightly together. Her hands fisted at her sides when his circled her wrists, tugging her toward him.

"Dance with me. Sit with me. Have a drink with me."

She twisted her hands free. "I don't want to do anything with you."

"Charlotte," he coaxed softly, unable to keep from touching her. Her hair, her cheek, her shoulder, her waist. And just when she began to thaw a bit, her stare slipped beyond him and she froze up solid. He glanced around to see Amber sliding his jacket about her shoulders as she settled at his table, waiting for him to rejoin her. His grip tightened on Cee Cee's upper arms as he heard her breath suck in through her clenched teeth.

"Take—your—hands—off—me—right—now." Each word was wielded like an eviscerating slash. He let her go and she jumped back into a combative stance.

"It's not what you think."

She gave a taut laugh. "So now I'm blind as well as stupid." She swallowed hard. "I made a mistake coming here. I won't make it again."

"Don't—"

"I have some questions for you. I'll stop by your office tomorrow at three."

His features stiffened. "I see. On the record."

"Yes."

"Your game, your rules, detective." He turned and started back to his table, stopping when he heard the soft snag in her breathing. By the time he looked back, she was gone.

"CHARLOTTE!"

She increased her stride, dashing the tears from her face with the rough swipe of her hand. "Leave me alone," she snarled when Max caught up to her outside. He put his hand on her elbow. She shook it off violently. "Leave me alone!"

"Charlotte, I'm sorry. I didn't mean to hurt you."

She flung off his attempt to put his arm about her shoulders. "It doesn't matter. *You* don't matter. Get away from me."

He hurried after her. "We need to talk. Please. Come home with me."

"I don't want to talk to you now. I don't want to go home with you. I don't want you, Max."

"Yes you do. You do want me. You *do*. You told me you did. You told me you always would." He spoke with urgent insistence, finally grabbing her shoulders and turning her to face him. He was breathing in quick, anxious snatches. "Tell me you still love me."

"I can't." She couldn't make eye contact. "Let me go, Max."

"Tell me, Charlotte. I need to hear you say it."

Her eyes squeezed shut. "No."

"No you won't tell me, or no you don't love me?"

"No I don't—"

He clamped her face between his palms and kissed her, a long, deep, sweetly tormented kiss that was devastating. She didn't resist. Nor did she respond, but that didn't seem to bother him.

"You taste so good. You smell so good," he whispered against her lips.

"You taste like a cigarette butt floating in a stale glass of beer," she told him bluntly.

He grinned, remembering when he'd told her the same thing. "That's because I've been smoking and I'm drunk off my ass. And I want you so bad." He folded her in close to him, pressed her face into his shoulder. She sighed, inhaled, then went rigid.

"And you smell like one of your new girlfriends." She shoved him hard, making him stumble. "Save your sweet talk for them."

He blinked at her. "My what?"

She had her car keys out. Her tone was hard, angry, like steel. "Stay away from me, Max. I don't like what you've become, and I don't want to be with you anymore."

He was so stunned, she managed to get all the way to her car before he came after her.

"You don't mean that. I *know* you don't." He stood on the passenger side while she unlocked her door.

She glared at him over the rooftop. "Read my lips, Savoie: Leave me the hell alone. I don't want to see you again unless it's work-related."

He just stared at her, expression blank. Then he shook his head. "You're just saying that to hurt me because I hurt you."

"And you keep *on* hurting me."

"I said I was sorry."

"It's not enough, Max. This isn't working. *We're* not working. I can't be what you want me to be."

A look of confusion crossed his face. "But, Charlotte, you're everything I want."

That only made her angrier. Needing to protect herself, she attacked. "But you're not what I want. You can never be what I want. You're a criminal, a killer. You're not even human. I don't know *what* you are. You went from someone I thought I cared about to this . . . this monster in Armani. You lie to me, you hide things from me. You stand there in your shiny shoes and say you love me, but you don't know what that means. If you knew what it meant, you wouldn't have that woman's smell all over you. You wouldn't be out every night drinking and screwing without giving me a second thought. Without caring that I might need you. Just like my—" She broke off, gulping for breath, for clarity of thought.

Max just stood staring at her, the look on his face so blank and stunned, so horribly wounded. Yet she couldn't keep herself from going on.

"I can't do this anymore, Max. I can't do it. You won't stop pushing me. I can't . . . I can't look at you without seeing every painful thing that's ever happened to me. My heart's so raw, it bleeds. It hurts too much to be with you. Leave me alone, Max. Just leave me alone."

She slid into the car. The sound of the door slamming woke him from his stupor. He pulled on the passenger side handle. The door was locked.

"Charlotte, open the door. We need to talk. I'm not letting you just drive away. Talk to me. Dammit, *talk* to me!"

She started the engine, the roar drowning out his voice. She had her hand on the gearshift when an explosion of glass showered across the seat from the impact of Max's elbow.

He reached through the broken window to unlock the door and slid in. No longer the wavering injured party, he was all dark control and determination. The sound he made was a low, dominating growl.

"Get out!"

His eyes glittered. Hot green, gold, flickering furiously. Dangerously. "No. Talk to me." He dodged the slaps of her hand and jerked the keys out of the ignition. But by then she had the door open and was running.

She knew she couldn't outrun him, but she had to get away, to escape him while her emotions were so exposed and out of control. If she could evade him, maybe he'd be drunk enough to give up and let her go. She glanced back, surprised and relieved to see he wasn't behind her, then burst out onto the next street—right into his arms. She lunged back and his grip tightened.

"Don't run. Charlotte, *don't run.*"

On the periphery she heard the pleading, the warning in his voice, but at the same time, she was writhing, squirming, striking him with her elbows until his hold loosened just enough for her to slip free. Then a hard push toppled him to the sidewalk, where he rolled off balance for just a second, struggling to get his feet back under him. She grabbed her keys from his hand and darted into the parking structure that connected the two streets.

Even though the workday was long ended, the

ramp was still fairly crowded with vehicles from the night owls who prowled the city's hot spots. She wove between them, crouching low, finally stopping to listen, hearing nothing but the hoarse pulls of her breathing. That's what he'd be listening for, too. She had to get control of herself.

She crouched behind the rear tire of a parked SUV and struggled to slow her breaths. Then she heard soft thumps, coming closer, closer. He was traveling across the roofs of the parked cars, like an animal on the high ground stalking his prey. Another sound, one that made the hair on her arms stand up.

A growl.

A low, throaty vibration so fierce and menacing that she forgot all about Max Savoie and saw Sandra Cummings and Vivian Goodman fleeing for their lives. Panicky instinct took over.

She lay down on the cold concrete and rolled beneath the vehicle. On her back, staring up at the drive train, she unsnapped her holster and eased her weapon free.

Max. It's only Max.

The suspension gave a slight bounce. Cee Cee held her breath and waited. Waited.

It's Max. It's only Max.

Again, the deep, threatening rumble.

She held her gun up between her breasts, seeing those empty eyes so filled with shock and horror. Those torn-out throats forever holding their screams silent.

Please, Max. Please just go.

She heard the soft sound of his feet touching down on concrete. Then the rasp of his breathing. The quiet snuffle as he took her scent.

And then he started to move away, footfalls light and quick toward the front of the vehicle. Then silence.

Cee Cee released her breath slowly.

The clamp of his hand around her ankle shocked a cry of alarm from her. He jerked her out from under the SUV. As she tried to twist under the chassis, trying to grab on, to kick free, she lost her grip on her gun and on her composure.

Scream all you want. Shout and curse, it don't matter. Ain't nobody gonna hear you. An' even if they did, they wouldn't help you. So you can lie there quiet and let me take what I want, or you can scream and fight and I'll take it anyway. And probably enjoy it more.

Help me!

But she'd never said those two words out loud. Not once.

She was facedown as Max's shadow loomed over her. She stopped fighting, tensing at the feel of his weight settling over her, heavy and insistent as he moved against her. Her mind closed down, becoming empty, blocking out the fear, the knowledge of the pain to come. Then came the feel of his hot breath on her neck, followed by the slow rasp of his tongue.

A small, helpless sound escaped her.

Max went completely still.

Slowly he rolled her over onto her back. Her fisted hands came up to cover her face protectively. When he didn't touch her, she slit her eyes open cautiously. There was no awareness in them, only a defiant readiness to accept what she couldn't escape.

"Go ahead." Her voice sounded as if it was scraping over gravel. "Take what you want. I can't stop you."

"Just say 'Stop.'"

"Stop. Please stop." Fright shivered beneath the gruff command.

Max rocked back onto his heels, at a loss as to how to deal with her. "I'm sorry. I didn't mean to frighten you. I would never hurt you. I would never—" He reached out his hand, halting when she shrank back to avoid contact. "Charlotte, I'd never hurt you."

"Just don't touch me. All right? Just don't touch me."

"I won't. I promise."

Cee Cee crawled under the vehicle, retrieving her weapon. They both got awkwardly to their feet, Cee Cee strung tight with remembered terror, and Max beginning to weave with the effects of confusion and booze.

"I'm sorry. You ran and I had to chase you. Can't stop myself. Have to chase when you run. Don't be afraid. I wasn't going to hurt you."

She stared at him as if he was something foreign and awful.

"I wasn't going to hurt you," he said plaintively.

"Just stay away from me. Stay away." She started to back up. When he didn't move, she turned and hurried toward the street where she was parked. She heard him follow, his steps unsteady. By the time she exited the ramp she was breathing normally again, the residue of helplessness and terror replaced by anger once again. And a riptide of sorrow.

Max stumbled out onto the sidewalk beside her. His gaze was bleak, his expression broken.

"Don't leave me."

She took a shaky breath, because his eyes were welling up and her throat was tightening up.

"Please, Charlotte. Please let me explain."

"It's too late for that."

His breathing quickened as he tried to get his jumbled thoughts around that statement. He turned it over and over in his alcohol-muddled mind, and finally said with quiet disbelief, "That can't be true. I have nothing without you."

She didn't answer.

He started to say something more, but the words wouldn't come. His legs gave out with a graceful ripple, dropping him onto the curb where he sat, head between his knees and arms crossed over the back of his neck. He didn't move or make a sound, so Charlotte finally forced herself to start across the street.

A glance showed that Giles was no longer there waiting. He'd probably assumed that she and Max would leave together and had gone home.

Not her problem.

She got in the car, scowling at the shattered window and the pebbles of glass all over the seat. Dammit, now she had two broken windows. After brushing the glass off with an impatient hand, she started the car. And glanced at the opposite curb where Max still huddled.

With a fierce curse, she executed a sharp U-turn and pushed open the door. Though furious and hurt, she wasn't about to let him go back inside the club.

"Get in, Savoie. I'll take you home."

He crawled into the car without a word, slumping in the seat, eyes closed. He didn't even grab for the dash when she spun the car around a second time to take the spot Giles had vacated in front of the club.

"Wait here," she said.

Leaving the car running, she strode back into the smoky darkness, back to Max's table. A man she recognized as the third man in Cummings's office looked up in surprise, then amusement. He had his arm about an intoxicated redhead. The other woman stared up at Cee Cee in annoyance.

"Let me extend Max's apologies. He won't be rejoining you. I've come for his coat."

The woman's eyes narrowed. "You can't be serious."

"Serious enough to shed blood if you don't take it off right now. Is it worth that much to you? Because it is to me."

Pouting, the woman stripped off the jacket and extended it. "Have Max call me later. He has my number."

"So do I." Taking the coat between thumb and forefinger as if it was something offensive, Cee Cee drawled, "I'll give him the message. I can't guarantee he'll be in any condition to hear it once I'm through with him."

As she walked away, she heard the man, Rollo, chuckle and say, "Okay. Now I'm impressed."

At the bar, LaRoche hoisted his glass and smiled wryly.

She climbed back into the car, throwing the jacket at Max's immobile form, gritting her teeth because of the expensive fragrance that filled the interior. A scent that was not her own. She tore out of town without a glance in his direction.

The electronic gates opened when she pulled up. She sped down the long drive to Jimmy Legere's front porch and fishtailed to a stop nearly on the first step.

Max made no move to get out. His eyes were still closed, and she guessed he was unconscious. She leaned over to push the door open, then with a hard shove toppled him out onto the steps.

"They can have you. You're not my problem," she told him as she shut the door. She drove about ten feet, slammed into reverse, and stopped again to fling his coat out the window. "Your girlfriend wants you to call."

She drove off in a temperamental spit of gravel.

Surprisingly there were no tears. Only a deep, dark emptiness weighting her soul.

At home she crawled into her bed still dressed, shivering with the effort of holding her emotions inside. Only in her dreams did they escape her: clawing, gnashing nightmares that had her weeping and whimpering in her sleep.

She was so exhausted, she imagined he was there to comfort her, could almost feel the gentleness of the arms holding her close, hear the tenderness in his low voice as he crooned, "Don't be afraid. I'd never let anything harm you."

Believing him, she sank into much-needed slumber, not waking until her alarm went off.

When she awoke she lay in bed, puzzled, but not sure why. Something was different. Then she noticed that the suit in its dry cleaner bag and the red shoes were gone. And the tears she'd held back the night before came in a flood.

Twelve

"GOOD AFTERNOON, DETECTIVE. Right on time. Marissa, I don't wish to be disturbed. Thank you."

Cee Cee had spent a ridiculous amount of time getting ready for this meeting. She'd stood looking in her closet and all she could see were all of his things mingling with hers. His gorgeous Armani jacket, his gray silk tie, two of his silk shirts, his T-shirts, even a pair of his shiny shoes.

And then there were her things that had him all over them. The bronze dress she wore on their first date, the short leather skirt he loved to see on her—and take off her, the sexy undergarments she'd bought to tease him, and the beautiful raincoat he'd bought her to make her think of him. *Everything* made her think of him.

The bastard.

She was so in love with him, her fillings ached.

She finally opted for black. A loose black T-shirt and slim black jeans. And boots. No open toes. She slung a silver studded belt about her hips, glazed her short hair into an aggressive bristle, circled her eyes with heavy smudges of liner, and put a coat of bright red on her lips.

She thought she was ready to tangle until she went downstairs and saw a glass company finishing with the new windows in her car doors, just as the first fat raindrops began to fall in what became a deluge by the time she pulled into his office lot. Finding no empty spaces up close, she was a soggy mess by the time she reached the building.

Pride wouldn't allow her to wear the raincoat. So that pride was dripping miserably cold down the back of her neck by the time she stood on the other side of his desk, her hair gooey and misshapen, her eyes smeared, and her shirt stuck to her.

"Would you like some coffee? A towel?"

"I'm fine. This won't take long."

"Have a seat, detective. Where's your partner? I thought he'd be glued to your side for the sake of propriety."

"The sensitivity of my visit took precedence over public opinion."

"That's a first. What can I do for you, detective?"

He engaged in the expected banter, but there was no life in it. Just as there was no animation in his expression, in his voice, or in his eyes. His cheeks were still stubbled but neatly edged. He wore a Saints muscle shirt under one of his tailored suit coats with jeans. And his red Converses. The effect should have been sloppy, but he managed to appear carelessly elegant.

"I need to wrap up this case. You're still on the top of the list of those we're looking at."

"I know that."

"We both know you didn't kill those women."

"Do we?"

"Yes. But I think you know who did."

"Do I?"

"Who are you protecting, Max?"

"Why would I protect a killer, detective? If I knew who it was, why wouldn't I have told you?"

"Because this murderer is one of yours, not one of mine. I've been searching and searching for some kind of link, for some reason for this man to target Cummings—either on his own, or for someone else. But there's nothing Cummings is involved in at the moment to warrant that kind of intimidation. There's no purpose in these attacks, unless they're motivated by vengeance. Or unless the killings were accidental."

There was no change in his expression when he asked, "You're suggesting these women were killed and half eaten by accident?"

"You told me not to run because you couldn't help but chase me. Why is that? Some sort of animal behavior? Some primitive instinct?"

"Something like that," he answered carefully.

"The chase is like the hunt. Pursue, bring down, kill."

"Something like that, yeah."

"Can it get out of control?"

"I suppose it could. It's intoxicating, exciting. It's power. It's something dark and passionate at the soul of what we are. I can't explain it any better than that."

"Suppose he didn't intend to kill them. But they got scared. They ran and he chased them, got caught up in it, reverted to the wild or however you describe it. And he killed them. Is that possible?"

"Perhaps."

"But you don't think so?"

"Power is balanced with control. We're not beasts, detective."

"Then maybe he did it because he likes it. Because he likes losing control."

Max said nothing.

"But I still need some kind of motive. Some reason why. These weren't random acts. And now that Cummings's older daughter has been threatened—"

"What?"

"You didn't know that?"

"I hadn't heard." He looked away, but not before she caught the sheen of concern in his eyes. Then he met her gaze with a flat stare. "I'm afraid I can't help you. I don't know what's behind these killings."

She rose from the chair and began to pace. His eyes tracked her restless movements. Finally she circled in close to slap her palms down on his desk.

"Why won't you help me?"

He regarded her unblinkingly. "What's in it for

me, detective? Why should it matter to a criminal, a killer, a monster like myself?"

She chewed on her own words for a moment, then went right for his throat. "Even if you don't care about me, you care about them—about your kind. You'll want to do whatever you can to protect them and yourself. Imagine what Karen Crawford could do if she had just a hint about what killed these women. More and more people suspect, but can't quite come to terms with the reality of such creatures existing. How could you keep them safe, yourself safe, if the truth got out?"

Something flickered in his expression, a deep, desperate panic. Then it was gone, glossed over by a hard stare and a harder tone.

"You would do that? You would lead them to me with pitchforks and torches?"

She went right after the fear, sensing it as keenly as he would have.

"I don't want to. Don't force me, Max. I want this killer. He's dangerous. He's careless. And if he isn't stopped right now, he's going to expose you all for what you are, and I won't be able to prevent it."

"Detective, I'm afraid that's all the time I can give you today. I'm sorry I couldn't be of more help," he drawled smoothly.

"Fine." She straightened, shoulders squared, her expression nearly as sharp-edged as his own. "I have some of your things. Do you want me to have them sent here or to the house?"

He absorbed that kick in the gut without a flinch. "I don't care. Whatever you want to do, detective." He held her stare for a long minute, then his slid away. He lifted an unsteady hand to rub at his eyes. "Keep them, burn them, mail them. I don't care."

Beneath the shading of his palm, he watched her hand stretch over his desk. It opened slowly, setting the keys to the car he'd given her on the blotter. His speed startling, he grabbed her hand, pushing the keys back into it and closing her fingers tightly around them.

His voice was a low throb of fury. "You don't have to shove it all back in my face, Charlotte. Keep the car. It's a debt I needed to pay. I wouldn't want to owe you anything." He pushed her hand away and spun his chair so his back was to her. "We're done here. See yourself out, detective. You know the way."

He closed his eyes as she went to the door, then hesitated, to address him softly.

"I was so proud of you at Cummings's office— the way you held your ground with him and Crawford. You were magnificent, Max."

An involuntary spasm in his throat cut off any possible answer.

The door closed quietly.

Max gave himself over to the emotions shaking silently through him for long, tearing minutes. Then he took a breath and scrubbed his face dry with the back of his hand. A hand that was steady when he reached for his intercom.

"Marissa, have Rollo meet me in the gym."

HE WAS WORKING the bag with short, hard strikes when he felt Rollo watching him. He was in no hurry to acknowledge the other, continuing to pummel the stiff canvas and leather with his bare knuckles until they stung and began to bleed.

"Keep your elbow in tighter to the body. That's it. Nice form. Who taught you?"

Max stepped back and steadied the swinging bag with his fingertips. "I don't remember his name. I was only about eleven. Some fellas roughed me up and Jimmy thought I needed to know how to defend myself the conventional way. Jimmy was always bringing in folks to teach me things. Boxing, martial arts, gymnastics, Latin, calculus. I can even play the piano. The perfect pet to perform at social events." A quick jab sent the bag spinning. "T-John tells me you used to fight down on the docks."

"That was a long time ago."

"Were you any good?"

"The best."

"Now I am."

Rollo smiled tightly. "Perhaps."

"Shall we see? Just a friendly go-round. I find myself in need of working off a little aggression this afternoon."

"You and your girl didn't patch it up last night?

I would have thought so, the way she came plowing into the club like an Arctic icebreaker to demand Amber surrender your jacket or lose her jugular."

"Did she? Didn't know. And no, we're not together."

"So you want to beat me up over it? Okay. You can try, but I only fight when there's a wager involved."

Max smiled, baring his teeth. "What do you want?"

Rollo shrugged. "A percentage. Think of it as retirement for your old man."

"Okay."

"How 'boutchu?"

"The truth."

"About what? Your mama and me?"

The smile never faltered. "For starters. About anything I want to know. About all those secrets you never got around to telling me. About why you killed those two women."

He didn't even hesitate. "Fair enough. You're not going to beat me, you know."

Max's fist took him squarely on the jaw, sending him staggering back. As Rollo touched a hand to his bloodied lip, Max began to bounce lightly in his Converses.

"We'll see. Consider me highly motivated."

"You're on, boy." He charged in, looping an arm about Max's neck and smashing him to the padded floor. With an agile twist, Max was on his feet. He was lighter and faster, but Rollo struck like a runaway cement truck. His fist caught Max just below the ear and sent him stumbling.

Max shook it off and snapped off a sharp kick to the side of his opponent's head, following it up with elbows to the body in quick succession.

Rollo shoved him and rubbed his ribs, grinning. "You're pretty damned good, kid. Shall we take the gloves off?"

His hand fisted in Max's shirt, yanking him forward so the top of his head took Max in the face. Then he flung the younger man into the free weight rack, where he slumped to the floor, momentarily dazed. Rollo picked up a twenty-pound dumbbell and swung it at Max's jaw.

Max slid down onto his back to dodge the shattering blow and caught Rollo with a scissoring of his legs, flipping him hard into the bench press. Then they were both up, eyeing one another with respectful wariness.

"Why didn't you marry my mother?"

Rollo weaved around the fast jabs Max flashed out at him.

"I asked. She wouldn't have me. I wasn't good enough for her family. They had other plans for her." He pounded Max with a series of hard hits to the midsection, then sent him reeling back with an uppercut. "So I convinced her to run away with me. They never forgave either of us for it."

"I have family? Where?" His heel connected with

Rollo's sternum, then sharply beneath his chin, top-pling him like an imploded skyscraper.

On his way down, Rollo knocked Max's feet out from under him with a sweep of his own. Then he was astride Max's chest, his forearm pressed against his throat.

"They're dead, boy. All of them. Your entire line was slaughtered. Every man, woman, and child—except you. And they'll kill you if they find you."

Max hooked his leg around Rollo's neck, pulling him off and reversing their positions. "Who? Why?"

"You want any more answers, you'll have to earn them." His elbow socked Max in the temple, send-ing him sprawling. When Max came up on all fours, his eyes swam with red and gold. "That get your hackles up, son? Come on, then. Let the fur fly."

A deep reverberation worked up through Max as the hands splayed wide before him began to change. His lips curled back from sharp teeth in a ferocious smile, and he lunged.

There was no finesse as they grappled on the floor; it was all about power and the willingness to inflict damage.

With a huge hand clenched on the thick cords of Max's throat, Rollo leaned close to growl, "And what would your tough little Upright girlfriend think of you if she saw you now?"

Using his feet, Max flipped the older man over his head and rolled into a crouch. "She thinks I'm magnificent."

That took Rollo by surprise. "She knows what you are? She's seen what you've become?"

"Yes. And she's not afraid of me."

He chuckled. "I take it you haven't tried to mate with her yet."

"I don't care to discuss my sex life with you."

"I'm not talking about sex, Max. I'm talking about howl-at-the-moon mating, when the need to claim her in the old way drives you mad. You won't be able to think of anything else, and she won't want any part of what you have in mind."

"What are you talking about?"

Rollo laughed. "Nature. I don't want to spoil the surprise for you. Or should I say for her."

Distracted and alarmed, Max allowed a hard punch to get through his defenses. Then he was all lethal focus.

"Is that what you did to those women?"

"Once you try it, you'll crave it like nothing else you can imagine. How do you think you were conceived? In a nice hotel room on starched sheets? In the dirt, Max. On the ground on all fours, like the animals we are. And your mama, she was howling, too."

Max plowed into him, rage overwhelming restraint or care. It was the reckless move Rollo had been waiting for. One big hand clamped over Max's face, holding his jaws shut while his own huge teeth went for Max's neck.

Max lurched to one side but couldn't evade the

attack altogether. Sharp agony stabbed through his upper arm just below the shoulder. He dropped to his knees, his world going black.

"Time to pay up, you cocky little bastard," Rollo said smugly.

Max drew a deep breath. "Not yet."

He struck with every ounce of his strength. The heel of his hand drove into Rollo's Adam's apple, dropping him onto his back with a gurgle of surprise. Then Max was on him, pounding with his right fist because his left was numb and useless, pounding until Rollo was no longer moving. He crawled off the unconscious figure, his head swirling as he examined his torn shoulder. He bound the savage wound as best he could, then gingerly put on his coat.

He didn't remember leaving the building or the long reeling walk through the city. With his dark glasses on and his head down, he could have been just another weary visitor on the crowded streets. Except he left a trail of blood dripping off his fingertips.

HE SLUMPED AGAINST the doorframe, vaguely seeing the figure of a man straightening from his work under a bank of bright lights.

"Are you Devlin Dovion?"

"Yes. Can I help you?"

"Charlotte said I could trust you."

"You must be her Max."

Her Max.

His knees began to give. Then he was aware of supporting hands under his armpits.

"Good lord. You need to see a doctor."

"I need to see you. I need you to do something for me."

He just managed to get it all out before his eyes rolled up white.

CEE CEE REACHED for her desk phone. "Caissie."

"Charlotte, this is Dovion. I need you to come over here, please."

"Dev, I'm right in the middle of something."

"This can't wait. Now. And don't say anything to anyone."

Provoked by the mysterious summons to the morgue, she told Babineau she was going out for coffee.

More puzzled than alarmed, she left the bustling halls where lives could still be saved to travel down into the refrigerated realm, entering Dovion's lair.

"Dev, what's going on—"

She drew up short, her breath catching on the upward lunge of her heart. She made a small, injured sound as Dovion caught her by the elbows.

For there on one of his stainless-steel tables, his face as pale as the sheet draped over his motionless form, was Max.

"No. God. *Please.*"

"Charlotte, he's not dead. He's *not* dead."

She looked at Dovion through wild, frightened eyes. "What?"

"He's lost a lot of blood. He's weak. I don't know how he managed to make it here."

She rushed over to Max, not daring to take a relieved breath until she felt his chest rise and fall beneath her hand. She touched his still features, noting the bruises and scrapes in surprise. What had weakened him so quickly he hadn't had a chance to use his almost instantaneous healing powers?

She looked at the snug wrapping on his arm, then up to Dovion. "What happened?"

"He showed up here, bleeding buckets, and asked me to check his wound. Not to take care of it, but to document it."

"What? Why?"

"He had me chart the bite radius and take photographs."

"Why?"

"Because whoever sank their teeth into him also killed Sarah Cummings and Vivian Goodman."

She absently stroked his cool cheek, his hair, his chest, her hand shaking as her mind spun ahead. "Did he say anything about who it was? Did he mention a name?"

"No. He was pretty out of it by the time I got him on the table."

"Is he going to be all right?"

"By the time I see them, I usually don't have to give odds." When her eyes filled up, he added hastily, "He's fine. I got the bleeding stopped, but you need to get him to a hospital."

"Did he ask you to call me?" Her voice was oddly fragile.

"That was my doing. Like I said, he was out of it. I figured you'd want to come get him."

She nodded. "Dev, I need you to work up the results, but keep a tight lid on it, okay? I want to get Max's statement first."

"You're the boss."

She pressed his arm. "Thanks, Dev. I owe you big."

She made a quick call. Within ten minutes, Giles and Teddy arrived. They asked no questions, quickly doing as she instructed. Max was wheeled out a back entrance and loaded into the vehicle Giles backed in. She gave Teddy her keys and told him to follow with her car. Then she climbed into the backseat, cradling Max's head and shoulders in her lap. As Giles piloted them into traffic, her control came apart in small fractures.

"What were you thinking?" she scolded Max quietly, her fingertips caressing his battered features. "If you had died, it would have *killed* me."

His Adam's apple moved in a slow swallow. "I'm sorry."

"It's all right, baby. I'm here. You're going to be all right."

His eyes blinked open to regard her as if he couldn't quite believe what he was seeing. "I'm sorry, Charlotte. I didn't mean to hurt you. Please don't leave me."

Her throat tightened up painfully, making it hard for her to answer. Her voice was hoarse with tears. "I'm not going anywhere, Max. I'll be right here. Close your eyes. I'll keep you safe."

He smiled faintly as his eyes slid shut.

She met Giles's worried gaze in the rearview mirror.

By the time they reached the house, Max was stirring. Though disoriented, he was able to walk between them on wobbly legs. Cee Cee directed them into Jimmy's office, afraid he'd never be able to make the stairs.

"Helen, I need some blankets."

The ever-present housekeeper hurried off without comment.

Max slid bonelessly onto the leather couch, letting Cee Cee ease him down onto his back. He watched through half-closed eyes as she unlaced his shoes, then tucked the blankets Helen provided around him. When her hand got close enough, he curled his bloodstained fingers around it. His grip was surprisingly strong.

"Don't leave me."

"I won't."

"I love you, Charlotte."

Her other hand stroked through his hair. "I know you do, baby. Should I call Dr. Curry?"

"Not yet." He was shifting restlessly, his breath

coming quick and shallow. His fingers clenched about hers.

"What is it, Max? Why haven't you thrown it off?"

"I can't," he panted softly. "I don't know why."

"I do."

Cee Cee looked up to see Rollo in the doorway. "What's wrong with him?" she asked. Then, as he drew closer, she got a good look at him. At the blood on his torn clothes. And she knew who Max had been protecting.

What she didn't know was why.

Thirteen

ROLLO KNELT BESIDE the couch, brushing Cee Cee aside as inconsequential. He put a hand on Max's brow.

"Listen to me, boy. Are you listening?"

Max gave a jerky nod of his head, but his eyes wouldn't focus. He was panting in quick, restless snatches.

"Remember when I told you about the silver, about how it couldn't hurt me? Remember that?"

"Yes."

"That's because I built up an immunity to it by ingesting larger and larger doses of it. At first I thought it would kill me, but it didn't. It's in my system, Max, and it transferred to you through that bite. That's why the wound won't heal. That's why you feel so sick. You're going to have to ride it out. It won't be easy, but you'll make it. Don't fight it. It's easier if you relax and let it run its course. Do you understand?"

Again, the fitful nod.

"You'll be all right." His voice pitched slightly lower as his blood-encrusted knuckles rubbed down the side of Max's face. "You got the better of me, boy. No one's ever done that before. You surprised me." Lower still. "You pleased me. We'll talk when you're stronger. Get your questions ready."

He stood, regarding Cee Cee with a mixture of suspicion and mild contempt. "So, you're back."

"I am."

"For how long this time?"

"For as long as he needs me." *For as long as he wants me.*

"He doesn't need you, human."

"Then why did he come to me?" That was true in a roundabout way. He had to know Dovion would contact her. And he'd been sure enough of her to trust her to come for him.

Rollo smiled. It wasn't a pleasant one. "Keep him quiet. He may try to hurt himself. Don't let him. He may try to hurt you. It's the silver. It makes us go a little mad."

"I'll keep him safe."

"You do that." He stared at her for a long silent moment, studying her distastefully. Then he shrugged and left the room.

Cee Cee turned back to Max, touching his fevered cheek, and repeated, "I'll keep you safe."

Easier said than done, she discovered, as his system reacted violently to the invading toxin over the long hours leading to night. He alternately thrashed with fever, then was taken by fierce chills. He didn't know her. He didn't respond to her voice as he twisted and fought through the darkness of his delirium.

She sponged his face and chest with the cool water Helen provided and bundled him up in blankets, her arms around him, to warm him through the worst of his shivering. She tried to keep him still, but he was so strong. He began an awful wailing, that strange howling sound that was both mournful and terrifying, pounding his fists against his head until she had to shout for Giles to help her restrain him.

She leaned close, clutching his face between her hands, to say low and steady by his ear, "Max, stop it. Stop. Stop."

He must have heard her on some level, because his body went limp and he lay still except for the hurried panting.

She rocked back on her heels, closing her eyes, perilously close to weeping. How much more could he take? How much more could she watch him endure?

"Detective, get some air."

"I'm fine, Giles."

"It wasn't a suggestion. I'll sit with him. Go on."

Reluctantly Cee Cee went out onto the side porch. She was surprised by how dark it had gotten, by how much time had passed. As she leaned against the rail, looking out into the peaceful shadows, shock and exhaustion began to shake through her. She took out a cigarette, but the hand holding the match was too unsteady to light it before the flame went out. After two more abortive attempts, she gave up.

"Coffee, detective?"

She gave Helen a faint smile. "That would nice." She watched as the older woman set the service down on the wicker table where Jimmy Legere used to have his breakfast and read the financial news. Where Max Savoie would stand motionlessly at his back, watchful and silent during her many visits to the sprawling antebellum home, his eyes on her, smoldering.

Helen filled two cups with a thick, fragrant chicory, then laced both with a liberal dash of brandy. Cee Cee took the cup, brow raised in surprise as the woman joined her at the rail to sip the calming brew.

"Have you been here a long time, Helen?"

"Most of my life. My husband worked for Jimmy. Jasmine is my daughter."

"I didn't know that."

"Jimmy always took care of his people, like family. Max learned that from him."

Cee Cee took another sip and studied the woman's profile with interest. She was a handsome woman, large, rawboned, and capable. And more than a little imposing. Her blunt-cut black hair was unlined by gray, her steely eyes stern and clear. She dressed casually, neatly, like she was waiting to tee up at a country club with collared shirt, walking shorts, and shoelaces that matched the piping on her crisp piqué outfit. She was the only strong female influence in a house of rough, brutal men, and she ran it with an iron fist. Admiration snuck in uninvited.

Taking advantage of their tentative truce, she asked, "You were here when Jimmy brought Max home?"

A soft, sad sound. "Such a pitiful little thing, nothing but filth and bones and those big eyes. So timid and silent. You never even knew he was in the house, except when the nightmares came. Poor little boy. It broke the heart to hear him. His mother was shot, you know."

"I know."

"And he killed them, the two men that took the mother and son out into the swamps. He was just a little boy. A child. My Sam was with Mr. Legere when they found him. He'd torn them to pieces. That's all that was left. Pieces."

Cee Cee hadn't known that.

"Such terrible dreams. He'd wake the whole house. Jimmy sat with him. He wouldn't let me do it. Night after night, for almost the entire first year, even after Max started sleeping through the night. Just in case the boy woke up, so he wouldn't be alone in the dark. He loved that child."

"I know," Cee Cee whispered.

"Such a solemn, strange boy. He'd never let anyone touch him or hold him. Just Jimmy. He never smiled, never laughed, rarely spoke, not for years and years. Not until you." Helen looked at her then, catching Cee Cee's surprise.

"Something about you brought him to life. It was like a light came on inside him every time you were here. It drove Jimmy crazy. He was so afraid of you, afraid you were going to hurt him, break his heart; afraid you were going to take Max away from him."

Cee Cee swallowed a wad of emotion that went down like broken glass. "I did. That's exactly what I did."

There was no accusation in the other woman's expression this time. "I don't think Max could have survived Jimmy's death if you hadn't been here for him."

Tears scalded Cee Cee's cheeks. "But I wasn't. I wasn't here for him. I've never been here for him, and he's always been there for me, every time I needed him. I *did* hurt him, Helen. I broke his heart. I've been such a selfish bitch."

"If you say so, detective." But she was smiling wryly in agreement. "He likes that about you, you know. He likes the fact that you're tough, and independent, and don't mind going nose to nose. That's the way it was with me and my Sam. They love a good fight when they know you're not afraid of them. When they trust you to love them, no matter what. Men with that much power can become hard and heartless when they don't have someone to keep them humble. Like Mr. Legere."

She chuckled. "Being tossed out on the front steps was quite a humbling experience for Max. I think that's when I started liking you."

"But I *am* afraid of him, Helen. He scares me to death. I'm just a coward."

Helen took the empty cup from her. "If you were, you wouldn't be here with him, would you?"

When Cee Cee went back into the office, Giles looked up at her in relief.

"See, Max. Here she is. I told you she was here."

Wide green eyes flashed up and fixed on her with a desperation. "You *are* here. I thought I'd imagined it." He lifted his hand and she laced her fingers between his, letting him draw her down to him. She settled on her knees next to the couch, nodding a dismissal to Giles. Then she combed the fingers of her other hand through Max's sticky hair.

"How are you feeling, baby? Any better?"

He groaned. "I feel like gum on the bottom of football cleats. It hurts to think."

"Then don't think about anything. Just close your eyes."

They slipped shut for a moment, then snapped back open. "Don't go."

"I'll be right here."

"Promise you'll be here when I open my eyes."

"All night. I promise. I'll be right here with you."

"Thank you," he muttered, eyes closing again.

"Happy to do it for you," she told him quietly, holding his hand, resting her head upon his chest, letting her own eyes close.

When Max's restless movements woke her some hours later, it took a minute to realize where she was.

The room was dark, the house quiet. Moonlight made a silvery path across the center of the floor, where old bloodstains gleamed black upon the wood. She sat up slowly—stiff, sore, and groggy—until a low, anxious sound from Max woke her completely.

His cheek was warm to the touch, wet near the corners of his closed eyes. He was dreaming. The feel of her hand on his face quickened his agitation. His head tossed fretfully.

"No. Don't," he said.

"Shhh. It's all right."

"Don't. Don't hurt me."

"It's all right, Max."

"Jimmy, please. Please." His anguished words were barely a whisper. "Jimmy, please. Don't let them hurt me. Don't let them hurt me. I'll do anything. Don't let them find me. Don't let them hurt me."

Torn between the need to comfort him and the desire to discover more about his past, she stroked his brow and asked, "Who's trying to hurt you?"

"I don't know. I don't know. I don't know. Hide. Hide. Hide so he won't find you." His voice got higher, sounding younger. Scared. Terrified.

"Who, Max?"

"My fault. It's my fault. I wasn't supposed to. Wasn't supposed to. Please. Please don't. I didn't know, I didn't know. I'm sorry, Mama. I'm sorry, Mama. Don't make me. Don't. Don't make me." His voice trailed off into a plaintive whimper.

"Make you what, Max?"

"Red shoes. Red shoes." His breathing stopped, then started up again, slow, deep, and shuddering. His eyes opened, glowing, sightless. "I took care of it. I took care of it, Mama. I'm sorry. Don't cry. I'm sorry. Please. Jimmy, please."

She soothed the dampness from his face and leaned up to kiss his eyes closed. After a few shaky breaths, he was back to sleep.

"He wasn't even four years old."

The sound of Rollo's voice gave Cee Cee a nasty start. She hadn't been aware of him, and now saw the faint glow of his cigarette where he stood just inside the open French doors.

"Amazing kid. Shifted at four and killed his first man. I couldn't change form until I was thirteen. Amazing. Without anyone to show him how. Just instinct. Pure instinct. No wonder they wanted him so bad."

"Who?"

"His people. His family. They were offering a fortune for him. I sold him to Legere, him and his mother. Jimmy was supposed to keep them safe. I should have stayed long enough to make sure, but I wanted to lead his people off.

"But the men I hired must have gotten wind that there was more money to be made. They only wanted Max; Marie was just in the way. He killed them, too, those two greedy fools." A low grim chuckled. "They must have been so surprised."

"Who are you?" Cee Cee demanded. "What do you want with Max?"

"I want him to be ready. I want him to be strong and prepared. He didn't have anyone to teach him, and now there's so little time."

"Before what?"

"Before they kill him. They'll have to, now. He's too much of a threat. He's powerful and he's smart, but he's just not ready. And you, detective, are going to get him killed."

Alarmed spiked. "What are you talking about?"

"He's soft where you're concerned, and he can't afford to be. He has to be fearless. He has to be invincible. He cares for you. They'll find that out and they'll use you to trick him, to trap him."

"I won't let them."

He chuckled again at her bold claim. "What are you going to do? You don't know who or what they are. You don't know what *he* is, what he's capable of becoming. But he won't, because of you. He won't save his own life, because he's afraid of what you'll think of him."

"That's such total crap." *Was that true?*

"Oh, yeah. You've got the hots for him when he's on his hind legs, but what about what he really is? You're not going to want any part of that. You don't know anything about what we are, what we need."

"What does he need that I can't give him?"

She saw the flash of Rollo's teeth. "How can I put this delicately? Our kind can only procreate in our natural form. There'll come a time when he'll have to. It's bred in us, that need to mate. It becomes an obsession. Until he does, he'll be one unpleasantly dangerous and aggressive fella.

"Now, our females don't enjoy it much. Sometimes they don't even survive it, which is why the lines have become so diluted by human stock. But Max, being what he is, *who* he is, won't have any trouble finding a dozen who'll be willing."

"Let's say I'm willing." Her tone held a low, possessive fierceness.

He laughed at her. "Let's say . . . let's say you don't find the idea of mating outside your species repellent or the actual act distasteful, and can actually survive it. It's quite violent, you see. Then there's the bonding."

"Bonding?"

"You know we can sense one another. Mates have a deeper, more intense link. We only take one mate and the bond is for life. It requires the male to bite right here." He tapped the juncture of his neck and shoulder. "The marks never fade. Like a brand."

"Marking territory," she concluded.

"Exactly. Crude and painful, but an efficient way to protect one's mate."

"And that bond can't be broken?"

"Only by death. So you see, detective, you have no future with him. It's not a matter of if but *when* that urge is going to take him. It won't be a matter of choice for him. And I can't see you letting him roam to scratch that particular itch with someone else."

She was silent for a moment, picturing Max and the voluptuous woman dancing at the club. Her long fingers sliding up into his hair. "Can your kind bond with a human?"

Rollo took a long drag on his cigarette, the smoke clouding his silhouette. "I don't know. I've never heard of it being done. That would require a great deal more courage than I've ever seen in you Uprights."

Her thoughts flew ahead—quick, practical, unflinching. "If Max and I were bonded, I would know if he was in danger and I could protect him."

"Theoretically. *If* he didn't kill you in the process. I'd give it some serious thought if I were you. Good night, detective."

HOURS LATER, CEE CEE stirred, reluctant to give up the sense of comfort. Sunlight was bright on the inside of her eyelids and she blinked, looking about in confusion.

Jimmy Legere's office. She was stretched out on his leather couch, curled up in a blanket. Alone.

"Max?"

She sat up, squinting at her watch. Seven o'clock. She got to her feet, stretching the kinks out of her back.

"Good morning. Coffee will be ready in a few minutes."

Cee Cee blinked at Helen, who smiled.

"He's upstairs. He asked me not to wake you. He's all right."

But she had to see for herself. She took the stairs two at a time.

The shower was running. He slumped under the spray, hands on the tiles, head down, letting the water beat on the back of his neck and shoulders. A low, indescribably content sound escaped him as her hands slipped around him to begin lathering his chest. More than willing to place himself in her capable care, he stood motionless while she shampooed his thick black hair and eased over his upper arm, where there were scars but no longer open wounds. Then she soaped and gently scrubbed him, working her way down the strong, lean line of him, kneading, stroking, soothing until he was relaxed and limp. Well, *almost* all of him. One part of him pressed hard and insistent against her belly when he turned.

She shut off the water. "All clean," she announced.

"But my mind is still dirty."

She laughed and pulled open the curtain. "Out."

He had to hold on to her for balance stepping from the tub, evidence of lingering weakness. She didn't mind, liking the feel of him all slick and naked and provokingly aroused against her.

"Are you going to dry me?" he asked.

"Part of the service."

He stood with eyes closed, almost dozing, as

she blotted off the moisture, then gave him a push toward the bedroom. He trudged obediently to the bed and sat down heavily on its edge.

"Are you going to dress me too?"

"No. I prefer you like this."

He looked up to have her frame his face in her hands. The playful mood was gone between them.

"When I saw you lying on that table, I thought I'd lost you." Her voice cracked painfully. "And I wanted to die, too."

"Don't."

She sank down at his feet, her head resting on his lap as he'd once done in this same place. "All I could think was that I'd said such terrible things to you, and I'd never have the chance to take them back."

"Do you? Take them back?"

Her tears fell unashamedly as she clung to his knees. "I'm sorry. I didn't mean them. I didn't expect— I didn't know you would be with someone else. It shouldn't have been such a surprise, but it was. I was so hurt and angry, I couldn't think. I know I have no right to expect so much from you when I give so little."

"Charlotte, don't."

"You're *mine*, Max. I don't want to think of you with anyone else. I don't want you to *be* with anyone else. It's not fair for me to ask—"

He gripped her by the elbows and lifted her up. She couldn't meet his gaze.

"You don't have to ask, Charlotte. I don't want

anyone but you. I've never wanted anyone but you, and I never will. You're it for me. I'm sorry if that scares you. I know it's not what you want to hear from a criminal, killer, monster, but it's the truth. You are my every dream, and that will never change."

Her eyes lifted slowly, glazed with fragile hope.

"You can thank me, detective." He tapped his mouth with two fingers. "Right here."

She said his name, her voice soft and choky, as her arms circled his neck tightly.

He held her close, his face buried in her hair. Then he complained, "My kiss. Now, if you please."

The taste of his mouth was like coming home. All the anxious, edgy panic fell away in an instant, replaced by glorious sensation, familiar yet exciting.

Max took her down to the mattress beneath him, where his tongue played about hers and his heart beat fast, answering the hurried tempo of her own.

"I apologize," he breathed into her kisses.

"For what?"

"For how quick this is going to be. I'm embarrassed to say that just the smell of my soap on your skin has just about finished me."

She drew in his lower lip, worrying it gently with her teeth before moaning, "I'm right behind you on that."

Her body shuddered deliciously, welcoming his. His breath shook, his eyes closing, then opening, so his stare could fall into hers as he withdrew, then slowly sank home again. Just watching him, feeling him come apart before he concluded that claiming stroke was enough to push her over with him.

And then he was laughing softly against her lips. "I'm sorry. That didn't even last long enough to be called quick."

She made a contented noise. "It lasted long enough."

His fingertips fanned along the strong angle of her jaw as he promised, "Tonight we'll take that ride to the Grand Canyon. I'll have you for hours and hours, until you beg me for mercy."

She was smiling. "Make me beg, Savoie." She carried him on the strength of her happy sigh. "I love being here with you."

"Move in with me. I get so lost in this place when you're not in it." His words were quick and impulsive, surprising him as much as her. But he didn't take them back. His gaze searched hers with a hopeful intensity.

Cee Cee wanted to cave in just to see him smile, because leaving him was suddenly too awful to contemplate. But part of her still held back.

Her lips pursed. "Now that was quick." She knuckled his cheek tenderly.

"I'm serious."

"We'll talk about it." Before his mouth could form a frown, she kissed him sweetly and gestured toward the door. "How about a compromise?"

He glanced over to see a duffel bag.

"I brought some clothes." Her voice grew shy and nervous as she admitted, "I've been carrying them around in my trunk for the past few weeks. Teddy brought them up for me. Can I unpack?"

"Absolutely."

He lay sprawled and naked on the bed, watching her pull out her belongings while a feeling of complete and utter bliss got so big, it made him shiver.

After she carelessly heaped her things on the corner of his dresser, she returned to his arms for a long, urgent kiss. Then she glanced back at her clothes. "That wasn't so bad. At least now you won't have to borrow underwear for me from the staff."

"I love you, Charlotte."

He said it so easily, with such warmth and depth, her soul trembled. She ran a fingertip over the shape of his mouth. "Max?"

"Charlotte?"

"Tell me about Rollo."

Fourteen

*H*E REGARDED HER with a cool, remote stare.

She gave him the benefit of the doubt, taking a moment to slip away to pull on a fresh set of clothes while he had time to mull over his answer. But when she turned back to him, he was still silent.

"Max, you talk to me now. How long have you known he's the one I've been looking for?" It was hard to keep anger from her tone, but she managed. They were trying to shore up a relationship. It wouldn't do her any good to start poking holes in their precarious levee.

"Yesterday."

"And how long had you suspected?"

"Suspecting isn't the same as knowing, detective."

"Words, Max. Just words. Find some better ones."

"Since the night you arrested me."

"And you didn't think that was something I'd need to know before I snapped the cuffs on you?"

"I didn't want to spoil your bondage fantasy. I knew you wouldn't let me stay behind bars for long.

At least there you wouldn't have to worry that I'd start seeing someone else."

Hurt scissored across her expression, then her jaw set tight. She snatched her stack of belongings off the dresser, but before she could turn he was there in front of her.

He pulled the clothing from her hands, jerked open one of the dresser drawers, shoved his things to one side, and carefully deposited hers beside them before shutting the drawer.

"Not an option," he told her quietly. "Why can't you trust me, Charlotte? Why can't you ever believe that I'm trying to do the right thing?"

"Are you?"

"Yes."

"You could have told me."

"I tried. I tried to talk to you. I tried to get you to listen to me."

Yes, he had. The rest of her argument fell apart into miserable, petty pieces. "I was . . . too busy believing the worst."

"What else were you supposed to believe when I rubbed your nose in it? I'm so sorry, *sha*. You were never supposed to see that. I tried so hard to keep things from you so you wouldn't be hurt by what you didn't understand." When her brow furrowed in upset, he put his arms around her. It took a minute of struggling to draw her in close. When he got her there, he had no intention of letting her squirm away until things were resolved between them. "I had to convince him that you weren't important to me. That's the only way I could get close enough to find out what I needed to know."

"So you were just pretending to enjoy having that woman in your arms?"

He smiled into her hair. "How could I enjoy her when she didn't feel like you?" His embrace tightened. "Or smell like you." He nosed behind her ear. "Or taste like you." His tongue slid down her neck, inciting a shiver. "She did have a really nice rack, though, and some interesting ideas about what she wanted to do to me." He quickly sidestepped her knee. "I'd better get dressed before you decide to neuter me."

She held her scowl until his back was turned, then did a slow, appreciative sweep of his bare posterior as he pulled on loose-fitting jeans. Her gaze jumped up to his face when he turned back to her.

"Now, where were we?"

"I believe you were trying to feel up that waitress."

"With a jealous girlfriend who carries a gun? I don't think so." He rooted through the dresser looking for a shirt, making a mess that was very unlike Max.

He was still distracted, still holding things back that she needed to know. Things she wouldn't like. More things that would hurt her? More secrets that would push her away?

She placed her hand on top of his shoulder. He

went still beneath her touch even though he didn't look at her. Her palm circled slowly, over smooth skin and sleek muscle. Nothing had ever felt so arousing as that inviting warmth stretched taut over hard, deadly power. He was so deliciously made, it was all she could do not to bend over to taste him. She turned her hand so the backs of her fingers and short nails grazed down the ripple of his rib cage. He released a stuttering breath.

She could be distracting, too.

"Speaking of trust, Savoie, you weren't overflowing with it, either."

His gaze flickered to hers, wary and worked up over the brief physical contact. "I trust you. I trust you to do your job. I didn't want to compromise that, detective."

"Hmmm. A tactful way of telling me you wanted me out of the way until you got what you wanted."

He paused, choosing his words carefully for fear he would be choking on them later. "It wasn't business. It was personal."

"I see. I can respect you wanting to keep business matters to yourself, but if you can't share the personal things, then there's no reason to continue this conversation—or anything else—is there?"

He grabbed a silky black pullover and yanked it on. Her hands were on his chest and the soft fabric pooled over her wrists. He met her uplifted gaze, then slid his away in agitation. His heart hammered against the flat of her palm.

What the hell was he keeping from her? What could be so awful, to have him wound this tight and distressed? She wasn't going to let him back away from her. Not again. She'd drag it out of him with the brutal finesse of an inquisitor if she had to.

"Talk to me, Max."

"He knows things about me, Charlotte. Things about who and what I am."

"And you think he's going to tell you? Can you trust him to tell you the truth?"

"I have to. I don't have any other choices." He caught her hands, holding them tightly, kneading them anxiously before letting them drop. "I need a few days. Will you give them to me?" He met her stare, his intense and desperate.

What the *hell* was it?

"What if he kills again?"

"I'll make sure that doesn't happen. Please, Charlotte. I need the time. I wouldn't ask if it wasn't so important."

"What is, Max? What's so important about him that you're willing to risk . . . everything?"

"He's my father."

She couldn't react at first, then finally murmured faintly, "My God."

He pulled away emotionally as he watched her expression. And he held himself very still as she reached out to him, her fingertips gliding across the back of his hand, curling into his palm to squeeze gently.

"What does that mean to you, Max?"

"I don't know. I—I don't know."

She stepped into him, holding him as he rested his head on her shoulder. "Oh, baby, why didn't you tell me?"

And just like that, her tender empathy melted away all the panic and uncertainty of the past weeks. He let it go with a soft exhalation, and relaxed in her embrace.

"What are we going to do, Max? What do you need me to do?"

He couldn't speak through the sweet ache in his throat. He lifted his head and looked down into the dark eyes usually filled with passion and fire, now steeped in dewy concern. At the wide mouth so often curled back in a combative snarl or ripe with sultry invitation, now softly parted. At the bold, exotic features so frequently shaped by fierceness or pride, now left naked of all but the most vulnerable emotions. For him.

He touched her cheek, rubbing his thumb over the swell of her lower lip. Her eyes glistened, close to overflowing. How had he gotten so lucky? Why had this tough, practical woman thrown all logic away to give him a second look, a second chance? What had she seen in his dark, solitary soul that convinced her to look beyond his lengthy rap sheet, past his vicious deeds, over the insurmountable differences between them, to take a risk on him so unwisely?

He could still feel the stroke of her fingertips on

his altered face, on his ferocious, inhuman face, and hear the quiet awe in her voice as she whispered, "Oh, Max. You're magnificent." All the lonely fetters around his heart had fallen away at that moment, and he'd known with certainty that he would love her until the day he died. He wouldn't risk her, not for anything.

Puzzlement rose in her expression when he was silent for so long. There was just a hint of wariness, always swimming below the surface, that shadow of anxious readiness—just in case. She said she wasn't afraid of him, that she didn't fear his touch the way she had every right to. And perhaps she believed it. But he could sense it—that slight pause, that infinitesimal jerk of her heart, when a movement would catch her by surprise. Amazingly it had nothing to do with what he was, but what had been done *to* her. And he would spend the rest of his days trying to quiet that jump of fear, trying to convince her that she would never have cause where he was concerned to expect harm to come her way.

He leaned toward her, waiting until he read anticipation in her expressive dark eyes, letting her meet him halfway. He sank into the luxury of her kiss, his mouth shaping to the pliant sweetness of hers. Marveling, as always, at her eagerness to pursue that thrill of reacquainting need that rose whenever they touched.

A pragmatist, he always expected to find she wanted him just a little bit less, to discover her passion a bit cooler. But he never did. If anything, he found more urgency, more greed in the way her lips parted, in the way her tongue chased his in an intimate tangle. The sound rising up from his soul was a contented, rumbling purr.

The sound of his cell phone ringing was an annoyance.

He groped about the dresser top, then flipped it open.

"Savoie."

"I'm becoming familiar with the sound of being a third wheel. Let me talk to her."

He handed the phone to a puzzled Charlotte. "It's your conscience calling."

She took the cell phone and immediately started to complain. "Babineau, you have the absolute—"

"Worst timing. Yeah, whatchu gonna do? I was beginning to wonder if you were going to Aruba for that coffee."

She shifted the phone to her other ear, and eased slightly out of Max's arms.

He understood. Duty called. He took a few steps back to give her privacy, but wasn't too proud to eavesdrop.

"I had an urgent personal emergency come up."

"If you're talking about tending to Savoie's sex drive, that's not an emergency."

"No."

His voice lowered slightly. "Everything all right?"

She reached out her other hand to rub Max's

shoulder. "It is now. Why are you calling on this phone?"

"Couldn't get through to you on yours. Figured if you were distracted enough to forget to put it on the charger, I could guess where you'd be."

There was a funny pitch to his words that put her on guard. "Alain, what's going on?"

"Ceece, how long have you been with Savoie?"

"Why?"

"How long?"

"From the time I left my desk until this minute. Again, why?" Her hand fisted in Max's shirt.

"Noreen Cummings was attacked."

Cee Cee cursed fiercely. "When? Was she killed?"

"Apparently she'd gone out into their backyard this morning a little before five when their dog didn't come back to the door. She was slashed up pretty bad, but apparently her screaming brought her husband out and the attacker fled on foot. She's in surgery now." His tone toughened. "Cee Cee, Hammond's on his way over to Savoie's. I'm meeting him there. I'd suggest you not be. You don't want to be caught in the middle of this."

"Thanks." She shut the phone and lifted her somber gaze to Max. "You heard?"

"He's right. You need to go."

"Max, I'm not leaving. They'll arrest you if you don't have an airtight alibi."

"And if you give me one, your career is as good as gone. And that's what I'm going to be."

Her other hand gripped his wrist. "What do you mean?"

"I can't let them take me in. I've got no time for it. I have to find him. I have to get my answers now, while I still can."

"Max, you can't run. They'll swear out a warrant and put an APB out. They'll hunt you down."

"They can't take me if I don't let them."

"Max." She cuffed both his wrists with the circle of her hands, terribly afraid of the cold determination she saw in his face. The "they" he spoke of so savagely were her friends, her colleagues. "Don't do this. I don't want anyone getting hurt."

"Charlotte—"

"*Please,* Max. Please. For me."

He gave a heavy sigh. "I suppose Giles and Helen can give statements. If I call D'Marco now, he can start on the paperwork. But you stay out of it. Your car's in the garage, out of sight. You do the same. Stay up here until I'm gone. All right? Charlotte?"

Her palms glided over the sides of his face. "I love you, Max."

He didn't look pleased. "Why are you telling me this now?"

"Because it's true."

"What are you up to, detective?"

There was a tap at the door.

"Mr. Savoie, there's a police person downstairs."

"Put him in the parlor, Helen. I'll be right there." His suspicious gaze never left Cee Cee's, even as she pulled him down for a deep, soft kiss. His response was hedged with caution.

"I've missed you, Savoie," she whispered gruffly against his mouth. And he was lost.

He crushed her to him in a fiercely possessive way he didn't quite understand, but when it got a hold of him there was no reasoning with it. He wanted to growl over her, a dog with a tasty bone he didn't plan to share. He wanted to sweep her up and away from the dangerous lives they both led, and closet her away with him someplace where he'd have her to himself and have time to explore all the things he'd fantasized about during those unrequited years before their first kiss. But for right now, he'd settle for a quick feast off her lips and the feel of her poured against him. A taste of Charlotte Caissie was better than a seven-course meal of anyone else. Still, he let her go reluctantly.

"Charlotte?"

"Max?"

"Are we okay?"

His question startled her. "I hope so, because our underwear is commingling inside that drawer." Then, seeing how serious he was, she smiled. "I'm okay. How 'boutchu?"

"I am now. I'd better go make nice with my company."

"You'd better put on some shoes, then." She bent and picked up his Converses. She studied them for a moment, a perplexed frown building.

"What?"

"Red shoes. You said something about red shoes."

Alarm leapt in his eyes, so sudden and obvious she was instantly on guard. "When?"

"Last night. You were talking about your mother."

His face drained of color. His eyes went flat and dead. "I don't know anything about that. It doesn't mean anything."

But when she extended the shoes to him he took an anxious step back, unwilling to take them. If he'd been in his animal form, he'd have been bristled up from head to tail in a defensive posture.

She set the shoes on the floor and he continued to stare at them as if they were something frightening and foreign to him, as if half expecting them to launch an attack upon his bare feet. Perplexed, Cee Cee brought him a pair of socks and his boots from the closet, keeping her tone quiet and casual to soothe whatever had provoked him into the strange, tense skittishness.

"Here, baby. Wear these. You'll probably be wading in it up to your ankles for most of the day."

He took an unsteady breath, shaking off the shock and horror he wouldn't explain. He looked at her, his eyes wide and glossy with something she didn't understand. Dammit, how could she understand when he wouldn't tell her?

But instead of demanding a truth he obviously

wasn't ready to confess, she pressed the battered work boots into his hands and went up onto her toes to rub her cheek against his. She whispered, "It's all right. Don't worry about it now." By the time she settled back, he was himself again. Eager to move past whatever had scared him into the jumpy animal behavior, she stroked his face gently. "You still look a little bit woozy from last night. Have you had anything to eat?"

He blinked, then gave her a faint smile because she wasn't pressuring him. For the moment. "No. Nothing. Maybe I'll chew on the unpleasant Detective Hammond for a while." He quickly put on his boots, keeping a nervous eye on the shoes. Then he straightened and pointed a finger at her. "You stay put. I'll take care of this."

He didn't realize until later that she never actually agreed or disagreed with that.

Clever girl.

JUNIOR HAMMOND WAS a poisonous toad of a fellow who disliked Max only slightly more than he loathed Charlotte. When Max entered the room, Hammond glanced about with a smirkiness that just begged slapping.

"Looks like you been keeping up the place, Savoie. Haven't been out here since they were scraping Legere's brains off the floor in back. All but the ones splattered all over you, that is."

Max bared his teeth. "Always a pleasure to see

you, too, Detective Hammond. Still sniffing after Charlotte's leftovers in hopes of getting that grade raise?"

"I believe you're the only one sniffing after Caissie. Now. You think you're the first she's twitched that short skirt around? She worked her way through the squad room before lowering herself to those in lockup." He grinned slyly.

The innuendo stung Max like a sharp smack on the snout. He reared back slightly, his eyes narrowing, darkening into a ruby red glimmer that was almost black. Charlotte and Hammond? He assessed the man, then snorted. No. It was too ridiculous. His smooth voice betrayed none of his irritation.

"I'm not going to discuss Detective Caissie with you. I wouldn't soil her by association. Do you want something, or are you just here to whine over what I've got that you'll never have?"

Hammond's features reddened and his aggressive step forward was halted by the arrival of Alain Babineau.

"Let's make this professional, shall we, gentlemen?"

Max slid him what was almost a welcoming smile. "Good morning, detective. Care for some coffee or do you want to proceed right to the handcuffs? I assume that's why you're here. What have I supposedly done this time? Pissed on somebody's shoes?"

Babineau became all crisp efficiency. "Noreen

Cummings was attacked at her home at approximately five this morning, And you were where, Mr. Savoie?"

"Here, detective. I fell ill at the office yesterday and left around four o'clock."

"And I brought him here and have been taking care of him all night."

Max and Babineau spoke the same aggravated oath as Cee Cee entered the parlor. Helen was behind her carrying a tray with coffee. Hammond simply stared, jaw loose.

Meeting the fierce green eyes, Cee Cee smiled. "Max, a word with you. Helen, Detective Babineau likes cream and sugar, and Hammond takes it any way he can get it."

Max stalked over to where she stood with her back to their company.

"What are you doing?" he growled softly, but he was quickly distracted by an enticing scent.

"I thought you might need a little something to tide you over."

She brought up a hand filled with fresh cubes of meat from the kitchen. Raw meat. The fact that she would think to do so, as if there was nothing odd about feeding him like a wild thing, as if it was nothing more than bringing him a quick bite of breakfast, stunned him into a moment of astonished gratitude.

After a blink of surprise, he fed swiftly and ravenously from her palm, then licked and sucked her fingers clean. By the time he placed a kiss on her knuckles, his color was already better. He murmured, "I'm still angry," before stepping away to put a more impartial distance between them. He rubbed a swift hand over his mouth and chin.

"We have to take him in, Ceece. You know that," Babineau stated as he stirred his coffee and tried one of the pastries on the tray. He nodded to Helen. "This is outstanding. Did you make these? Could I get the recipe for my wife?"

"Of course, detective."

"This isn't necessary, Babineau," Cee Cee countered. "He hasn't been out of my sight. Helen is a witness as well. Giles St. Clair"—she gestured to the big man who'd just entered the room—"drove us here from the city and was present throughout the night. Giles, give Detective Hammond the security tapes that document our arrival and the fact that no one has left the grounds since.

"Mr. Savoie was not in the city this morning, nor did he attack Mrs. Cummings. I'll give my statement to that effect, on record, right now."

"Charlotte, you don't need to do this," Max cautioned quietly. "They have nothing. Don't involve yourself."

She stared him straight in the eye. "It's the truth. It's not as if I've done anything wrong. Or anything to be ashamed of."

Then she looked to the others. "Because I love him that much."

"Oh, fuck me sideways," Hammond growled.

"I don't think an official statement is necessary," Babineau decided, recovering from her blunt declaration. He slanted a piercing look at Hammond. "Do you, Junior?"

"If it's not him, who the hell is it?" Hammond grumbled. He clearly wanted to arrest someone, anyone. And he clearly preferred it to be the obnoxiously smug Savoie.

"Any insights on that, Savoie?"

"Sorry, detective." His gaze slid to Charlotte, betraying no hint of how much he depended upon her answer. Surrendering no clue as to whether or not he expected her to back him and the promise she'd made.

"Cee Cee? Anything to add?"

She looked away from Max to state calmly, "I'm following up on some things, but nothing we can jump on yet. I want this to be rock solid when we make our move. I'm tired of Cummings snapping at my ass."

Junior's gaze dropped in contemplation of that particular part of her anatomy, then collided forcefully with Max's on the way back up. Their stares held, growing heated and intense.

"I hear you there," Babineau concluded, hoping he wasn't going to have to separate the two aggressively posturing males with more than just words. He slapped at the back of Hammond's high and tight haircut. "Junior, let's roll. You coming with us, Ceece?" Her partner's gaze went from her to Savoie, hoping to convince both of them to make the smart choice.

"I'll meet you at the station in a few."

That was good enough for Babineau. "Max. I suppose I'll be seeing you."

"I would assume so, detective. Thank you."

"I'm not doing you any favors."

"Heaven forbid that I would ever jump to that conclusion."

Babineau almost smiled. "Come on, Junior. We're spinning our wheels here."

As Hammond started to turn, Max stepped up beside him, placed a hand on his shoulder, and said quietly, almost conversationally, "I thought I warned you once what would happen if you made loose talk about my girl. Maybe you've just forgotten." Hammond started to squirm under his tightening grip. "And maybe you've forgotten who taught me all I know about settling up a score. If I were Jimmy Legere, I'd tear out your tongue and feed it to you mashed and fried. But I'm not. Maybe you ought to start worrying about what else I *might* be." He opened his hand and Hammond leapt away from him.

"You crazy son of a bitch. Who do you think you are, threatening a police officer?"

"I didn't hear anything," Babineau drawled, licking the pastry sugar from his fingertips. "Did you, Detective Caissie?"

"I *do* think I heard something about loose talk,

and it must have been directed at me. Maybe we'll have to have a little talk, Junior. Maybe you should be worrying about *me*, not Max."

Hammond scowled. "The two of you deserve each other."

She caught a restraining handful of the back of Max's shirt. "Yes, I think we do. I'll see you back at the shop, Alain."

After they'd gone, she turned to Max in a simmer of temper. "What exactly did he say to you?"

Max grabbed a handful of her hair and yanked her up to meet his hard, soul-sucking kiss.

She staggered back from it, mouth bruised, eyes glassy. "If he told you *that,* he was lying," she panted.

"Why?" His voice was tight and intense.

She knew he wasn't talking about Hammond. "Why, what?"

"Why did you come down here? It wasn't necessary for you to risk so much. I could have—"

"You came back."

Her soft statement tossed him off track. "What?"

"The night before last. After you followed me out of the club, after I refused to listen to you, after all the awful things I did and said to you. You came back to my apartment, because you knew what happened in the parking garage would bring my nightmares back. You came back to be there for me. Why would you do that, Max? How could you be so . . . kind to me after I'd hurt you so badly?"

"Because it hurt me worse to think of you alone and afraid."

His simple logic tore her in half. There were tears on her face when she launched herself at him, wrapping him up in a tangle of arms and legs.

"Take me upstairs and take me, Savoie."

"Whatever you want, detective. Happy to do it for you."

Fifteen

*H*E CARRIED HER, twined hot and eager about him, as far as the arch leading to the hall. Her mouth hurried over his face and neck, nipping, teasing, devouring, driving him wild. He stumbled into the wall, supporting his balance with one hand while trying to control her with the other. He couldn't do both.

"Excuse me, Mr. Savoie."

He looked over the top of Cee Cee's head to see a blushing Jasmine. "Yes?" His voice was hoarse and impatient.

"You have a call from—"

"Take a message. I'm in a meeting and don't wish to be disturbed." He gripped the edge of the pocket door and slid it shut.

"A meeting?" Charlotte chuckled against the side of his throat.

"Meeting all your needs, *sha*. I think that deserves my undivided attention."

"Here?"

"It's my house. If I want to roll around naked with my woman on the parlor rugs, I can, you know."

"I'm feeling very needy."

"I'm feeling very obliging."

"Max?"

"Charlotte?"

"Kiss me."

From the way his heart was beating like crazy, she expected a rough savaging, which would have been just fine with her. But the touch of his mouth was soft and poignantly sweet upon hers. She made a helpless sound of wonder, of surrender, of encouragement as his tongue danced lightly along her lips. Then the exquisite seal of his upon hers, the fit so perfect, so stirring and strong.

While he leaned her back against the wall and took that kiss to a level deeper, her hands were busy on the buttons to the shirt she'd just put on, at the zipper of her jeans, then of his. She wiggled down from him without breaking from their kiss, swiftly shedding her clothing to the waist, then reluctantly left his lips to shimmy out of her pants and skim his shirt over his head. Then her mouth made a searing trail down his chest, and lower. She dragged his pants down to the tops of his work boots. Undoing the laces brought her eye level to the aggressive and somewhat menacing jut of his sex.

She regarded him warily.

I suppose you and I will have to get better acquainted.

She'd never touched him with any serious degree of intimacy. Not the way he'd almost religiously explored and conquered every available inch of her body with an insatiable curiosity and profound appreciation. Her reluctance had nothing to do with him. Making love with Max Savoie was the single most explosive pleasure she'd ever experienced.

But she'd had other experiences, too. They had nothing to do with pleasure, and everything to do with why the mere thought of a touch from anyone other than this man filled her with icy dread. Which was why she held herself back, just a bit, in case things were too good to be true, and all that remembered darkness was lying in wait behind the deceivingly beautiful delight.

Coward.

She finished with the laces. Max levered out of his boots and kicked free of his pants, leaving her to confront this last remaining barrier between her past and her future. *Dammit.* She wasn't one to run from what scared her, and that fear was wrapped up around all the passion she felt for Max like an invasive, deep-rooted weed that would choke out her chance for happiness. If she let it.

She eyed that powerful, impatient length of him as a not-insurmountable roadblock to what she wanted.

I'll make you a deal. You don't hurt me, and I'll take very good care of you.

She touched him lightly. He jerked against her palm. Smooth, warm. Not quite as terrifying as she'd imagined.

"Deal."

"Did you say something to me?"

"Indirectly."

She licked him. Strong and alive, like the rest of Max, only hotter.

"Charlotte, you don't have to—"

She slid her mouth down the length of him.

Max's knees buckled. His palms slapped against the wall as she continued to touch him, stroke him, weigh him in her palms. Though he wanted to, he didn't dare touch her. And then there was the sharp, glassy fire moving up and down him, burning, tearing, pulling through him until he couldn't catch his breath. Until he thought he'd gone deaf, dumb, and blind. Until he caught a glimpse of Heaven.

Having brought him right to the edge, she straightened, rising up between the brace of his arms to meet dazed green eyes. She filled her palms with his roughly beautiful face and told him with soft ferocity, "You're mine, Savoie. Every piece of you is mine. Every breath you take is mine. And I want you madly."

Heat and dark desire flared in his eyes. "I'm yours," he agreed, his whisper raw and harsh and shaking. "Remind me to send a thank-you note to those fellas in lockup. Later." His hand slipped behind her knee, bringing her leg up over his hip bone, opening her to his sudden claiming thrust. Pinning her to the wall as he drove into her, drove the breath from her body and the awareness from her half-shuttered eyes. And he drove them both to a climax that shattered time, space, and sanity.

CEE CEE LAY stretched out naked on the ornamental sofa. Max sat on the floor, his cheek warm and a bit scratchy on her abdomen. She toyed with his hair with the fingers of one hand while the others were laced through his.

His head shifted so their eyes could meet, his smile lazy and smug with contentment. "I can't move. I think you've paralyzed me."

Her hand clenched in his hair, shaking his head slightly. "Good. Then I can use you mercilessly at my leisure."

His eyes closed. "Okay."

"We're going to be okay, Max."

She felt a slow gathering of tension in his shoulders, a tightening of his hand about hers. She waited, giving him time to pull up whatever he needed to say.

"I was very young, Charlotte—three, possibly four years old, and so alone. You can't understand that kind of loneliness, the kind that comes from being different. I kept hoping I could find someone else like me, so I'd reach out with that sense we have—secretly because I wasn't supposed to ever let anyone know what I could do. Like casting out bait in a pond. Until one day I got a nudge back, and I was so excited. Then I got a tug. So I pulled back and there was another tug, harder this time. So I pulled back again as hard as I could, and it kept getting bigger and stronger and I got scared, so I stopped.

"But it was too late by then. He came to the door of our house. I could feel him, like a tingling in every part of me. My mama knew him. They started arguing, arguing about me. And then he hit her, and kept hitting her. Hurting her." His voice broke off and the sound of his quick panting breath was filled with his fear and fury and confusion.

"I don't know how it happened. I got so hot and cold inside, and all I could think of was stopping him, keeping him from hurting my mama. So I struck out at him and kept hitting him with my hands, only they weren't my hands anymore." He lifted his free hand, turning it to and fro as if he'd never seen it before. "He stopped, and at first I didn't know what I'd done. And then everything inside him started to spill out, and there was so much blood. Blood on his shoes." *The red shoes.* He stopped again, his breath shuddering as the horror caught up to him.

"But he wasn't dead. Dying, probably, but not dead. He grabbed me by the hair and started dragging me toward the door. My mama knocked him to the floor, and she . . . she tore out his throat with her teeth. Only it wasn't my mama; it was the same awful thing that I'd become. And then she was my mama again, and she rolled him up in our good rug and said, 'Help me, Max. Help me get rid of him so they'll never know he was here, so no one will know what we've done.'"

Charlotte sat up to put her arms around him, holding him fiercely as she listened to the rest of his flatly delivered recitation. Seeing it through the traumatized eyes of the child he'd been. Mother and son dragging their burden out into the moonlit swamp, filling the carpet with rocks and branches to make it heavier. And then standing there in the damp, in the dark, waiting for the evidence of what they'd done to sink out of sight.

"We went back home. I was so tired and so cold. And I started to cry and she— And she—" His body jerked sharply. "She told me I wasn't to cry. That now I knew what I was—what *we* were. And that no one could ever know, or someone else would come to kill her and take me.

"So I didn't cry, and I watched her scrub the floor all night until the stains were mostly gone. And I kept seeing those shoes—those red shoes. When I thought of them, I knew that there was something inside me that could protect us and keep us safe. I knew that I didn't have to be like everyone else, and that the secret I had to keep was that I was stronger, more powerful then any of them.

"And I still am, Charlotte. For some reason, I am the best of what we are."

Cee Cee pressed a kiss on the top of his head and laid her cheek there.

"And there was another secret I was never supposed to tell. Our females aren't supposed to be able to shift. They have a bit of the glimmer, the extra sense, but not the ability to change shape. But my mother did. I don't know what that means, but I think my father does. I have to find out why it's so important to those who are trying to find me."

"I can't give you much time, Max. Not after what's happened."

"I know. How much do I have?"

"I'll meet you tonight at the club."

"Charlotte—"

"For a date. I have some great new shoes."

"Yeah?"

She smiled at the interest perking up his tone, rubbing her cheek over his hair. "We'll talk and decide then. Okay?"

He nodded.

"Max, don't trust him," she warned. "And don't let him hurt you."

"And you promise me one thing." He lifted his head to look at her, deep worry in his eyes. "Promise you won't try to take him unless I'm there. *Please,* Charlotte. For me."

There wasn't much she could deny him at that moment. Plus, she hadn't quite figured out the logistics of bringing Rollo to justice. *"They can't take me if I don't let them,"* Max had said, and she was just beginning to realize how true that was. If he hadn't been inclined to go with them, the NOPD never could have brought him in to the station. She remembered the way he was that first night at the club, ripping through those of his own kind to prove dominance. What chance would ordinary humans stand against him? Against Rollo, if he decided to be uncooperative? And there was damned little to convince her that he might be otherwise. If she was going to take down the maverick shape-shifter, she needed Max at her side.

But could he, would he, turn in his own father?

"All right." She brushed her hand over the healed punctures in his arm. He rolled his head to the side so he could nip at her wrist and suck on her knuckles. Her other palm scooped under his chin, lifting him for the slow, luscious sampling of his lips.

"I want you, Savoie," she murmured with a smoky curl of desire twining about her words. "I'm just out of time and energy at the moment."

A smile, slightly smug, faintly uncertain. "You'll come back here tonight? You'll stay here with me?"

"Yes." Oh, yes. The department be damned.

That satisfied his heart, just as she'd already satisfied his body. "I have to go." He stretched up to kiss her lightly. "Don't feel you have to hurry off."

"Ummm, yes. I think I'll just lounge around naked on your sofa for a while."

His gaze caressed over her as he stood. "It could be your sofa if you wanted it to be."

She smiled and lay back on the cushioned arm, her eyes closing as fatigue settled in. She'd just rest a minute. She drifted until the soft touch of his mouth on hers made her stir, and then she heard the sound of the pocket door sliding closed.

What had he meant?

Her eyes popped open. What had he meant by "your sofa" if she wanted it to be?

Fluttery panic set in around her heart. She sat up, pressing her palms over it to quiet the anxious beat. He hadn't meant anything other than her staying here with him. That was all. She refused to read anything deeper into it.

Still, she scurried off the couch to gather up her scattered clothes, which Max had stacked neatly on a chair. She crushed them to her chest, her emotions bobbing crazily up and down in her throat.

When she thought of the anguished story he'd told her, she wanted to weep. But tears wouldn't help him. Answers would. He was going to find his the only way he could, and she would discover her own to back him up.

She dressed quickly, then left the parlor and went into Jimmy's office. She stood in the doorway, her gaze settling on the computer. What had Dev Dovion said about things getting ugly when it was personal?

She'd looked at Simon Cummings's life from every angle and had found no reason for Rollo to attack his family with such methodical viciousness. But maybe the reason went back farther than she had researched. Back to when her father had put Etienne Legere away and Rollo had disappeared. But had something else been going on? Something deeper then she'd already discovered?

She sat at Jimmy's keyboard, studying the blank

screen. What secrets were stored on that hard drive?

"Can I help you with something, detective?"

The sound of Helen's voice made her jump, but she didn't try to hide her intent. "I was wondering if Jimmy had anything on here that would shed some light on this case I'm working on."

"Simon Cummings, you mean."

"Yes. But what I'm looking for would have been a long time ago."

"Mr. Legere was a meticulous record keeper. He hired someone to come in and scan all his old files and clippings, from this year back to his father's time. He was a firm believer that history repeated itself, so one had to keep an eye on the past."

"An eye on the past. Yes. Would you happen to know his password?"

"Does Mr. Savoie know you're looking into his private papers, detective?"

"He told you to give me anything I wanted, didn't he?"

"It depends on which means more to you: your job or his trust."

Cee Cee scowled at the housekeeper. She hadn't wanted to look at it that way, but now that she was, she had to address it. With a curse, she pushed away from the desk. Not seeing Helen's smile.

"It's Etienne."

"What?"

"The password. I trust you'll only look where you need to, and will disregard the rest."

Cee Cee grinned. "I'll be the soul of discretion."

The second Helen left the room, she pushed the power button and went to work. Digging, searching, sifting through Etienne Legere's almost illegible notes, finding her father's name, then Cummings's. She glanced up when Helen set a tray on the desk beside her.

"Your eggs, detective. And some fresh coffee."

Surprise left her momentarily speechless.

"Don't let them get cold."

"Thank you, Helen."

"Thank *you*, Charlotte."

She made a quick call to Babineau, asking him to cover for her while she followed up on something. He caught the shiver of excitement in her voice and kept his questions to himself. She forked up the excellent egg dish while jotting shorthand notes onto a legal pad from the desk drawer. And slowly the story emerged.

Her ambitious father going out on his own to tap a civilian, Cummings, to assist in a dangerous game after information leaked out about Legere's intentions. The slick and clever Etienne caught between his caution and his greed, cutting in Cummings in an effort to squeeze out his brother. The sting, sharp and devastating to Jimmy's father.

But it wasn't the money he'd lost, or even the chance he might go to prison if his lawyer couldn't make the claim of entrapment stick. It was the fact that someone close had betrayed him. And since he could think of only one person who was close enough to know his plans, he struck out viciously, killing his brother. Who was as innocent as he was surprised.

Rollo. That was the only answer. Rollo had turned on his boss and had run before the consequences could catch him.

So why was he back? Why was he going after Cummings after all these years had passed? She had the connection but no reason. She still had no proof.

She'd make another hard run at Cummings. For some reason, her father had kept the young developer's name out of his reports, away from the media. Why? One would think an ambitious businessman would love the chance to appear the hero. She needed to ask him why his involvement was silent, and why Rollo was out for his blood.

"Detective, a call for you."

She glanced up at Jasmine, noticing the young woman's discomfort around her. How had Max been able to win them all over, to inspire such loyalty when he was such an outsider, so isolated, so alien? How much did the household know about what he was? Would he be surprised to learn of their devotion?

She supposed he would. He always seemed so terribly confused as to why anyone would care for him. Well, that was something he'd just have to get over.

She responded to the young woman with a smile;

she had some winning over to do herself. "Thank you." Cee Cee picked up the desk cordless.

"Ceece, Noreen Cummings has made a statement," Babineau charged right in. "She got a good look at him. She ID'd that new fella shadowing Savoie."

A mixture of relief and regret sliced through Cee Cee. Max was off the hook, but that gave him little time to tie up his loose ends.

"Babs, can you sit on it until tonight? There's more here, something going way back to Etienne Legere. Let me work through it."

"Does this have to do with Savoie? Is he going to get in the way of you bringing one of his own down?"

"No." She spoke with a lot more confidence than she felt. "He'll let me do my job."

"I'll get the paperwork started, but I'll wait for your call. Her condition is still guarded, so we don't have to worry about the press for now." But she could tell by his tone that he was worried about her.

"Thanks, Alain. I'll stay in touch." She clicked off.

She looked at the phone for a long moment, arguing with herself between emotion and responsibility. She owed Rollo nothing, but Max too much to even consider. She dialed.

"Savoie. Leave a message."

"Max, time's up."

ROLLO LIFTED HIS cup of café au lait. "Been waiting for you. You look no worse for wear."

"No more games." Max drew out one of the plastic chairs beneath Café du Monde's awning and sat. "Time for our Q and A."

"All right, Max. You earned it. Fire away."

"Cummings. Why are you after him?"

Rollo smiled faintly and sipped his coffee. "Her business before yours. Interesting."

"It's my business, too. I'm up for these murders."

"No you're not, boy. I saw to that for you."

"What do you mean?"

"Your little girlfriend should be slipping you free of that chain any time now."

"Why? Has this to do with the attack on his wife this morning?"

"I let her see me, Max. If you have any questions, you'd better ask them now."

"Why Cummings?"

"Are you sure that's what matters to you the most?"

No, but what he really wanted to know was too hard to verbalize. Why had Rollo risked himself to protect a son who meant nothing to him? Another move in the game he was playing? Or something else—something Max wasn't sure he was ready to consider? He didn't ask because he didn't want the potential answer to tie him to this violent, dangerous being.

He tried to force up the image of Rollo crouched

in the alley, grinning as he tormented that frightened, helpless bum with such heartless amusement. But he also felt the comforting weight of that big hand on the back of his head, the solid strength in the voice that said, *"I've got you."*

"Answer, please."

"A long time ago, I got restless being on Etienne Legere's leash. He didn't treat me as nicely as Jimmy did you. I saw a chance to better my lot and I took it. Simon Cummings wanted in on a project Legere was bankrolling. He wanted to make his mark in his daddy's company, and he didn't mind cutting legal or moral corners to do it. Don't be fooled by his sanctimonious pap—back then, he had no qualms about authorizing substandard materials to take an extra cut of the cream. For a percentage, I put Cummings and Legere together."

"There's more. Tell me everything."

"Some of it might strike a little close to home." He smirked. "Cummings wasn't the only one looking to make a name. Tommy Caissie was looking to come up in the world, too. He sniffed out Cummings's set of double books and had him up against the wall.

"There was something in it for everyone. Cummings got his daddy's approval. Caissie got his shield. And I was supposed to get my freedom—but somehow that didn't pan out the way I planned it."

Max sat and listened, hating it all. Some of it he

already knew, some he'd guessed at. And some cut through him like a blade because of the impact it would have on the woman he loved.

"Of course," Rollo drawled when he'd finished, "all that stays with me once I'm gone."

"Charlotte's not going to let you run."

"Maybe you should convince her to look the other way." His gaze grew sly. "Considering."

"She wouldn't listen, and I wouldn't ask."

"How about a little something to give your old man a head start, then?"

Max harbored few illusions about decency in the hearts of others. He knew exactly what Rollo was and what he wanted. And it wasn't the chance to play daddy. "How much?"

Rollo stared at him, a bit amazed. "You don't want to dance around for a little while first?"

"I don't dance with other men."

Rollo named a figure and Max nodded without a blink. "I'll have it for you in cash within the hour. Then you'll disappear."

"Like I never existed."

Max studied him somberly. "Did you know she could shift?"

Rollo looked startled. "Your mama? How do you think she got away from me? I had plans for us, for us and the children she would give me. I wasn't sure of much, but I was sure we would have beautiful, phenomenal children." His eyes grew dreamy as he looked back, then he glanced across the table and smiled wistfully. "She didn't exactly run away with me of her own free will."

He saw Max's hands grip the edge of the table top and hurried on. "Oh, she loved me and wanted to be with me, but I couldn't convince her to break ties with her family. So I took her, and killed some of them along the way. She couldn't go back, then—but she couldn't forgive me, either. I would have been more careful if I'd known you'd already been conceived. She probably figured that out, too. So imagine my surprise when I came home one night and she was waiting with her eyes bloodred and fangs dripping. Hell of a temper, your mama. But she did love me, so she left me alive. Barely.

"I didn't know where she'd gone until I heard whispers about you sending out that glimmer. The minute I heard, I knew you were my son. I went to Legere; figured he'd look after you in a way I couldn't. Because they'd never given up looking for me."

"And Jimmy gave you money. He bought me from you."

Rollo shrugged. "He had his conditions that went with the cash. He was a clever one, always working the angles. As much as he wanted you, he wanted me gone—out of your life and away from Cummings. He'd stepped into his daddy's shoes by then, and wasn't about to get them dirty over the likes of me.

"Cummings owed me, and he hadn't paid up like he was supposed to. Because of that, I had to live some pretty lean years, doing stuff I'd rather not recall just to survive. I figured I could bide my time, then take what was owed me in blood. But Jimmy wasn't having any of my kind of vengeance. He wanted to bleed Cummings slow and steady for the long haul. If I wanted his money to get away clean, I had to cut all ties to you and forget about getting even.

"It's not the deal I wanted, but I took it. I had to. He kept you safe, and that's what mattered. They'd have found out about you if I'd stayed around, and I couldn't take you both with me, even if your mama would have gone. Jimmy kept you under the radar, just like I asked. And then he went and got himself killed, and there you were, front-page news. So I figured I'd better drop by before someone else recognized your mama's eyes."

"Why?"

"Because you're my son. The only one I'm aware of, anyway."

Max stared at him, his expression conveying his disbelief.

"I wanted to make sure you could handle yourself." A prideful smile. "Guess you answered my question."

"Motivated by fatherly love, I presume."

He laughed at Max's dry delivery. "You're a smart one, boy. No, there's no goodness in this black heart. Just self-interest. I was curious, though. I wanted to get a look at you. I wanted to see what you'd made of yourself. And I like what I see."

"Your approval, coming so late in my life, is so very important to me."

Another chuckle with just a touch of regret. "I came back for Cummings—I won't lie to you. I had to wait until Jimmy was gone to get him, but I did." A slow, fierce smile. "Yes, I did. But there were also things I needed to tell you. I didn't know about Marie, or I would have come a long time ago. I would have found a way to get around Jimmy. I came here for you, too, Max."

Sixteen

THEY LEFT THE Square and began to walk in the cool drizzle that blew across the river.

"Why are they so interested in me? I don't even know who they are," Max said.

"Think of it like horse breeding: the best stock with the best stock to improve the breed. Your mama—my, oh, my—she was a pure thoroughbred all the way. Beautiful, tough, refined, skilled, and smart enough not to let them see all that she could do. Me—my family can boast of a line just as long, but a bit darker and rougher around the edges. Over the centuries, there were fewer and fewer houses that could make that claim. And the school of thought was, the longer and purer the line, the greater the skills and the power. Power and position: that's what it's all about." He laughed at Max's baffled expression. "You're thinking small, Max. You're thinking local muscle, like Legere. This is big. Bigger than you can imagine. International. Global."

Max made a disparaging noise. "Why? Who cares? I don't understand."

"We're commodities, bought, sold, and traded because of what we do better than anything else. We're killers. That's what we are. What's inside us. We're raised and trained and controlled to serve, to kill, to fight. But Marie ran with you and slipped you past the system. You've never been processed or registered. You don't realize how amazing you are. How rare. How dangerous. How . . ."

"Valuable," Max supplied, frowning. "I don't like this. I don't want any part of this."

"You have no choice, boy. Someone else is making those choices, and making a lot of money off of them. Marie was worth a fortune to her family. But she was disgusted by the idea of being sold to some stranger for breeding purposes, to improve her family's status. Think royalty, Max."

"So I'm what—like a duke or a prince or something?"

"No."

The way he said it made the hair bristle at Max's nap. "What then?"

"You're *it,* Max."

"What?" He laughed. "Like a Shifter king?"

"Yes. Exactly like that."

Suddenly there was no humor in the situation at all. Just a deadly absurdity. "Can't I just tell them thanks but no thanks, I'm not interested?"

"It's not like sitting on a board of directors, Max. These Chosen, these controllers, they don't care about you. They care about what you pass on to the next generation. There are those who would pay a ransom for such an offspring."

"Like a . . . stud fee?" Now he was truly disturbed. "No thank you."

"They don't need your participation for that, either. *Or* for you to be alive. A smart man would make a deal and take a hefty cut."

"And if Charlotte got wind of that nonsense, that first cut would put an end to any progeny."

Rollo shook his head. "The first thing they'll do is kill her, Max. They can't have you polluting the line. If you bond to her, your seed could become worthless."

Max abruptly stopped. "That's not going to happen. None of this is going to happen."

"Again, your wishes won't matter much."

Max's eyes narrowed. "I'm surprised that you, being a smart fella, haven't tried to sell me off to them."

Rollo smiled wryly. "I'm not above admitting to the temptation. But one has to be alive in order to spend money, and they want me dead in a big way. Which is why I need to be out of here as soon as you can get to a bank."

"You said they wanted to kill me. Why, if I'm so valuable?"

"Not everyone thinks so. If you're dead, the next in line would have all the prestige and position."

Max shook his head and started to walk again, his stride betraying his agitation. "This is insanity."

"This is coming your way, and soon. So you'd better start preparing for it."

"What do I do? How do I recognize them? What do they want from me?"

"It depends on who finds you first. If it's my family, the Moytes, they'll try to catch you and trade or sell you, to restore the family name. If it's the Terriots, they will kill you like they did the rest of your family, for cheating them out of the contract your grandfather made selling them your mother. If it's the Guedrys, they will kill you so their own son can take your place. If it's trackers sent by the Chosen, they'll want you brought to them. Then they'll test you, break you, breed you, and kill you. If there are any of your mother's people left, they will hold you up as the rightful leader of our clan."

"Lovely. If they find me and kill me, I'm fucked. If I cooperate with them, then they'll kill me and I'm fucked. If Charlotte hears about any of this, she'll go fuckin' nuts and I'll be fucked." His head was pounding. "How long before they get here?"

"Days, weeks, months maybe. As I said, you're in the public eye now, and not exactly hard to find if they start looking."

Now he knew why his mother, then Jimmy, had insisted nothing official be traced to him. But when he'd taken over for Jimmy, his attorney had established his identity in every possible data bank, making him available at the click of a mouse.

"Can I protect myself?"

"You can try. No one can beat you in a fair fight; you have skills none of us has ever even imagined. But they won't play fair and they'll come at you when you least expect it, through ways you won't expect. Or you can run. Run far and fast and hide who you are, what you are."

Max shook his head. "I've lived alone almost all my life, afraid of what I am. I won't do that again. Everything that means anything to me is here, and I'm not in the mood to hide."

"Then for God's sake, don't advertise so loudly! You give off energy like a nuclear reactor. Shut down. Stay silent. Disguise your true strength. Then, if they come, you'll have the advantage of surprise because they won't know what you're capable of. Hit them without mercy, with everything you have."

Max was silent, thinking of those red shoes.

"They'll use silver so that they don't have to get close. Build up your immunity. Surround yourself with those you trust, or at least those who can't be bought. Keep yourself from being an easy target. Suspect everyone, even your friends. *Especially* your friends. They'll use them to slip through your defenses."

"You make it sound like I'm getting ready to defend against an army."

"You'd be a fool to think of it as anything less than a war. These trackers they'll send for you, they're cold and clever, and they won't stop until they have you or you have them. Don't be afraid to discover what you are inside, what you can do. Sharpen your senses, boy. Practice reaching out without giving off a glimmer."

"Can that be done?"

"You won't know until you try."

They'd come full circle, back to the Square. It was flooded with tourists, even in the miserable weather. Max stood in the center of them and cautiously sent out a whisper, feeling for the presence of one of his kind. He picked up some low-level signals a few blocks away.

"Good. I'm standing right next to you and hardly felt a flutter." Rollo smiled hopefully. "You're a smart boy. You'll be all right."

"You're fucked" was what they both knew he was saying.

"I don't understand this. Who controls this buying and selling of our kind? Why aren't LaRoche and his people bothered by them?

Rollo laughed. "They're nothing, Max. They're crude, unskilled, and untrained. Discarded and forgotten. Beasts with no worth. You and I can adapt and learn and blend. We can hide what we are from the rest of them. And we carry a secret they'd rather we not share."

"What secret? Who is this *they* you're talking about? These Chosen—what are they? Are they the ones my mother feared?"

"They own us, Max. They rule us Shifters. They were us, and what they don't want known is that some of us are still a part of them. You and I are a part of them."

A truck close by backfired, startling Rollo. He gripped Max's arm, pulling him away from the high visibility of the Square into deeper shadows.

"I can't stay any longer, boy. I can't tell you any more. There are those who help our kind. They might have answers for you. I'll see if I can put them in touch with you."

"I'll be careful." *I'm fucked.* "My bank's down Chartres."

"Be happy to accompany you there."

The bank manager took care of the withdrawal personally, handing the money to Max without question or curiosity. Max put the bundles into a backpack Rollo purchased at the souvenir shop on the corner.

Rollo shouldered the heavy bag and, once they were out on the sidewalk, regarded Max with a faint smile. "It was good to finally meet you. Your mother would be very pleased with what you've become."

An unexpected surge of emotion hit Max. "Where will you go?"

"If I told you, it wouldn't be much of a secret, now would it?"

Knowing it was unlikely that they'd meet again made for a bittersweet parting. "Take care of yourself," Max said.

"That's what I'm best at, boy. If you're smart, you'll send your Upright girlfriend as far away from you as possible. She'll get torn apart in the crossfire."

Though alarm leapt, Max smiled. "You don't know Charlotte like I do. There's no one I'd rather have at my back."

"Well, good-bye, then." Rollo unexpectedly took Max in a hard embrace, holding Max's head to his shoulder for a long beat, then pushed him roughly away. "Don't think too badly of me, son."

And he was gone, swallowed up by the crowd.

MAX SAT ALONE in the back of the club, waving off any who tried to approach. He stared at the door with an unblinking focus, his features expressionless until awareness washed over them like moonlight splitting clouds. He rose up and waited for her to come into sight, anticipation rising along with the corners of his mouth. When she paused on the opposite side of the dance floor, his eyes darkened as they caressed her, from the punky spikes of her hair and boldly accented features, along the camisole of bronze silk and lace under his leather jacket and the snug wrap of her short suede skirt, down the long plunge of her splendid legs to leopard-print open-toed shoes with pencil-thin four-inch heels. She struck an arrogant pose and waited for him, her bright lips pursing as his swaggering stride brought him through the crowd as if no one else existed.

He took her hand, touched it to his lips, then lifted it high to twirl her under the bridge their arms made. She ended up pressed against him. His arms slid under the loose jacket to tug her in tighter and hers went around his shoulders. As they burrowed their faces against each other's necks, their bodies moved in sync to Norah Jones's bluesy moaning about waiting for her man to come home and turn her on.

"How do you like the shoes?"

She felt his smile. "The entire package is almost too hot to handle. But the shoes make me want to do you right here, right now."

"Then they were worth every penny I paid for them." She nuzzled him, sucking at his earlobe until he shuddered. "Handle me, Savoie."

"Handling you has always been my fondest wish and greatest frustration, Charlotte."

Her arms clinched tighter about his neck, hugging his head as she whispered almost apologetically, "I love you, baby."

His posture stiffened. "What have you done, detective?"

"Enjoy the moment, Max. Business can wait a few minutes."

Though he still held her close enough for her to feel the teeth of his zipper pressed into her hip, tension began to wedge between them. When they ended the dance that unfinished business followed them to the table, though they linked hands to try to prevent that separation.

The buxom Amber was waiting to take their order.

"Buy you a drink, detective?" Max asked as he seated her.

"I'll have what you're having."

"I'm having water."

Cee Cee looked up at Amber with a killer smile. "I'll have that, too, with some Jack Daniels to keep it company."

The two women locked stares until Amber smiled thinly. Cee Cee watched her assess the situation, not missing the significance of Max's jacket on her shoulders. Or the fact that Max's gaze never lifted to acknowledge her. When her gaze returned to Cee Cee's, it held resigned understanding. Her chance with Max Savoie was gone. She slipped silently from the table.

"Tell me," Max insisted the second they were alone.

"Can it wait until I get my drink? It's been a long day."

"You're stalling, detective. Why?"

She met his stare with a sniperscope directness. "Noreen Cummings ID'd Rollo." A pause. "You don't look surprised."

"I'm not."

"Where is he, Max?"

"Gone."

"What?" She cursed and reached for her phone. Max stopped the move with his hand around hers. "Let go. I have to get something out on the wire before he's halfway across the country. Dammit, Max!"

"He's gone, detective." Something in his tone was so very final. She allowed him to take her phone and return it to her pocket. "Gone as in never existed. Like I used to: no past, no records, no identity. You'll never find him. You wouldn't know where to start looking. And before you ask, I don't know, either."

"Why didn't you try to stop him?" she accused, furious and frustrated.

"It wasn't my job. All I promised I'd do was help you find a killer. And I think I did my part there."

She sat back in her chair, her expression grim. "How could you have let him go?"

He regarded her unapologetically. "Are you very, very angry with me?" Cool caution edged his tone.

"Yes. You know I am. He killed two women. He's not the kind you let walk."

"I can't bring them back. I wish I could."

"He's going to do it again, someplace else, and it will be my fault for trusting you." She muttered a curse, then took a long swallow of the drink Amber placed on the table.

"No, detective. It's case closed. He got what he was after. There'll be no more souls upon your conscience."

"And that's supposed to make what he's already done okay? How could you think so?"

"I don't. I'm sorry." When she didn't respond to the stroke of his hand over hers, he leaned forward and kissed her.

She tried to pull back, but his tongue slid silkily between her lips and she forgot why she was struggling. He was too good a kisser to allow her mind to wander anywhere, except maybe to a horizontal plane with a lot less clothing between them.

Sensing her reluctant surrender, he sat back, a slight, chastened smile on his damp mouth.

"You're not off the hook," she grumbled, but her fingertips were charting the prominent angles of his face in adoration.

"I'm sorry," he told her, his quiet sincerity almost making his treachery forgivable.

"You're *not* sorry, Max. You had no intention of letting me take him in."

"So where does that leave us?" he asked casually, but there was anxiousness in the way he kneaded her leg. This was no small thing with her, and he knew it. He'd known it when he'd watched Rollo walk away. She might understand his motives, but could she forgive him for his actions?

As if in answer, she slapped his hand aside. "I'm rethinking wanting you to handle me tonight."

When he appeared suitably repentant, she sighed and leaned back in her seat. She studied him for a moment, working up her own courage for confession time.

"I found the link between Rollo and Cummings. I was digging around in Jimmy's computer," she admitted.

Max blinked. "Who gave you the password?"

"I'm sorry. I can't reveal my sources." She tried to sound flippant, but she watched his expression closely. Not much to go on.

"Helen gave it to you? Why would she do that?"

"Because you told them all to give me whatever I asked for."

A pause. "I'm glad it was helpful."

Now it was her turn to blink. "You're not angry?"

"What good would it do? I can't expect you not to be a policewoman." He brought her hand up for a kiss. "We can't change our spots, detective. We are what we are."

He kept her hand in his, very visibly displayed on the tabletop. His thumb charted the ridge of her knuckles in back-and-forth sweeps, the movement restless. Something more was wrong than just a little residual guilt.

"Did you find out what you needed to know from Rollo?"

He glanced at her, momentarily blank and uncertain. "What? Oh. As much as I could." He looked away. "I gave him money, Charlotte."

"To make it easier for him to hide from me?" She couldn't keep the anger from that question.

"It's not what I'd planned."

"You just had a sudden gush of sentimentality, is that it?"

He met her snapping glare with one steeped in murky emotional waters. "Yes. I guess I did. To protect what matters to me."

Suspicion nudged at the edges of her temper, making her frown. "Max, what—"

He kissed her softly, the barest brush of his mouth over hers. Enough to make her heart jump and silence her objections.

He eased back to hold her gaze in his. "This is one of those times, detective, where you look me in the eye and tell me, 'I trust you, Max. I know whatever you've done is because you love me.'"

She looked at him, into those gorgeous green eyes, and made a rude noise. "You're blowing smoke up my skirt, Savoie."

"Am I?" His smile was small and mysterious. "And that excites you, does it?"

"That you're sitting there lying to me? No."

"I don't lie to you, Charlotte. I just don't offer to tell you everything unless you ask me the right questions."

"Why did you let him go?"

Again the smile. "Because I love you." With a slight tinge of annoyance, he asked, "You don't believe me?"

"I believe you think by saying that I'll get all gooey and foolish and let you get away with anything."

His voice was a low caress. "Would I be right?"

She glared at him, then looked pointedly away. "I haven't decided."

He chuckled and leaned back in his own seat, but he held on to her hand.

For a while, they just listened to the music while Cee Cee contemplated the situation. What was done was done. She couldn't rescind choices already made. And she would just have to trust him. He made it sound like it was such an easy thing, that trust.

But as her mood settled and mellowed, she was surprised to discover that maybe it was simpler than the alternative. She thought of Babineau's prophetic words about drawing that line that could never be crossed again, and she wasn't ready to make this into that moment. She had enough difficulties to overcome in their relationship without dropping an ultimatum on top. Including the obstacle playing out right in front of her.

He sat beside her, communicating on a level that excluded her completely. His gaze moved in a quick flicker around the crowded club, settling briefly like a mental handshake, a pat on the back. Or, she wondered as several lovely females smiled at him, on the butt. She took a long swallow of her drink, and tried not to let it matter that everyone around her conversed in a silent foreign language.

Max might be the intuitive one, but she wasn't so thick that she was unaware of the thinly veiled hostility bristling about her. She wasn't of them; she was an intruder. And she was taking something from them that didn't belong to her. Something powerful and important. She knew their secrets and was in a position to reveal or exploit them. That made her too dangerous to simply ignore. And unlike Max, they had no reason at all to trust her.

There were few situations that scared her. She'd wade into a biker bar fight, confront hard-core felons with her bare hands, or face a ticking bomb without breaking a sweat. But sitting among these beings, she felt a tremor of fear. They were so strange, so strong, so beyond the scope of anything she'd ever imagined. They didn't recognize her laws or her authority. Hell, they didn't even follow the laws of nature.

And they'd managed to sink their emotional claws into the man she loved. To have him she'd have to be tolerated by them, if not welcomed. It was one thing to sit at Max's side as if she belonged there. It was another to walk alone among them. They could smell fear, and they could undoubtedly smell it on her now. That simply wasn't acceptable.

Max's attention snapped up to her as she stood.

"I'm going to the ladies' room."

"I'll go with you."

She laughed and pressed him back into his seat. "No thank you. I've been going by myself for quite a few years now, and I think I can manage."

"I only meant—"

"I know what you meant. If I'm not back in ten, come looking for me. Knock first."

He didn't share her smile or her levity. He was measuring the distance to the hallway that would take her out of his sight.

"Relax, Savoie. It's not like they're going to try to eat me right under your nose." He looked so solemn. "Are they?"

"No. I won't allow it."

"There. Now I feel safe and special." She was teasing him, but she shared his caution. She put her palm on his cheek, bending to touch a light kiss to his lips. "I'll be right back."

His hand covered hers, gloving it tightly until she pulled gently away.

"Don't grope any waitresses while I'm gone."

His smile was grim.

She left the table and started through the gauntlet of glowering stares. She kept her head high, her step aggressive, and her hand close to her silver-loaded weapon. Unexpectedly a corridor seemed to open for her. Couples stepped aside and waited; chairs moved back. Then she understood: Max was clearing the way like parting the Red Sea.

She turned back to him and scowled slightly, letting him know she didn't appreciate the almost smothering mantle of protection being thrown over her. He just smiled and waved her on her way. She continued past those who would wish her harm but wouldn't act on it. She belonged to Max Savoie, and no one dared touch what was his. And at the moment, that was a good thing.

IT WAS LIKE the interior of any bar bathroom she'd ever been in. The air hung thick with smoke and strong perfumes. Several females stood at the sink, reapplying their makeup. Conversation stopped when they saw her. She nodded in acknowledgment and went into a stall. The moment the door shut they began to talk again, this time in low whispers.

". . . like she owns the place."

"Like she owns him."

Catty laughter.

"If he wanted her for more than a toss or two, she'd be wearing his mark."

"That still wouldn't make her one of us. She can't give him what we can, and he'll realize that soon enough. And when he does, I'll be the first in line."

By the time Cee Cee emerged from the stall, simmering and ready to go toe-to-toe, she was alone in the restroom. As she washed her hands, she glanced at her reflection. Max had made a mess of her mouth, something none of those nasty little creatures could claim. She drew on another glossy coat. As she tucked her lipstick away, her attention shifted. She drew the collar of Max's coat away from the smooth skin between her neck and shoulder.

No mark. No link to his other life, to the deeper, darker desires Rollo hinted at.

She scowled fiercely. "No line forms behind *me*, bitches."

She opened the door and went out to stake her claim.

Seventeen

*J*ACQUES LAROCHE WAS standing at the table talking to Max when Cee Cee returned. She nodded to him, then asked, "Is there someplace Max and I can talk without being interrupted? It'll just take a minute or two."

LaRoche gestured behind him. "My office. Max knows where it is."

Max got up wordlessly, cued by her strained intensity, and led the way into the back. LaRoche's office was a surprise, all chrome, black, and red, as sleek and stylized as LaRoche was not. One whole wall was a one-way mirror looking out over the revving-up club scene, which made for a voyeuristic privacy. But it had a lock on the door, and that was all Cee Cee was interested in.

Max regarded her, his brows elevated. "What's this about, Charlotte?"

Her mouth was on his with such ferocity, it knocked him back a step. He managed to haul her back so he could gasp for air and answers. "Not that I'm complaining."

"Then don't. Shut up and put out, Savoie."

"You are so romantic, detective." She chained rough kisses about his neck. "What if I can't perform under this unexpected pressure?"

Her hand dropped below his belt for an assessing fondle. "Just my luck. Appears to be high performance all the way."

He chuckled and began to nuzzle and nip at her rather roughly, his attention supercharged by her aggression. "And what kind of handling are you looking for?"

"Fast and reckless."

He dropped down on both knees in front of her without another word, dragging her panties down along the way. His head ducked under her short skirt and, tilting her hips forward, he used his mouth to rocket her off the starting line to a quick, shattering climax. While she reeled from that release, he tugged her down atop him and plunged deeply inside her.

"You drive, *sha*. I love to watch you shift gears." His voice rumbled low and throaty, like a powerful engine.

Their kisses were hard and hungry. They moved together with fierce urgency, demanding, taking, pushing sensation to the limit and beyond to where pleasure was a hot wind-tunnel ride, ripping away restraint. His hands clutched the backs of her thighs the way he hung onto her dash when she was driving the muscle car. She was just as tough and powerful as that street machine, boldly rushing, roaring toward a goal just out of reach until she gripped him like the Jaws of Life and they both flashed over the line. Photo finish, winners all. She slumped against him, her arms dangling limply down his back, her chest laboring against his.

"Call for road service, baby," she sighed. "I think I just blew an engine."

Out of breath, shaky and grinning, Max kissed her, stunned by the force of their impromptu coupling. He kissed her mouth, her cheeks, her eyelids with all-consuming tenderness, so filled up with love for her that there was nothing beyond the feel of her in his arms, the taste of her on his lips, the scent of her in his nose. He laughed softly as he breathed in the hot, wild smell of well-enjoyed sex.

"Everyone out there is going to know exactly what we were 'discussing' back here."

Cee Cee smiled. "Good." There was a hint of grim satisfaction in her voice.

"Is that what this was about?" His tone was soft and even, but she wasn't fooled.

She touched his cheek, but he moved back from her placating caress. "You brought me back here so the scent of you would be all over me."

There was no use pretending, so she said it plainly. "I didn't want there to be any mistake."

"Mistake on whose part? Do you still doubt me, Charlotte?"

"No."

He began to frown. "Did someone say something to you? Is that it? Tell me."

Her gaze shifted away to conceal the anxiousness gripping inside her. "No one had to, Max. I'm not part of what you've found out there. I never will be. They have a part of you that is beyond my reach, and . . . and it scares me. Because I'm afraid of losing you to them. Jimmy was one thing. I understood him. But these . . . these . . ."

"Monsters?" he supplied quietly.

"No." She shook her head. "Family. Your family. That's how you see them. How can I compete with that?"

"Why do you feel you have to? What can I do to reassure you? Do you want me to stop coming here?"

"Don't be silly."

"I'm not. I don't think it's funny. I don't know how many times, how many other ways I can try to convince you how important you are to me, if you won't believe it. What do I have to do? Wear a collar with a tag that says, 'If found, return to Detective Caissie'? Have a shirt claiming, 'Hands off, I'm with her'? Wear a ring through my nose?" His voice lowered. "On my hand? You are everything I need or want. Charlotte, look at me. I love you. That's not going to change just because the things around us change."

She nodded, miserable and unconvinced. She reached out to him again, wanting the comfort of his embrace. He evaded her touch. "Now you're angry with me."

He didn't deny it. His tone was fierce when he told her, "I love you, Charlotte. There is *nothing* I would not do for you. I would let you walk on my naked body with those wicked heels. I would trail behind you on a leash or on my knees, if that's what you wanted. But there *are* differences that keep us from being an acceptable part of each other's worlds. You need to push me out of yours to placate your bosses. I understand that, even though I don't like it. The situation is the same here. I can't make my kind embrace you just because I do. My position with them is tenuous at best, yet you think you can force yourself into their private places and not upset or offend them."

Her tone cooled. "Are we talking about them or you, Max?"

He shook his head in frustration. "What do you want? What can I do?"

"Put your mark on me."

For a long moment, he simply stared at her. "What?"

She pulled the collar of his jacket aside to expose her skin. "Make me yours in a way they'll understand and respect."

He didn't move. Finally he said, "You don't know what you're asking."

"Yes I do."

"Who told you about such things?" Irritation warred with anxiety in his tone.

"Rollo. He told me I could never hold on to you

because there were others who'd give you what I can't." Her eyes began to glimmer with fright, with desperation. "There's nothing that you need that I can't give you, Max. Nothing. I'm not afraid of what you are."

"But I am." He stood abruptly, dumping her from his lap onto her rump, straightening his clothes. He took an unsteady breath. "We won't talk about this again."

And he left her there, sprawled and exposed on the floor, with her raw emotions and fearful heart.

It took her a minute to gather her courage. Then she got up and went into the small private bathroom off LaRoche's office and washed herself clean of Max's scent, scrubbing it away as if that would erase the taint of her insecurity. She touched up her appearance as best she could, drew back her shoulders, then went back to the table, where Max was talking to LaRoche and Philo Tibideaux. He didn't glance her way so she sat quietly, chin up, her expression set while her insides shook to pieces. Carefully she touched the back of his hand where it had come to rest on his thigh. Just a brush of her fingertips, quickly withdrawn.

He gave no sign of having felt it. The arrogant tip of her head began to sink until she stared at the glass rings on the table, their interlocking circles beginning to blur.

She didn't need any special gift to know they were the center of attention. Max Savoie's Upright cop girlfriend, claiming what could never be hers, sitting where she didn't belong. Keeping him from seizing all that he could be. Putting him on a short chain to control him, just like Jimmy Legere had, to use him for her own benefit.

She'd brazen it out for the moment, but she would never return here with him. He'd made it very clear that she had no place on this side of the threshold. This was his world. And if she kept pushing him to share it, she was going to lose him that much sooner.

What was she going to do when he was gone?

She listened to his tone as he talked. Such authority, such confidence. No longer Jimmy's shadow. No longer the silently smoldering enigma who'd chased after her with unflagging devotion, who'd challenged her to dream of him. He'd become her every dream, and now she could no longer hold on to it.

His gaze came up when she stood.

"I'm going to take off, Max. Tomorrow's going to be busy and I'm really tired."

She saw him realize her fatigue was from being up all night caring for him.

"I'm sorry. I wasn't thinking. Of course we can go."

She put a hand on his shoulder when he started to rise. "No need for you to cut your evening short. I know my way home."

"To mine?"

"If you like."

Her subdued reply made deep furrows gather between his brows. "I like."

"All right. I'll see you later, then." Her fingertips brushed lightly along his jaw, then she nodded to the other two at the table. *Take care of him for me.*

The hardest part was taking that first step away from him. She walked purposefully, putting an extra kick in her stride so they wouldn't think they'd driven her away. Even though it was true.

She was edging around the dance floor when his hand met the small of her back, warm and familiar. She looked up, unable to prevent the sheen of wetness in her gaze.

"They're playing our song, detective."

She wasn't aware of any music. She wasn't aware of anything but him.

He gave a slight tug, bringing her into the circle of his arms. She hid against his shoulder, unable to face him when so foolishly vulnerable. Her hands rested in a neutral position on the sway of his hips as he moved her to the crooning melody: "*By My Side.*"

When he felt the first suspicious hitch in her breathing, his grip on her tightened, one hand cupping the back of her head as his mouth brushed her brow. "Don't cry, *sha.*"

"I'm not. I'm just tired and I don't want to fight with you anymore. And I'm sorry. Let me go, Max. I want to go."

"Letting you go is not an option. Not ever. Stay here with me and we'll finish our date. If you're tired, you can sleep on my shoulder. If you want to go, I'll go with you and we can sleep together. I want to spend all night with you and wake up with you in the morning. For the rest of my life."

When she didn't respond, he nudged his head against hers. "I'm not angry with you, Charlotte. I was flattered to think you were so hot for me that you simply couldn't wait another minute to have me. My ego was a bit deflated is all. You know what a gigantic ego I have."

She turned so that their gazes met, but she wasn't smiling as he'd hoped. "I'm so hot for you, I simply can't wait another minute to have you. There's *never* a time when that's not the truth."

His eyelids lowered, his stare glittering like a cool green flame. "Yeah? And what exactly do you find so irresistible about me? I want specifics."

She touched behind one ear. "The way your hair curls just a little right here. That's sexy as hell."

He looked surprised and a bit perplexed. "Yeah? Okay. What else?"

"Here." She pressed her lips to the side of his neck. "Where your skin is so warm and smooth, and I know I'm making your heart beat fast. The way it is now."

He swallowed. "What else?"

"Your voice. Just the sound of it, all deep and mellow, melts me like butter."

"Really. Is there more?"

"Your hands." She slid a kiss across his palm,

then fit it to the side of her face. "So strong, so clever, so amazingly gentle. I've never let anyone touch me the way you do. Not ever." Her voice lowered, softening. "The way you stop when I ask you to. I trust you, Max. And I love you."

His kiss reached all the way to her soul. Then he held her in his arms, smiling as he rocked her to the tender ballad. There was nothing in the world he looked forward to more than spending the night beneath his sheets with her. And waking up to her for the rest of his life.

He felt Philo Tibideaux's approach before he saw him.

"I'm going to cut in here," Tibideaux told them. "Max, Jacques needs to talk to you. It's important. I'll finish the dance for you." He smiled, not without charm, when Cee Cee scowled at him. "You're not gonna bite me again, are you, detective, darlin'?"

Max glanced over at his table, where LaRoche was speaking urgently to someone he didn't recognize. The mood was unmistakable.

"I'll be right back," he told her, passing her to LaRoche's second, then quickly stepping away.

"No grabbing my butt," she warned the grinning redhead.

"Yes, ma'am. I mean, no, ma'am." He handled her very carefully through some sassy turns. "'Sides, Max done told us what would happen if anybody put a hand on you in a way he doan like."

"Oh? And what would happen?"

"Let's just say identification by dental records and leave it at that."

That possessive bit of ruthlessness pleased her enough for her to relax.

She watched the table, studying Max's posture for clues as to what was going on. It was something serious; she could tell by the way he stood—still, straight, braced. LaRoche rose, placing his hands on Max's shoulders as he spoke earnestly about something. Max staggered back as if he'd been struck.

"Philo, what's going on?"

"Let them handle it, *cher*." Tibideaux's somber expression said more than his words.

But she couldn't heed his warning. Not when Max pulled free and wandered in a tight circle, his hands laced behind his head, his movements jerky with pain and upset. She planted her feet, refusing to move as she glared up at Tibideaux.

"What's wrong?"

"It be business, detective. It doan involve you."

"Anything that hurts him involves me in a big way. Now, *what's going on?*"

Even as she made that demand, Max looked at her. The revolving dance floor lights caught his gaze, flashing brightly on the sheen in his eyes. His features might well have been set in stone. Then he turned briskly away and followed LaRoche toward the rear exit, with several others trailing close behind.

Tibideaux allowed her to leave the dance floor, but caught her arm once they reached Max's table. "I'm to keep you here until they take care of things."

"What things?" She threw off his hand.

"It woan take long." Again, that grimness that suggested terrible deeds. "You stay put. Doan make me get unpleasant about it."

"You haven't seen unpleasant yet."

He jumped in surprise when her gun barrel poked beneath his ribs. "Detective, you doan want to do this."

"Oh, but I do. And let me assure you, the bullets in this gun were specially designed with you in mind. You *will* take me wherever they're going right now or I will blow a hole right through you. One that will never heal."

"Max will kill me."

"Max will not. He understands how . . . formidable I can be when it comes to him. I'll determine whether or not it involves me."

Unhappily Tibideaux led her out the back door. Wet tread marks were still on the alleyway pavement, where a large vehicle had driven through standing water.

"Where are they going?"

Seeing no point in staying silent, Philo mumbled, "To the docks."

"My car's out front."

At the prodding of her barrel, he led her around the building. "That's a nice car!"

"You're driving." She tossed him the keys. "And Savoie won't be the one you have to worry about if you put a scratch on that paint job."

Philo Tibideaux believed her.

"*And* you still owe me a camera."

MAX ENTERED THE cavernous warehouse with all senses tingling. Though it was dark they didn't bother with lights, their eyes adjusting to the blackness. The sounds and scents of a small group somewhere in the center drew them onward through the maze of stacked goods. The air was redolent with the odors of brackish water, fish, starchy produce, oil, and machinery. And blood. That last aroma had them all on edge.

"T-Beau, coming in," LaRoche called out, his voice echoing back eerily.

"Come ahead."

As they entered the central hub of the building, light flared, illuminating a dozen men armed with pistols or machetes, each cold of eye and attitude. On the floor, on his knees, was a single figure bound in heavy chains, a rough sack pulled over his head. That head came up from where it had sagged to a bloodstained shirtfront.

"LaRoche, I should have known your treacherous hand was on this," came a low, slurred snarl. "Who's that hiding behind you? Show yourself, coward." His voice shook slightly in uncertainty.

LaRoche nodded to one of the men guarding the

prisoner. The sack was pulled off his head. Rollo blinked against the light, then stared.

"Is this your doing, boy?" Shock gave way to a shaky laugh. "I wouldn't have guessed you had it in you."

"Where did you find him?" Max asked LaRouche emotionlessly.

"Drinking away a wad of money up in Baton Rouge, right out in the open like he didn't have a care in the world. Or like he was waiting for someone to find him—just like you figured when you sent us to tail him."

Max fought to control the feelings rioting inside him, betrayal not the least of them.

"Didn't I pay you enough?" he asked, his voice as sharp as the blade thrust figuratively into his heart.

When there was no answer, his hands fisted at his sides. "How much?" he asked with lethal softness. "How much did it take for you to sell your own son?"

Eighteen

I T WASN'T LIKE that, Max."

"Tell me what it was like, then. What did they offer you, if not money?"

"My life. And while that may not have much worth to you, it's quite valuable to me. Cummings owed me, but that greedy bastard wouldn't come clean with the money, not even for the lives of his family. I had no choice, Max. I owe some dangerous people who are very unforgiving. It was the only card I could play."

"And now your miserable life has no value at all, fool," LaRoche growled. Then he regarded Max somberly. "You know what must be done and quickly."

Max continued to speak to his father. "Why didn't you come to me first?"

"I didn't know you. Why would you care if I lived or died?"

"Because you're the only family I have."

Rollo finally saw the magnitude of his mistake, and the only way to escape its consequences. "Let me make it up to you, Max. All those years. All that loneliness. I haven't had anyone, either."

"The police know you killed those women. Noreen Cummings gave a statement."

Rollo shrugged with a callous indifference. "Easily remedied if she never makes it to court."

"Charlotte knows, too. Would you kill her as well?"

Rollo was smart enough to be very careful there. "She would never say anything that might endanger you. She's no threat to us."

"He endangers us all, Max," LaRoche cut in coldly. "He brings attention to us from the news, from the police, from the public. He's careless and he's stupid. He brings your enemies to our door. For what? His own selfish business. He can't be trusted. He's already been judged. It's only out of respect that we brought you here—not to ask your permission."

Max stared dispassionately at the kneeling man before him. The man who shared his blood, who'd given him life and precious little else. He was everything LaRoche described and probably worse. There was still defiance in his eyes, but behind it, the fear of a man knowing he was about to die. They must have drugged him somehow, to have him at their mercy. And now, Rollo was at his.

Max had killed countless times, without hesitation, without regret. Many of those deserved it less than Rollo—but they hadn't been his family. And suddenly that made all the difference.

"Let him up."

Rollo expressed a huge breath of relief.

LaRoche stared at him, aghast. "Max, don't be foolish."

"I'll take responsibility for him."

LaRoche shook his head. "It's too late for that. He'll destroy us all."

"I'll do anything you want, boy. Anything you want." Rollo was nearly laughing at his good fortune. He lifted his shackled wrists to the silent sentinel beside him. "Uncuff me, you sorry son of a bitch. Didn't you hear my son?"

The man made no move, his questioning stare fixed on LaRoche.

"It's done, Max. He has to be dealt with. Don't force us to include you in that judgment," said LaRoche.

"Oh, that would be a big, big mistake. And the last one you'd ever make," said Charlotte Cassie.

A small smile touched Max's lips as she emerged from the darkness with her gun at the back of Philo Tibideaux's head. "Excellent timing, as usual, detective." He smirked at Rollo. "I told you there's no one I'd rather have at my back."

Cee Cee shoved Tibideaux away from her and filled her other hand with her throw-down piece. "Where do you want me, baby?"

He glanced at his fierce warrior mate with her sexy shoes, fists filled with firepower, and eyes hard as bullets. And he wanted her straddling him, riding him like a Grand Canyon pack mule.

"Right there is fine. I trust you've armed yourself for the task at hand?"

"With enough silver to make some great jewelry. Enough to take down anyone who makes a move on you. Any one or all."

"I love you, *sha*."

"Right back at you, Savoie. What am I interrupting?"

LaRoche hadn't reached a position of power by being an idiot. "Charlotte, don't misunderstand the situation. Max isn't in danger here. We just need him to make the right choice. Or to do nothing at all."

"Fill me in."

La Roche said, "This liar, this traitor to his own family, his own kind, sold Max to his enemies to save his own life. Enemies who will come here to kill Max."

Cee Cee studied Rollo for a moment. "You are dead."

LaRoche pressed on. "He's dangerous, Charlotte. He has no loyalty except to himself."

"I know what he is." She was remembering two bodies on Devlin Dovion's table, the horror of their last minutes imprinted on her memory, on her abused and broken body, in that corner of her heart Max Savoie hadn't quite yet conquered. The corner where fear and pain resided. "And I'm here to arrest him for the rape and murders of Sarah Cummings and Vivian Goodman, and the attempted murder of Noreen Cummings."

"Detective, if he was anything other than what he is, I would step aside and let you do your job. But I want you to think carefully about what would happen if you do. If, and that's a big if, you could contain him long enough to actually bring him to trial, how long do you think it would take your superiors to discover that he is more than your average rapist and murderer? Do you think he'd go silently to his fate, or would he try to bring all of us down with him—Max included? And what do you think the reaction of the press and the good citizens of New Orleans would be?"

Flaming torches and pitchforks. Now she understood what Max had meant.

"Charlotte, I'm not making light of those women who lost their lives." LaRoche's expression was firm, his eyes betraying empathy. "We don't condone the slaughter of innocents. Not *ever*. We'll see he pays for them."

Cee Cee stood down. "You were right. This doesn't involve me. This is your business, and as long as it doesn't involve harming Max I'll stay out of it." She met Max's flat stare with unwavering support. "Unless you ask me to make it my business, Max. Then I'll step in with both feet—hard. Max? Where do you want me?"

She hoped her words would make him take a step back from pure emotion to think, to consider what he was doing and why.

He didn't ask or answer.

She'd worry about what was behind his silence later; for now she had a serious problem to tend to. She turned back to LaRoche. "He needs to disappear."

"I'll give him everything I have," Max said quietly. "Enough so he'll never surface again."

Rollo jumped on that with desperation. "I'll disappear. And before I do, I'll lead them away from here, away from you, Max. I'll tell them I was wrong. I'll tell them I couldn't find you. And you'll never hear from me again."

"Let him up," Max said again with hard authority.

"I'm sorry, Max," LaRoche told him. "That's not going to happen."

Frantic because the chance of escape was narrowing around his neck like a noose, Rollo cried, "You don't even know who they are. You don't know who they'll send. If you kill me, you'll never know what to look for. You'll never know when it's coming. Max, I didn't have to stay here as long as I did. I wanted to make sure you could protect yourself. I tried to protect you and your mother. Let me do what I can to save you now."

LaRoche warned, "Don't let him deceive you, Max. He doesn't care what happens to you or to us. He's only thinking about his worthless hide. We don't want to take steps against you, but we will stop you."

Cee Cee shifted subtly into a more aggressive pose, her cool stare in constant motion.

"You can't," Rollo gloated. "You have no idea how powerful he is. You won't stop him; no one can. He'll tear through you and spit you out. They're nothing to you, Max. I'm family. You're above all of them and yet they won't obey you. If they kill me now, do you think you'll be able to stop them when they decide your girlfriend is a threat?"

Max's gaze shot over to Cee Cee, alarmed, then incredibly dangerous when he looked back to LaRoche. "Do what I tell you and let him go. Right now."

"Max, don't listen to him." LaRoche kept his tone reasonable, but around him his men were tensing, getting ready to take on a force they knew they couldn't defeat. "We stood behind you because we believed in you, in your willingness to put us first, ahead of Petitjohn, Vantour, and those like them. To put our needs ahead of your own wants.

"And you have. You've earned our respect and our loyalty. Detective Caissie has nothing to fear from us, because she is honorable and would lay down her life for you. As we would, without hesitation. As we do now with this danger that threatens you. We will fight to protect you, die for you if need be. Don't ask us to die for the likes of him. Don't ask *her* to. He would not do the same. Think about what you're doing, what you're risking."

"Kill them, Max," yelled Rollo. "Kill them all! Who do they think they are? We are their gods. You are their king! They deserve to die for defying you. Destroy them, or they will destroy you."

The cold sheen in Max's eye grew hot and golden. A low, vicious rumbling started deep down in his chest, rising like a fierce unstoppable tide.

"Charlotte," LaRoche called quietly. "If you can control him, do it now before we all die. We can't back down from this—not when we know it's right. He'll know it, too, as soon as he's thinking with his head instead of his heart."

"You don't need them, Max," Rollo called. "You don't need any of them. They will crush you because you're too strong and they fear you. I'll stand beside you. Together we can rule all."

Charlotte put herself in front of Max, seizing his face between her hands even as it began to change. Lips curled back from the rows of sharp teeth, teeth that could tear through her like tissue paper. Until what she held on to wasn't Max at all.

No. That wasn't true. It *was* Max.

And Max would never harm her.

She leaned in closer, until his hot breath scorched her skin. Until the foreign fury in his bloodred eyes burned right through her. She stroked her fingertips over those altered bones, her touch gentle and gentling.

"Max, please. Don't do this. Don't let him come between you and what you know is right. Between you and me. Please."

"You'd stand against me?" The deep, harsh growl was edged with raw anguish.

"Never." Her arms went around the neck that had thickened into a powerful ruff of soft black fur over bunched muscle. She drew him down so her cheek pressed to his, so his jaw and all those razor-sharp teeth were against her vulnerable throat. "Don't let this hurt you. He doesn't deserve your mercy, and he doesn't deserve the loss of any more lives—not after the ones he's already taken. Make it business, not personal, Max. For Sarah and Vivian. For Mary Kate. For me. We need justice, Max. Let it be done."

He took a deep breath, then everything about him was familiar once more. He leaned into her, his face tucked into her shoulder as she kissed his brow.

LaRoche acted quickly, emotionlessly, crossing to the ever-defiant Rollo.

"You wouldn't dare," Rollo spat up at him. "I'm of pure blood. You can't kill me. You can't harm me with your silver bullets. Max!"

With a deadly swish of sound, LaRoche's machete took his head.

Feeling Max recoil, Cee Cee clutched him tight, whispering, "Don't look, baby."

But he was already straightening, drawing himself up to his coldly formidable height.

Standing next to the headless body, Jacques LaRoche let the wicked blade drop to the cement floor. His hands spread wide. "Take me, Max, but let them go. They were only acting on my orders."

Max made no move toward him. There was no bitter heat of vengeance in his heart, just emptiness, as he turned and walked out of the light into the shadows.

When Cee Cee started after him, LaRoche called to her. "Charlotte, what should we do here?"

She took a reluctant breath and faced the group of grim men who'd acted to save their clan. And Max Savoie. Then she looked down at the lifeless form of one who would have destroyed them all with his rage and greed.

"Take him into the swamps and sink him deep with all his secrets." She was thinking of the red shoes, and a small child and his mother seeing to their own survival. "I've got to call in my report. I followed him here. I ordered him to surrender and he tried to attack me. I called for him to halt, then fired two rounds into him." She fired twice into his still form. "He was seriously wounded but he managed to get away. And as far as I know, he's still on the loose, probably crawling off to die somewhere. Somewhere where we'll never find him."

LaRoche surprised her with a smile. His voice was low and rich with admiration. "No wonder Max trusts you so. You are a wise and fierce creature, Detective Caissie. He's lucky to have you."

But did Max feel the same way?

She stared briefly into the darkness, then reached for her phone to make the call that would close the case.

HELEN OPENED THE front door. "I'm glad you're here, detective." The woman's tight expression of concern alarmed her.

"Where is he?"

"In Mr. Legere's office. He's . . . he's not himself."

What did that mean?

It was after midnight. She'd waited alone at the warehouse for Babineau and an investigation team. She walked them through her story, then had finally gone home to shower, change, and feed her pets. Her mood settled into an odd blend of relief, satisfaction, and regret, all stirred together in a bittersweet gumbo. She saw to her duty, then all she could think of was seeing to the fragile heart of Max Savoie.

"Evening, detective." Giles stood outside the closed doors to Jimmy's study. He looked as relieved as Helen at her arrival.

"How is he?"

"Been pretty quiet for the last half hour or so. Tore through the place like a hurricane when he first got here. Don't know what he was doing. Sounded like remodeling with a ten-pound sledge."

She reached for the doorknob, and Giles sidled in to intercept her.

"He said I wasn't to let anyone in."

"He didn't mean me."

"He said you specifically."

She refused to be discouraged. "Tell him I'm here, Giles."

He rapped on the door, calling, "Max, Detective Caissie is here."

A long silence, then his oddly muffled voice. "Tell her I'll come in to make a statement in the morning."

Giles shrugged and didn't move aside.

"Step back, Giles. I don't want to hurt you, but I will."

He stared at the whipcord tough girl he dwarfed by one hundred pounds and almost a half a foot. And he chuckled, moving out of her way.

The room was dark, moonlight ribboning across the surprising destruction of the parquet floor. Boards were broken, pried up, tossed aside with a singular violence of strength and determination. The boards stained by Jimmy Legere's abrupt death.

"Go away, Charlotte. I'm not fit company."

The sound of his voice, so hoarse, so weary, cramped her emotions, but she kept her tone low and easy. "That's all right. I don't expect you to entertain me."

He was tucked into the deeper shadows of the room, on the floor at the foot of the old chair Jimmy used to sit in while reading his evening paper. His arms were folded on the comfortably worn leather seat, his dark head pillowed upon them. He watched her through dull, eerily lifeless eyes.

She went to the big sofa and sat there, giving him

the space she sensed he needed to sort through his grief and guilt. When he saw she was going to keep her distance, the defensive line of his shoulders relaxed.

"You've made a mess of the floor" was her quiet observation.

"It's my floor."

"You've made a mess of your hands." As her eyes adjusted to the limited light, she could see the torn skin, ripped nails, and swollen knuckles he hadn't healed. Not because he couldn't, but because he didn't want to, punishing himself with the needless pain.

"They're my hands," he growled, daring her to make something of it.

She shrugged and sat back against the tufted leather cushions. "Far be it from me to object to your self-flagellation."

He eyed her suspiciously for a moment. "Are you here to take me in for obstruction of justice?"

"No. I'm here to get some sleep. If the offer of shared sheets is still open."

The terrible tension eased another slight notch. "Go ahead and go up."

"Shared, as in you and me under them together."

His expression spasmed, then grew cold. "I'm really not in the mood at the moment, detective. Sorry you wasted the trip out here."

"No need to get pissy, Savoie. It might surprise you to know that there are things that appeal to me beyond the incredible hot sex we have."

He blinked. "Really? Well, that's an unkind blow to my wilted ego." He smiled slightly, and she knew things would be okay.

"Things about *you*," she corrected with an answering smile.

"Oh. Yeah? Like what?"

"Come over here and I'll tell you."

He crossed the short distance on all fours, settling at her feet with his head on her lap. She felt his sigh when her hand touched his hair.

"You were saying? What appeals to you about me other than the incredible hot sex?"

"Well, for one thing, you never get angry."

He laughed, a startling but genuine explosion of sound. He didn't object when she took one of his hands, her touch gentle. Her kiss on his smashed knuckles was gentle. "Enough," she scolded. "I can't bear to think of you in pain."

He sighed again. "It felt good at the time, but now it really stings."

A long shudder ran through him, then she could feel the swollen joints and splintered fingers repairing themselves until he was able to lightly grip her hand.

"What else?" he prompted. He settled in, turning onto his left hip, his cheek nestled against the firm cushion of her thigh. His free hand began to move up and down her calf in slow, almost seductive repetitions. He studied her face, his own more composed and in control, but his eyes still holding vulnerability.

She let her steady tone and strong emotions build them both back up. "I love your sense of fairness, of what's right."

He snorted. "Yeah. And that's why I was endangering everything and everyone this evening. I could have killed them all, Charlotte, and for what? And I brought you into the middle of it, expecting you to back me even when I knew I was wrong. I *knew* I was wrong."

"But you *didn't* ask me, Max."

"Doing a wrong thing myself is very different from asking you to do it with me."

Her tone, her touch were tender. "The way you protect me—from the past, from yourself—even when I don't need to be protected. That appeals to me, Savoie."

He was silent for a long while, and she wondered what he was thinking about. He seemed so far away.

Finally he said, "There's nothing I wouldn't do to keep you safe. I failed you once. Never again."

"You've never let me down, Max. You've always been there when I needed you."

He straightened, turning away from her to lean back against the couch. She couldn't see his face, and when he spoke, his voice was neutral.

"Jimmy Legere was the only father I ever knew. Even though he didn't give me his name or share my blood, he gave me everything else. He was the one who loved and protected me—not this man who shows up after half my life is gone. Rollo was nothing to me, Charlotte. Nothing. So why do I feel—why do I feel—"

He waited for the agitation to leave his breathing before saying, "I don't understand. I don't understand how a father could do such things to his own son. I had him followed because I knew what he was going to do. I knew the money wouldn't be enough for him, that he would try to turn me in for a little more. I was hoping he wouldn't, yet I knew he would. I wanted him to be a little more . . . heroic. He was my father."

Charlotte bent to lay her cheek against the top of his head. "Sometimes the pain of guilt is so great, it's easier to escape it than to confront it. Once you know you've failed someone who depended on you, it's easier just to keep on letting them down than to accept that first failure."

"Is that what your father did? After your mother left?"

Cee Cee stiffened in surprise. She hadn't thought he'd remember that ragged Freudian slip during their confrontation outside the club.

So much of her hurt and anger had been focused on her own past, not on him. She didn't want to talk about it. She wanted it buried deep and forgotten. But she forced herself to answer because he was being so honest with her.

"Not at first. He tried. He really tried. But it got easier to stay away, to stay busy, to turn the burden I'd become, the reminder I would always be, over to someone else. To let St. Bart's care for me. By the time Jimmy's men took me and Mary Kate off the street that night, trying to force him to change his testimony, he'd fallen into a bottle and into the arms of a long line of faceless others that could never love him the way I did.

"After you brought me back, Max, he never touched me. Not a hug. Not a hand on the shoulder or a kiss on the cheek. Nothing. And that hurt for a very long time." Until Max Savoie filled all those lonely hollows in her life. She took a shaky breath. "I can't believe I'm telling you this. I never even told Mary Kate."

He came up on his knees to face her. "I will never do that. I promise you. I will never leave you feeling alone and unloved."

He brought her down to him, to kiss her slow and sweet with a tenderness that had tears wobbling in her eyes.

When he finally let her pull away, her hands slipped over his. "Thank you, Max. For what you did tonight. For what you did for me."

"Only for you."

"Max, who was he talking about?"

Max's heart dropped like a brick. "What do you mean?"

"Who did Rollo betray you to? He said they were coming for you? Who?"

He shrugged with pretended nonchalance. "It's some feud that goes back generations. Apparently he made it worse by running off with my mother. They were after him, not me. They don't even know I exist. LaRoche snatched him up before he could pass on that information. And I don't plan to bring myself to their attention.

"There's no threat, detective. LaRoche and the others will see no harm comes to me. Now let's go upstairs. I could hibernate for a month, as long as you're curled up beside me."

She rose up with him, her fatigue showing in the way she leaned against him. His arm curved about her waist, tucking her in close as they went out into the hall where Giles and Helen were loitering. He didn't miss their looks of relief.

"We need to have the flooring replaced in there," Cee Cee told the housekeeper.

"I'll call someone in the morning. Good night, detective. Mr. Savoie."

Max nodded absently, his thoughts and heart caught up by one word. *We.*

The bedroom was cool, scented by the rain that had finally quit falling. The sight of Charlotte undressing against the backdrop of moonlight had him staring, transfixed with fascination and possessiveness. She never stopped amazing him: with her courage, with her passion for what was right, with the love he still couldn't quite believe she felt for him. All deceivingly soft femininity and bronzed skin, she slid between his sheets, and it took him a minute to remember to breathe.

Snuggling down into the pillows, she glanced over at him. "Aren't you coming?"

A slight smile. "Probably not right away, but hopefully by morning."

He undressed and sank into her uplifted arms with a huge sigh. "I love having you here."

He felt her smile against his neck. "You love having me anywhere, you beast." She was fading fast, her breathing growing deep. Then she vowed softly, "I'll keep you safe, Max. They won't get by me."

Max's eyes snapped open, gleaming in the dark. She hadn't believed him for a second.

Nineteen

Simon Cummings checked the dark countertop for his keys, cursing softly. He liked to be at the gym before five so he'd have time for a two-mile jog through Audubon Park afterward. He was already running late. That would leave him with only a brief time to stop by the hospital without disrupting his schedule. He reached for the light.

A jingle.

"Looking for these?"

Cummings jerked up in surprise at the sight of a shadowy figure seated in his breakfast nook. His dangled keys and the man's eyes both glinted with quick metallic flashes. He snapped on the overhead light with an unsteady hand, knowing what was waiting for him. All he could do was brazen it out and hope to keep his insides where they were.

"What the hell are you doing in my house?"

"We need to talk."

"You know where my office is. Make an appointment. Now get out."

Max Savoie leaned back in the comfortable chair, swirling the key ring around his index finger. He glanced down at the loose jogging clothes he wore over the inevitable high-tops. "I'm not dressed for the office yet. And our conversation isn't the kind of business that you want to go any further than the two of us here in this room. We can talk now, or I can follow you to the park for your morning jog. Only if it comes to that, I guarantee you'll be running a lot faster than usual. And you won't get very far."

A healthy jump-start of alarm warred with the outrage in the businessman's expression. "If you're waiting for an apology—"

"I'm not the one you owe the apology to."

Cummings sneered. "If you're suggesting I should make one to your out-of-uniform slut of a girlfriend—"

Max's eyelids drooped slightly but his tone was still pleasant. "No, I'm not. And if I were, I certainly wouldn't allow you to address her that way and continue to breathe."

Cummings wasn't stupid or angry enough to mistake the line he'd just crossed. "Perhaps I do owe her one. It would seem she's found who was behind my daughter's death."

"No, I don't think she did. Her killer, maybe— but not the one responsible." A pause. "That would be you."

The sputter of furious objection died on his lips under Max's penetrating stare. "What do you know about all this, Savoie?"

"Everything. About how you cut legal corners in a development deal with Etienne Legere. How you underbid by using substandard materials, then took a hefty cut for yourself. And when an ambitious cop found out about it, you made a deal with him that would protect your future and guarantee his.

"You and Caissie bribed Legere's man Rollo to set up his boss and to make him think it was his own brother who soured the deal. Legere snapped and killed him, and no one was the wiser about your involvement and profit in it. Except Rollo. Caissie came out looking like a hero and got his grade raise. Legere went to prison, and Rollo disappeared with the promises you made to him. Caissie went on to become a solid cop and a real hero. You used your ill-gotten wealth to invest wisely and build a reputation as a brilliant businessman and philanthropist. Jimmy kept Rollo off you for occasional favors, and Tommy Caissie buried your name in the paperwork for the kickback. And then it all went bad."

"You can't prove any of this."

"Sure I can, or I wouldn't be here. Rollo didn't care that you were trying to cover your ass so you could run for office. All he knew was you were the golden goose, and he didn't want to end up with egg on his face. You never expected him to show up on your doorstep. You thought you could bully him into disappearing again. You underestimated him."

"He killed them before he even came to me. Just to get my attention, he said." Cummings dropped into a chair across from Max, his expression stark with grief and horror. "That's why I thought it was you, at first. I couldn't believe he'd show up after all these years to confront me. I couldn't believe he'd be that much of a fool."

"Or just that desperate for the money."

Cummings shook his head slowly. "The greedy bastard. I would have found some way to make it right with him. He didn't have to . . ." He covered his face briefly, then scrubbed his eyes to face Max with an all-business solemnity. "So, what now? Your girlfriend brings him in and tears everything out from under my wife and other daughter?"

"I don't want to hurt your family. They don't deserve that. They've been through enough."

A flicker of hope sparked in Cummings's eyes. Then he gave a wry smile. "How are you going to keep your tenacious little lady from doing that job she's so proud of? Or does she have a bit of her father in her?"

"No," Max snarled. Then his voice smoothed over again. "I wouldn't stop her. And I couldn't, if she knew the truth. She believes Rollo went after you because you blew the whistle on Legere and spoiled Rollo's comfortable life. She doesn't have any facts to the contrary. I made sure she couldn't find them."

"What facts?"

"Jimmy learned his habit of record keeping from his father. He made nice notes about his dealings with you. About the arrangement you made with

him, to have Tom Caissie killed when his conscience
and his drinking started to get the better of him. My
attorney took those files off the computer before
Charlotte got curious enough to see what was on
it."

"What's it going to cost me for those files to be
erased?"

"I don't want your blood money."

"You must want something or you wouldn't be
here."

"I want to make sure the truth about Tom Caissie never surfaces. I want to make sure Charlotte
never finds out that in a moment of weakness her
father made a wrong choice to provide for her. The
shame and guilt and disillusionment would kill her.
I won't let that happen. Protecting her is the only
thing that matters to me. I'm not one for the letter of
the law. I figure all of you paid a steep price for what
you did. There's no point in anyone else suffering
for it. Do you agree?"

"Yes. But Rollo—what if he surfaces again?"

Max gave a small, tight smile. "That's unlikely.
I'll make sure he doesn't, and I'll keep the truth
away from Charlotte."

"And? There's more. Spell it out, Savoie."

A shadow of Jimmy Legere crossed Max's expression as he leaned forward, a predatory gleam of
fierceness in his eyes, of having an exposed throat in
his jaws. "You and I will be doing business together,
Simon, a sort of unofficial partnership. Nothing

intolerable that you won't be able to live with. But certainly something you won't be able to live without. You see, I'm a businessman, too. At one time, I would have simply torn out your throat to keep you from telling Charlotte a truth that would wound her. But I promised her I would behave myself. So now I'm just going to sink my teeth into your reputation. I'm going to make sure you keep those promises you toss about so freely."

Cummings nodded, feeling the sting at his neck.

Max smiled. "I'm going to enjoy doing business with you."

AFTER LEAVING THE Cummings home, Max made one more stop, to a dark hospital room where he waited in shadow until groggy eyes opened and focused on him in surprise.

"Do you know who I am?"

"Yes."

"I wanted to tell you that I'm sorry. And I wanted to let you know that despite what you might hear, justice has been done for you and your daughters. You're safe now."

For a moment she just stared at him, then she smiled faintly.

"Thank you."

WELL RESTED, CRISPLY dressed, and carrying a cup of coffee, Charlotte Caissie started up the steps of the courthouse, thinking only one thing would have made the morning complete. Unfortunately waking to find herself alone nipped that possibility in the bud.

"Nice job, detective."

She glanced around to see Karen Crawford fixing a microphone to her exquisitely tailored suit. "Thank you, Ms. Crawford. It was your faith and support that sustained me." With the cameraman still fussing with his equipment, Cee Cee felt safe to linger to enjoy the crow eating.

"This man, this Rollo, how does he fit in with the murders?"

"That will all be covered in the commissioner's statement. He'll be making one later this morning, after I give him my full report."

"Come on, Detective Caissie. This is your moment. Talk to me. Get a little face time."

Charlotte followed the sudden shift in the reporter's attention and saw Max Savoie and his attorney exit the building. In his Armani suit and dark glasses, Max looked every inch the dynamic businessman, with just enough edge to make her heart stumble.

"Face time," she murmured. "Excellent idea."

Max paused at the top of the steps, waiting for her to come up to him. His voice was a low, intimate caress.

"Good morning, detective. How nice to see you again so soon."

"I expected to see you a bit sooner." She stopped a step below him. Her tone betrayed slight irritation, and an undercurrent of frustrated longing.

"I'm sorry. I had some business to attend to. Since I was out and about, I figured I'd drop in and get my statement on record. Your partner obliged me. A poor substitute, but who knew you planned to sleep half the day away?" His voice dropped to a whisper. "And look so gorgeous and irresistible doing so. I love waking up to you." He glanced at his attorney. "Thank you, Tony. I'll see you at the office."

"Max." A stiff inclination of his head, "Detective."

Then Max only had eyes for her. No one observing them would know the effort it took for him not to reach out to her, to touch her. But he wouldn't, because she didn't want him to. Not here. And so he stood, smiling as if to an acquaintance, when all he could think about was starting down the buttons of her silky white shirt . . . Damned if it wasn't *his* shirt!

"Where are you off to?" Her words were casual, while her gaze moved over him as if it was peeling off his clothes.

"I've got to go to the office. I've neglected things there for too long and Francis is probably embezzling all my money. I need to stand over his shoulder today and make him nervous. Or maybe I'll just have to kill him."

She pursed her red lips into a sassy smirk. "Decisions, decisions. I can think of several things you've neglected, like that Canyon tour we talked about."

"Careful, detective. I'll have you right here on these steps before Ms. Crawford can say, 'Roll tape.'"

"Ooo, I've always wanted to be in the movies."

He showed his teeth briefly, then was suddenly serious. "You showed quite a flair for the dramatic in your statement. Are you all right with that? I would never have asked you to."

Was she all right about making a false statement about the events of the previous night? Uncomfortably all right. It should have been tearing her up inside. So why wasn't it?

He had his answer. She would break her laws for him, for him and his clan of unnatural followers, to protect him. And to protect them, for him. As long as justice was done as it had been in that warehouse on the river.

Maybe later she would feel regret for the tarnishing of her ideals. But now all she felt was relief. Relief and an impatience to take back all those things she'd sacrificed to bring the case to a close. And a cautious acceptance of the fact that this wasn't the first or the last time she was going to be forced to hopscotch along that straight line of the law in order to be with the one she loved.

He hadn't asked her to step across that tenuous line. He hadn't asked her to make sacrifices. But she'd said, "Help me, Max," and he had vowed in that low, fervent rumble, "I would do anything for you." Anything to ease her pain, to serve her purpose, to see her precious justice done.

What had she been willing to risk for *him*?

"You shouldn't have to ask, Max." She took his hand. Such a simple thing. No grand or overly demonstrative gesture but he went suddenly still, his fingers remaining motionless as hers stroked over them."

Suddenly Karen Crawford was there, shoving her microphone between them.

"Mr. Savoie, I understand you paid a visit to Noreen Cummings this morning. For an apology?"

Max frowned slightly. "To express my regret over the pain her family has suffered, Ms. Crawford."

"Are you relieved now that the stigma of guilt has been lifted from you?"

"I was never guilty, Ms. Crawford. I'm relieved not to be hounded by those who were determined to make it seem so." His reply was so smooth, it took her a moment to respond with a slight narrowing of her eyes.

She turned to Cee Cee. "I understand Mr. Savoie was instrumental in your breaking this case, Detective Caissie."

"It was his information and Noreen Cummings's description that led us to the alleged killer."

"Who is currently still at large. Will you be heading that team as well?"

"No, Detective Hammond will be in charge. He'll provide you with details as they become available."

"And where will you be, detective?"

"Taking some personal days."

"What will you use them for?"

"As you suggested, some serious face time." She caught Max's tie and tugged him down to her, then tapped two fingers on her lips. "Step up, Savoie, and thank me."

There was no resistance in the way his mouth settled over hers. Firm, warm, and wooing. Her breathing was seriously compromised by the time she let him go, and the curve of his lips looked smugly satisfied.

"Detective Caissie, are you confirming rumors of your relationship with Max Savoie, right here on the steps of a New Orleans courthouse?"

"I don't need to confirm anything with Mr. Savoie, and I don't listen to rumors, Ms. Crawford." She straightened his tie and placed her hand upon his snowy white shirt, unable to resist the feel of him so hot and hard and male beneath the fabric.

Her voice lowered. "I'll see you later, baby."

"So you and Mr. Savoie are . . . ?"

"Busy, Ms. Crawford."

MAX STOOD IN the hall, glumly studying the new wood floor. Its gleam betrayed no hint of a violent past. Its polished surface held no memories, no dark reflections. And suddenly he wanted the old, stained boards back so he would never forget. So he would always feel close to the man who raised him.

Restless, he wandered back by the kitchen, where several of the men played cards while keeping an eye on the closed-circuit monitors.

Giles greeted him with a smile. "Hey, boss man. Play a few hands?"

"No thanks." He scanned the screens impatiently.

"You looked good on the news."

A couple of snickers.

"I did? What was I doing on the news?"

More chuckles and a few rib pokes.

"Sucking the lips off Detective Caissie." Max stared at Giles, jaw unhinged and so aghast, Giles had to run with it. "Real nice close-up, too. The voice-over from that fine little reporter was talking about the murder case being solved, but I think the real story she was after was the tongue action."

Max cursed. If Charlotte's superiors saw it . . . Of course they would see it. So much for being discreet.

"I made a recording of it for you, boss. If you ever want any other kind of video taken of Detective Caissie, just let me know. Happy to do it for you."

But Max wasn't listening.

His stomach lurched. No wonder he hadn't heard from her: she was probably being dressed down by her commander. What had they done?

"Here she comes. Nobody kicks up dust like your lady behind the wheel of a big block."

Max's gaze jumped to the screen, and some of his anxiety eased when the aggressive little green and black car raced into view. She probably wanted to drive it over him and park it up his ass. Or she was coming to pick up her clothes on her commander's orders.

He followed the different angles, through the gates, up the drive, screeching to a stop at the front porch. She climbed out of the vehicle and jogged up the steps wearing tight jeans, running shoes, and a skimpy tank top that offered some majorly suggestive bouncing. Then she was out of camera range.

He waited, listening for the front door.

Nothing. No knock. No sound of her letting herself in.

Then his cell phone rang.

"You look hot on camera, Savoie. Crawford must be creaming herself with jealousy. She's got it bad for you, you know."

"No, I didn't know." He turned his back on the others so they wouldn't see his foolish grin. "And how 'boutchu?"

"I want you bad, Savoie. Now."

He tightened like an overwound watch, but his voice remained casual. "Where are you? I didn't hear you come in."

"I didn't. I'm outside."

His brow lowered in puzzlement. "Why?"

"Come find me."

"Is this some kind of game?"

"Yes. And you're It. Chase me, Max."

A bolt of heat charged through him.

"Catch me if you can." On that sultry taunt, she hung up.

A rush of adrenaline revved Max's system. "Turn off the cameras," he told Giles.

"Do what, boss?"

"Turn off the cameras. Leave them off until I tell you otherwise."

"Sure thing. But what—"

Max ripped off his tie. His coat followed. And then he was gone. No sound of his Converse shoes on the hall hardwood. No creak of the door or slap of the frame. He was simply gone.

The fellows looked at one another with brows raised in speculation. Then up at the monitors expectantly. They grumbled when the screens went black.

"Don't you boys have things to do?" Giles ordered. As they slunk away, he grinned at the red Record light. Home movies they probably wouldn't want to show in mixed company.

MAX CROSSED THE lawn in an easy lope, his gaze sweeping the grass until he picked up the crush of her footsteps. Excitement, swift and visceral, kicked up his pulse rate. He ran in a low crouch, tracking her long strides until they disappeared into the woods. He grinned, the expression feral. If she thought she could lose him, she was mistaken.

Going by scent and sound, he plunged onward. Turning toward the snap of a branch, the sudden warm tease of perfume, he rushed in a new direction, feeling her close in the heavy stillness of the woods. Almost close enough to touch. To taste. To eat.

He felt movement, but looked around a moment too late. Swinging from a low limb, she hit him with the flat of both feet right between the shoulder blades. He flew forward, stumbling, falling facefirst to the ground. He tasted dirt and old leaves and heard her quick, laughing breaths as she sprinted away. He was on his feet in an eye blink and in pursuit.

She was fast and strong and clever. She vaulted up onto a stone wall and ran along its uneven top, swinging up into overhanging branches like a tomboy, leaving no path to follow. Dropping down into a swallow creek bed, then splashing upstream, slowed by her waterlogged shoes and pant legs.

He hit her from behind, a low tackle that knocked her forward but gave him time to twist to take the impact himself. She was up, off, and over him in an instant. He caught her ankle, bringing her down again to slap water and muck. She scrambled free, leaving him with a single shoe and a face full of mud. He lunged after her with a throaty growl, grabbing her around the knees, unprepared as she whirled about and dragged him down with her. She shoved his head underwater, using it to push herself back up to her feet to run.

Max came up on all fours, shaking his head to clear the water from his eyes, which now gleamed hot and gold. This time he didn't follow after her.

Instead, he veered off to one side, skimming through the woods, his heart beating hard and fast, his breath rushing light and quick. And he began to shift into something he barely recognized, something primitive and wild.

CEE CEE CURSED softly as a sharp twig stabbed into the bottom of her foot. She hobbled on through the deeply shadowed surroundings, not sure where she was in relationship to the house. Not sure where Max was, or if he was even following her. Wet, sore, and tired, she trudged on, the fun factor rapidly ebbing out of the adventure. Thinking it was time to call Max in and adjourn their sexcapade to a soft bed and clean sheets, she stopped—and heard a low, deep vibration of sound.

"Little girls shouldn't wander in the woods alone. Not when dangerous animals are on the prowl."

She started walking again. He was so close she could hear his breathing. "Some little girls can take care of themselves and are more dangerous than the animals."

A husky chuckle. "Not this animal. Not this King of the Beasts. Are you ready to give up?"

"Not quite yet."

She broke left and with a quick feint dodged right. But he was fast, so fast, and right on top of her. He cinched his arm about her waist, thinking to trap her close, but she reached over her shoulder to get a lock on his dark head, using skill and leverage to flip him. Then, because she didn't want to run anymore from what she so desperately wanted, she dropped down astride him, pinning his wrists to the ground.

"Gotcha, oh great King of the Beasts." She grinned down at him, breathing loudly with a hard-won satisfaction.

"Do you? I wonder." With a powerful move, he rolled, coming up over her, restraining her easily with his size and strength. She didn't struggle. Instead, her body bowed up to rub against his. His eyes went dark, the pupils swelling to swallow up any trace of color. His grip on her relaxed just enough for her to reverse the hold and pitch him over.

"I win," she gloated, lowering to take his mouth as her prize. Then she leaned back to meet his stare. "Do you surrender?"

He grinned. "Of course. Then we both win. I like this game."

His hands cupped the back of her head, bringing her down to him, to a kiss that wasn't sweet or safe or gentle. His mouth crushed hers, demanding, almost brutal. And because his claim of her was so quick and complete, she bit his lower lip to restore some of the balance. He didn't relent, his fingers fisting in her hair as he continued to devour her will. And she wanted him to.

Her hands tore open his shirt. He released her and enjoyed the way she nipped down his chest to his belly, toeing off his shoes as she slid down his zipper to use her mouth on him there until he couldn't stand it. His control fracturing, he sat up, hauling her to him for more fierce, urgent kisses. She stood to let him peel down her jeans, stepping out of them before settling back onto his lap, for a rough, elemental mating of tongues.

Then his head dipped lower and his mouth closed upon her sensitive breast. The breath exploded from her lungs. His name moaned from her as his hands pushed up her thin tank top so he could apply a direct assault on her soft skin and stiff nipples. The sharp tugs and soothing swirls of his tongue, that mind-blowing blend of tender and rough, had her shaking with a six on the Richter scale.

And then the feel of his palms on her thighs, rubbing, sliding upward until his thumbs stroked and teased and parted her. Slipped inside her. A spectacular release rumbled through her, and before the last of those splendid aftershocks ran their course she felt him press against her, rock hard and ready.

She palmed the mud from his cheeks. His stare fixed to hers, glittering a hot green and gold. His desire for her lasered from his eyes. Not just for the incredible hot sex, but for her. For her love, her acceptance, her loyalty. His hunger for those things burned deep and hot.

She understood it, having suffered from that hunger just as keenly. She took a wild joy in knowing it was the same for both of them, that only the other could satisfy that craving, could fill that need.

It would never be the same with anyone else. Max Savoie, her fiercely primitive, frustratingly mysterious, and desperately faithful lover, was It for her. Her chance to have everything she'd dreamed of. And what it would take to keep him quite simply scared her brainless.

But on this night, when passion steamed as hot and thick as the Louisiana woods, when lust and love and urgency overrode any practical reservations, she was ready to pay that price. For him. To have him.

"Show me your other face, Max. Your other beautiful face."

His surprise was quickly replaced by a flare of something bright, raw, and dangerous. She held his stare as she felt his skin and bone shift beneath her hands. Angles lengthening, growing hard and bold and bestial. Slipping her fingers into his soft dark hair, she kissed him and was rewarded by a shudder of need.

Eyes closed, she let her head fall back. She tensed slightly at the warm brush of his breath, then shivered deliciously at the light stroke of his tongue. Her fingers tightened. Her body arched as he licked and nibbled an erotically charged path down her throat, along the smooth slope of one shoulder. Hesitating there. She held her breath, waiting for his bite, for the pain that would forever bind them.

But she was rushing the ritual. Mating first, then bonding.

The difference in him was immediately and amazingly apparent. Scaldingly hot and huge, burning against her belly, probing between her legs, ready to tear into her. Images flashed in her mind before she could keep them out: Sarah Cummings, Vivian Goodman. Ripped, violated, savaged. Tumbling about with her own brutal memories were Rollo's taunting words: "*If you survive it.*" Tension snapped through her as his foreign heat breeched her. Even wet and more than ready, the shock had her clutching his shoulders, biting her lip. Determined as she was to see it through, a soft sound still escaped her.

He stopped. For a moment, there was only their hurried breathing.

Then he withdrew.

His soft kiss upon the side of her neck stilled her trembling. Her palms clasped to the familiar contours of his face. His human face. A slightly more aggressive kiss behind her ear had her shifting against him, relaxing, warming, seeking his mouth, feasting on his lips. Lifting, sinking, settling carefully over him. Taking in that well-loved part of him that promised never to hurt her. Riding him until the exquisite friction built into an unstoppable force that left them gasping, then clinging to one another in sated relief.

Satisfied and ashamed, she burrowed against the slick heat of his throat, soothed by the steady throb of his heartbeat. "I'm sorry."

"Look at me, *sha*. Open your eyes."

She did so with reluctance, to find him regarding her with concern. And love. So much love, it broke her. She buried her face against his shoulder again, her palms moving anxiously over his smooth, familiar body. "I'm sorry. I wanted you. I wanted to be with you. I wanted to please you."

"It doesn't please me to hurt you or frighten you." His tone was gruff. Then it gentled. "You always please me, Charlotte. In more ways than you'll ever know. It doesn't matter, *cher*."

Of course it did. She knew that the instant she'd seen the amazement in his eyes at the acceptance he yearned for. Then she'd snatched it away.

Coward.

And if what Rollo had said was true, soon it would begin to matter a whole helluva lot.

She leaned back, trying to ease the tension with a tease of a smile. "You waited twelve years for that first time. I won't make you wait much longer."

She saw the doubt flicker through his eyes, almost immediately followed by a cautious glimmer of hope. And there was damned little she wouldn't do to keep his fragile dream alive.

Her fingertips charted the unyielding line of his shoulders. Everything about his life had been that way: hard, ungiving, brutal. She'd change that if she could.

"I was thinking of taking a trip," she said.

"Oh?" His expression didn't alter, but she felt the objecting brace of his body. "Where to?"

She soothed her palm along his firm jaw until he leaned into it, butting like a faithful hound seeking a master's attention. A strangely submissive gesture for one who controlled a huge empire and a preternatural world. Yet here he was, nudging for affection from her as his eyes closed.

I'm not going to leave you, baby. I could never leave you.

"I'm thinking someplace hot and breathtaking." She paused until his gaze lifted. "Someplace like the Grand Canyon. You still interested in taking that tour?"

"You mean right now?" His voice rumbled like the takeoff of a 747.

"If you're up for it."

More than his interest began to rise, and his smile spread slow and sure. "It won't be a dry heat, *sha*."

Her smile was a naughty little curve of promise. "Hot, wet, and all night was what I had in mind. How's that sound, Savoie?"

"I love you, Charlotte."

She hugged him, kissing him gently behind the ear, where his short black hair curled slightly in the way she found sexier than hell. "I love *you*, Max Savoie. I need you and I want you. And I will have you. All of you. Every part of you."

His reply was soft and absolute. "I'm yours."

And for the next few hours, he was able to forget

the world that existed outside their intimate oasis. To forget that something dark and dangerous had been put into motion by his father's careless greed, and was even now readying to sweep down upon them.

Down from the north.